To

Justin Holley

May your nightmares be glorious...

BRUISED

Justin Holley
June 2015

A Shadow Play Books Publication

Shadow Play Books (Bruised Series) by Justin Holley

BRUISED

WEDNESDAY'S CHILD (October 2015)

THE GULLIES (December 2015)

All rights reserved. Published in the United States of America (2015) by Shadow Play Books. Copyright 2015 by Justin Holley.

Edited by Heather Jacquemin

Cover Art & Formatting by Novel Website Design

The Cataloguing-in-Publication Data is on file at the Library of Congress.

Trade Paperback ISBN: 978-0-692-43155-9

Shadow Play Books products are available for educational, business, and sales promotion use. Correspondence in regards to special pricing for bulk orders and general inquiries welcome:
customerservice@shadowplaybooks.com

Justin Holley enjoys hearing from his fans and is open to a variety of public speaking and book reading/signing opportunities. He may be contacted through his website:
www.justinholley.com

~To Devin

Your teenage brand of intellectualism propelled my writing to greater heights. Thanks. You're difficult to impress, but I'd like to think I have.

Prologue

The ivory skull gleamed as if it were polished moments ago. Black holes from where its nose once hung gaped like never-ending tunnels. From the silent scream of its mouth, the skull revealed its molars but its other teeth were mostly missing.

A human skull.

It flickered with blood-red candle flame, its eyes flashing like a deranged creature. We must've looked like zombies as we shambled and sloshed through the swamp toward the light.

We formed a ring around Harvey, who held the skull above his head. Harvey watched us like he had murder on his mind.

Maybe he did. Harvey chanted an invocation, exuding an economy and power I had no clue he possessed, like someone else—or something else—shared space in his head.

Then he sliced our palms across our life-lines, and the letting of blood began.

Chapter 1

I believe in love at first sight. I've experienced its crushing grip and survived to tell about it. But love is blind—nearsighted. I've been scared blind, too, if you wanna know the whole truth.

She had a slim body, red hair, pendulum arms, and bruises on her chalk-like skin. Long before Jewel parted her thin lips to utter a word to me, my world changed forever.

"You make my brain tingle," the girl said as she stared.

I rubbed at the gauze on my palm. A strange statement, sure, but it shouldn't have given me such a problem. To my credit, who had ever heard of someone's brain tingling? Still, at eighteen, I should've been savvier, caught on to her intentions a bit quicker. All my friends had, but I seemed to be the last bastion of resistance against the loss of innocence.

Unfortunately, that would change.

Ignorance aside, the whole brain tingling thing scared me. The girl's beautiful voice had poured from her mouth like butter. She could've told me she wanted to murder my family and eat their flesh for dinner, yet I would've remained calm and hypnotized.

"Are you talking to me?" I asked.

"Am I looking at you?" She jammed her fists onto her bony hips. Her blue torches for eyes burned through the thick strands of wind-blown hair covering most of her face.

"I—I think so." I immediately wanted to slap myself. I hoped she knew to blame my nerves for the avalanche of moronic words tumbling from my mouth.

Jewel pursed her lips. "Most people wouldn't have a hard time answering that. It's a yes or no question," Jewel said.

I shook my head. "It's—" My breath caught in my throat.

"You've never heard me speak to you," she said, answering for me. "Don't feel bad. I don't speak to anyone."

I really should keep my mouth shut. Jewel was new to our school, but nobody had befriended her because she was . . . different.

And cute.

My eyes widened at the thought, and the downward spiral of my youth slipped down the drain.

Jewel's eyes danced with electricity. "Good," she said. "Now, back to my original statement."

My gaze fluttered down to her bruised arms. I searched her eyes for mercy as I again picked at the gauze covering my own injury.

"You make my brain tingle," she said.

"What?"

"That's what I said to you, Jason. You make my brain tingle." She rattled off a cute giggle, like a sullen angel sighing, or a moth caught in white flames.

Her laughter fluttered my heart but I still had no idea what the hell she meant—or wanted. The woozy effect she had on me wasn't helping. "Oh, okay," I managed. "Is tingling good or bad?" I hoped to God it was good.

"Sure, it's fine," Jewel answered, as if her brain tingled daily.

I shrugged. This girl business was confusing the hell outta me.

A sneaky smile parted her lips. "My brain tingles when I find a kindred spirit."

Heat rose to my cheeks, not the only physiological reaction happening.

A sly smile erupted from Jewel as she wrung her hands and eyed me like a predator. She must've noticed my body's reaction to her.

"What's a kindred spirit?" I asked, nervous, wanting her words to replace the oddness coursing through my body.

"Someone who gets me," she said. Her eyes, portals to a world I now wished to live, widened with excitement but quickly disappeared beneath heavy lids.

"Oh," I said with a heavy breath, relieved. "Cool."

"Not cool!" she snapped. With zero warning, Jewel snatched up one of the Star Wars trading cards at my feet and waved it like a shank she hoped to plunge into my flesh. Jewel's abrupt change in demeanor threw me off kilter.

"Where did you get this?" Her cold, bitter tone of voice sounded as though a different girl had been implanted underneath Jewel's skin.

My heart dropped—I didn't want to tell her the truth. "Most people buy them at the store," I muttered, diverting my eyes. I'd tried for sarcasm but I reeked of deception.

Jewel steadied her eyes and conjured a wicked smirk. "You're eighteen. You didn't buy these for yourself. Besides, I didn't ask where they came from originally. I asked, Jason, where *you* got them?"

I didn't appreciate the emphatic use of my name. She sounded like my damn mother but possessed by the devil.

My delightful confusion at Jewel transformed into horrible discomfort.

"I got them from kids at the middle school," I answered. Our high school was located, conveniently, across the street from a campus full of little kids to extort.

Jewel lowered her head and peered from the tops of her eye sockets. Those eyes—blue-hot coals in her skull—scared the hell outta me.

"Did they give them to you or did you take them?" she asked, her voice way too grim for someone so young.

"They gave them to me," I stammered, wanting to escape Jewel's accusing eyes.

"In exchange for what?" she asked like a statement, bold and accusing.

"Nothing," I said. "I mean, I didn't steal them."

Jewel squinted as though she sensed my defensiveness. "No, I'm sure you didn't." She paused and wrung her hands, her arm muscles gyrating beneath her bruises. "I don't like people who control others, Jason."

I peeled my gaze away from her bruises. "I—I mean we—wanted—dang it." Frustration and guilt choked my words.

If Jewel caught on to my anxiety, she certainly didn't care about it. She relentlessly continued. "You and your buddies accept these cards from the middle-schoolers across the street in return for protection," she said. "I've watched you."

I opted to keep my mouth shut, thankful she didn't know about the blood oath. I feared what the gang might be capable of. We used to be a group of friends but now we were something else, bonded by blood.

She spoke slowly and carefully. "You aren't a cruel boy," she said. "But your friends are."

I shook my head but I had no idea which of my friends she considered cruel.

I should have.

"Like Harvey Kuchenbecker," Jewel said. "He's cruel. He treats little kids like possessions, like his own personal herd of cows. He gets more cards than you, too."

I agreed with a quick nod. She didn't know the half of it. "Harvey gets all the stuff and distributes some of it to the whole group," I said, pleased with the opportunity to deflect part of the blame. "He keeps a larger share for himself."

Jewel, however, kept me on the hook. "And you're stupid enough to go along with it."

I didn't reply. I stared at the ground instead.

"You know he's changing, right?" she asked, her eyes intense and scary like Harvey's had been the night of the ceremony in Buck Hill Swamp.

"Whad'ya mean?" I asked. But I knew—the whole gang knew.

Deep frown lines ran from the corners of her lips to her chin. She shook her head, long hair swaying back and forth, like she didn't want to bother explaining.

Our eyes locked, and a breath escaped my wide-open mouth. My hair stood on end as though an electrical current passed between us and zipped through my body. Scary but exhilarating—and somehow sexual.

"Come with me." She turned sharply and marched toward the swings, not even bothering to turn around and make sure I followed.

I trailed behind her like a lost puppy.

As I walked, I watched other teens talk in small groups, even saw Harvey shove a kid to the ground and yell at him. Harvey's head snapped up. I turned my attention back to Jewel and wondered how I'd managed to trap myself between two crazy people. Thankfully, one of them was beautiful.

With long, outstretched legs, Jewel leaped between the chains of the swing, over the seat, and onto the dirt ground. A graceful move, sexy and strong. She steadied herself and sat down, her narrow back to me. The swing didn't even sway.

I approached cautiously, afraid Jewel might pounce on me if I moved too quickly. I was excited but scared. I sat on the swing next to hers.

Jewel folded her hands onto her lap, long red hair shrouding her face. She turned to me, her beautiful yet terrible eyes boring into mine. Pupils big with a narrow ring of blue on the outside, Jewel wrung her hands slowly as if she were rubbing on lotion. "I know something about crazy," she whispered.

"What?" I uttered through a dry mouth, my swollen tongue stuck to my front teeth.

Jewel's shoulders slumped, pupils shrunken, and eyes sagged into their sockets. Why had her mood swung so wildly? I yearned to hold her and make her life better somehow, but I didn't know anything about her life. What could this pretty young girl possibly know about crazy?

She turned toward me, allowing her hand, which was attached to her bruise-ridden arm, to drift from her lap and onto my knee.

The butterflies in my belly responded immediately and I bent forward to ease the effect. Embarrassed and helpless about having zero control of my body, I took a deep breath.

A smirk played at her thin lips but didn't travel to her eyes, where sadness still dwelled. She stared down her arm straight to my midsection. Despite her despair, she had a spark of interest, like she knew.

I smiled and considered whipping it out so she could take a good look.

"What's so funny?" she asked.

I immediately squelched it. "Nothing."

She squeezed my knee. I thought she'd take her hand away but she didn't. "It's okay," she said. "I make you uncomfortable."

"Not exactly." I looked away. "Well, maybe."

A clipped laugh escaped Jewel's mouth. "At least you're honest—mostly."

"I didn't mean it like that," I said. "You don't make me uncomfortable. You—"

"I what, Jason?" she asked, searching my eyes. "Have you ever had a girlfriend?"

I shrugged.

"It's okay if you haven't," she whispered, squeezing my knee harder.

"Have you?" I asked. "Had a boyfriend, I mean?"

She shrugged. We were at a standstill, both afraid to answer a simple question.

At least I thought she was afraid but I had a great deal to learn yet about Jewel.

"Well," she said, "you'd have to shape yourself up before you could be my boyfriend anyway." But she hadn't moved her hand away from my knee. In fact, she had squeezed it a bit tighter.

My breaths were shallow, rapid gasps. Sweat oozed from my palms. Not knowing what else to do, I moved to place my hand over hers.

She yanked her hand from my knee and snapped it back to her lap. "I do the touching, not you. Please."

Feeling stupid and inadequate, I kept my mouth shut. I wondered if her reaction had something to do with the bruises plaguing her arms.

Sadness crept into her eyes. "Like I said, I know a little something about crazy. Stay away from Harvey."

She was beautiful—perhaps a little insane—but she made my heart thump all the same. My head spun with confusion and desire.

Jewel walked away, red hair swaying and eyes searching mine. "You're a nice guy," she said. "If you decide to ditch Harvey, I'll consider being your girlfriend. Because you . .?" She paused, waiting for my response.

I smiled, sheepish and ashamed. "Make your brain tingle," I whispered.

Jewel's thin lips cracked with the slightest hint of a smile. "Correct." Glancing over her shoulder as she walked away, she added, "I'll be watching."

Entranced, my entire being wanted to chase her and be the good guy. Unexplainable and never-before-experienced feelings welled up within me. *Jewel.*

Things were definitely changing.

I observed an angry, crazed Harvey watching Jewel walk toward the high school. Once again, I felt ensnared between two crazy people. Mom was a shrink, sure, but I didn't inherit her patience and nerves of steel to deal with the crazies of the world.

Harvey marched toward me, jaw set, hands stuffed into pockets. Harvey, always ahead of us in physical maturity, probably thought Jewel didn't bode well for his little thieving enterprise and knew it wouldn't do him well to lose me, one of his field-generals, to a girl.

I ignored him and watched Jewel walk away. I enjoyed the way she sauntered, her steps light and deliberate despite her internal voraciousness. Anyone who didn't know her would've thought her timid but I knew better. I wanted to be close to her, smell her scent, breathe her in.

Harvey grabbed my shoulder with fingers like icicles, even under the hot sun. Red stains under his fingernails and in the cracks of his knuckles stood out against his white skin. His soft voice belied his corpulent frame and manifested itself into a snake-like drawl. "You like that shit?" he asked. "Sniffing a little tail, are ya?"

"I ain't sniffing a damn thing," I said. I tried to find Jewel to make sure she hadn't heard me but she was already gone.

Sweat glistened off the top of Harvey's head, easily seen through his butch-cut hair along with scars from old beatings. "Then why you looking all red and flushed?" he asked. "You're either sick or in love—or both."

"I like talking to her."

"You're full of shit. She had her hand on your knee. Did she tell you I'm an asshole?"

I gave Harvey silence in answer.

"Did she tell you I tried to put my arm around her?" He chuckled. "I wanna give her more than just my arm, though." He grabbed his crotch.

Heat radiated from my face like steam. I remembered how Jewel didn't like to be touched. "She never said that." I clenched my hands into fists.

Harvey laughed. "You jealous? Gonna kick my ass, pussy boy?" He stepped closer until his chest touched mine.

"Leave her alone, Harvey," I said, surprising even myself.

Harvey grinned a malicious toothy smile. His breath smelled like old plastic and rotten food. "She ain't nothing but damaged goods," he said. "Didn't you notice those bruises on her arms and the scrape on her forehead?"

"Yeah."

"Did you ask her how she got them?"

"No, I didn't ask," I said, "and neither did you."

Harvey twitched as though something electric buzzed inside his head. "Don't need to," Harvey snapped. "Any idiot can see she's getting knocked around at home. Probably other shit too."

Harvey's greasy brows perspired like he enjoyed thinking about the cruelty. I almost slugged the dickhead but instead I said, "She probably fell down the stairs—or wiped out on her bike." I couldn't even imagine Jewel riding a bike.

Harvey sneered, apparently not buying it either.

"You better watch yourself," Harvey said. "One bad move and you're out of the gang, out of the deal, so start thinking about your allegiances. Bad shit happens to bad people who double-cross the gang. We swore a blood oath."

I considered kicking him square in the nuts. "I'll think about it."

Harvey blinked rapidly. "I'm warning you, choose carefully. This goes way beyond stealing from the kiddies over there. We're going big time!"

He spat, and his bile formed a bubbling sphere on the hot asphalt. Harvey stalked off like a lion in his domain, hands shoved into his jean pockets.

I remained where I stood, numb. Big time? My thoughts raced as I faced a decision about the mysterious circumstance I felt compelled to explore. The bruises on Jewel's arms and my concern for her dominated my heart, yet my loyalties to the gang ran deep.

I nearly screamed in surprise when Billy Stratham touched my shoulder, his fingers much warmer than Harvey's.

Billy smiled. "Whoa, take it easy. You look like you seen a ghost or something."

I let out my breath. "You scared the shit outta me. I didn't even hear ya."

"You were too busy arguing with Harvey. What's up with that?"

"He saw me talking to Jewel, and he thinks I like her."

"Do you?"

I gathered my thoughts with a deep breath. "She's okay."

Billy flashed a brilliant smile. "She has you turning to mush. You going for it?"

I pondered his question longer than I intended. I decided to take Easy Road. "No, I'm not gonna get all soft."

By his expression, Billy didn't buy it. He brushed his hair back from his eyes. "Yes you are. But that's good, maybe you'll get pussy-whipped."

"No girl's gonna tell me what to do—no way." I shot a quick glance, making sure Jewel hadn't overheard me.

"What're you looking for? Seeing if Jewel's around?" Billy made a crude gesture, repeatedly penetrating his closed fist with a finger. "Bet you wanna do this, right?" He winked and pounded his fist harder.

I grimaced. "Come off it," I said. "Harvey doesn't want me to hang out with her."

"He knows you'll get pussy-whipped, and she won't let you hustle cards no more."

"What makes you think she wouldn't let me hustle cards?"

"Settle down, dude. I figure she wouldn't on account of the beatings. You know, the bruises and all? She probably don't like shady deals."

Billy knew plenty about beatings. His old man had been beating him for years but his flippant disregard for Jewel pissed me off. "Fuck you, you don't know how she got those bruises. She could've fallen down the front steps." I cringed and my stomach cramped. I believed my story even less the second time.

Doubt painted Billy's face and he stayed silent for once.

"Look," I said. "I know you didn't mean nothing by it. She's beat to shit but I don't want anyone talking bad about her. She needs help."

"You gonna help her?" Billy asked.

I shrugged. "If I can," I said. "I mean, what can a eighteen-year-old kid do?"

"We're men now. We ain't little kids no more."

"I suppose." I felt way behind everyone else in a fundamental way. "It's none of my business but I'll help if I can. She's cool."

"Guess who else thinks she's cool," Billy said. His smile pissed me off.

"Who?" I asked, getting more pissed by the second.

"Who do you think, Romeo?" Billy asked. "Harvey."

"She would never let Harvey touch her." I felt powerful, able to handle anything, though I'd soon learn that covered more ground than I could bear. For good measure I added, "Harvey better leave her alone." A hollow threat but it felt right.

Billy grinned like he knew something I didn't—or like he wanted to watch a good old-fashioned fist fight. He said, "Forget about it. Let's go to Buck Hill."

Buck Hill Swamp, where a normal group of friends swore to a blood oath. My stomach ached worse than it already did.

Chapter 2

The slush from the ice splashed under my jeans and onto my ankles.

"What're you gonna do about Jewel and Harvey?" Billy asked.

I ignored him. I didn't even want to think about Jewel and Harvey at the moment. I wanted to crawl back into the womb of childhood and never come out. Mom always said, "Jason, you're eighteen going on eight sometimes." I shrugged her voice off.

I didn't care about the cold slush; the warm weather soothed me. The old waterways running through Buck Hill Swamp always thawed last, so every spring, Billy and I shared our last bike ride there on the icy swamp. As kids, Billy and I used the swamp as our playground, riding, sliding, and splashing water in the sunshine.

Now we used the swamp for more insidious purposes.

Memories of the blood oath in the dark of night filtered back to me. I tried to shrug them off but they clung to my mind. We had physically knelt before Harvey and given him our blood. He had mixed it together and asked for evil spirits to help us become one.

Goosebumps covered my arms.

When I didn't answer, Billy hopped back onto his bike and hit the ice. This would be our last summer using bikes since most of us would have trucks soon.

Billy pedaled off fast and hit a spring hole in the ice. His bike slid into the yellow grass and tossed him onto the ground.

Billy laughed. "Did you see my wipeout of the century?" Harvey and Jewel were already forgotten.

"Pretty good," I said. "Not the best one ever though. Don't forget about Harvey." My skin prickled as his name passed my lips.

"When his dumb ass fell through the ice? We had a damn hard time getting him out. Idiot should lose weight, seriously."

Billy stood up and brushed off his jeans, which had huge holes in the knees. A chunk of slush fell through the hole and landed by his shoes.

"You gotta cool it around Harvey. I mean, shit, he is the leader of our gang. He's looking out for us, ya know?"

This conversation was headed exactly the wrong direction. "Our gang don't have much longer anyway. We're gonna be all be scattered to the wind by next fall."

"We can still have a gang," Billy wailed. "We're bonded by blood."

"Fuck that, Billy," I said. I meant both the gang and his reference to the damn blood oath. "It's time to grow up, go to college." I paused then added, "Get jobs."

"We'll still be together in the summers. Harvey will make sure. We swore a blood oath, we got dark forces on our side."

I rolled my eyes. "Screw Harvey. He's trouble. If we let him, he'll bring us all down."

"What is wrong with you?" he asked. "Your mom been pulling her shrink tricks on you?"

"Have you seen how Harvey's been acting since the oath? He used to be fun but now he bullies everyone. He's all twitchy like his head can't relax. He made us cut ourselves and give him our blood. Seems like he enjoys being cruel, ya know?"

"No," Billy said. "Harvey's upping the ante. Extreme times call for extreme measures."

"Where'd ya hear that load of crap, Billy? Do you even know what that means?"

"Sure I do, saw it on Oprah. That's what gangs do, they escalate."

"Escalate? You don't even know what 'escalate' means."

"I know Harvey's doing his job. It'll be okay, roll with it."

"I can't anymore, and others feel the same way."

"It's Jewel, ain't it?" he asked softly. He knew me well.

"It's not Jewel, Billy. I've been thinking about this for a while. We're heading down a bad path into some bad shit."

"Look, bro, you either take shit or you have shit taken from you."

"No, it don't have to be that way."

"Not for you. Your family has money. And you're so far up Jewel's ass you can't think straight."

"Bullshit."

"Not bullshit. It's the truth, admit it."

"It's not her or money," I said. "Harvey's leading us to disaster, maybe to the devil."

"Then I'll have his back in hell too," Billy sneered.

"What about mine? I thought you were my boy."

"You don't need me covering your back no more. You got Jewel now. Enjoy."

Billy rode away, and my life changed. We woke up as mini adults, smaller versions of our dysfunctional parents.

Mom spoke about cycles. I was finally understanding.

Chapter 3

A boy's tree fort is his sanctuary. I was close to outgrowing it like most of the gang already had, but it's where I still harbored all my treasure, dreams—and nightmares. I sifted through the afternoon's events as I lay on my back, staring at the plywood ceiling and thinking about what Billy had said about Jewel.

I allowed myself to fantasize about where Jewel lived. I imagined Jewel showing up at my house, reaching out to me with her penetrating eyes. Excitement I'd never known before stirred inside me, scary and grand all at once. I shook my head, hard.

I needed to get a grip, like Billy said.

Heat radiated from my face into the pit of my stomach, and traveled down further. I ached with an anticipation I didn't understand. With tentative fingers, I explored the heat below. When it felt good, I pulled my hand away, startled by the visions and feelings about Jewel that accompanied the otherwise-familiar sensation. I'd masturbated before but this was different. I recalled Harvey's words about Jewel, and I hated him. If Harvey ever touched her—maybe even laid eyes on her—I'd beat him senseless.

Billy was wrong about Harvey, blood oath be damned. Harvey spelled trouble, and hell was coming.

The ladder rungs creaked, disturbing me from my happy thoughts. I hoped it might be Jewel, and that I had conjured her up like a medium.

"Jason?" Mom said.

I covered the growth which'd sprung up thinking about Jewel. "I'm up here."

"Are you coming in?" she asked from down below. "It's supper time." She poked her head through the hole in the floor. I must have blushed because she eyed me suspiciously. "What have you been up to?"

Mortified. "Nothing much. Reading rock magazines and comics."

For one horrible moment, I feared she saw right through the X-men comic hiding my manhood. "Let me feel your head," she said. "You look flushed. You getting sick?"

Relief spread through my body like a cool stream of water. "I'm fine, just hot. Gimme a minute to finish my comic."

"Okay but if you're still flushed when you come in, I'm taking your temperature."

"Sure," I said with a smile.

She gave me one last look and started back down the ladder.

"Mom?" I asked. The bruises on Jewel's arms burned in my memory.

She stopped her descent. "Yes?"

Silence dropped like an enormous weight, but the more I thought about the bruising, the more I convinced myself it was nothing. "I'll see you at supper," I said.

"Okay, see you at supper," she said suspiciously.

Nate, my little brother, stirred the mashed potatoes and peas around on his plate, the oldest and lamest trick in the book. You'd think he'd develop a better imagination. The family golden retriever licked up a few peas off the tiled floor.

I watched Nate with a half-hearted gaze, my mind elsewhere. I'd cooled myself off before coming inside for dinner, but Mom still eyed me with measured concern.

"Why aren't you eating?" she asked. "Is something bothering you?"

Nate snickered. "Probably a girl," he said.

Dad lowered his paper. A gentle smile tugged at his mouth.

My brother had no idea but his words had hit too close. I blushed, making my lie thin at best. "No way!"

"It's okay," Mom said, "if you have friends who are girls. No need to be ashamed. You're at the right age."

Mom's girls-can-be-friends line didn't explain what I felt about Jewel, a mixture of foreboding and lust. A wave of shame hit me for thinking about Jewel in such explicit ways, especially with the bruises on her arms begging for attention.

"Can I be excused?" I asked.

"I'm sorry," she said. "I didn't mean to embarrass you." Mom searched my eyes.

I averted my eyes, wanting to mask my deception.

Dad winked. "Let him go," he said. "Don't you remember what it was like when we were teenagers? It's about damn time he fell for a girl, anyway. Prom might be fun."

I didn't appreciate his insinuation, but if it earned me a getaway ticket from the dinner table, I would live with it.

Mom smiled. "Yes of course, all the mystery, and dreams of the future."

I stood, afraid I might lurch on the table. They talked about girls and boys like nothing bad ever happened, but those bruises weren't games—not fun ones, anyway. Neither was the blood oath.

I ran upstairs to my room, my bare feet pounding the wood staircase.

Behind my door, I sat against my headboard, staring at the popcorn ceiling. Jewel swirled through my mind. Fantasies of us laying side by side, fantasies interrupted by visions of dark blue bruises encircling her forearms—both fought for my attention like raptors and threatened to tear me apart. My stomach ached with anxiety and excitement. Did she truly wanna be my girlfriend?

A knock on my door pulled me out of fantasyland.

"May I come in?" Mom's soothing voice beckoned.

I paused, not wanting her to see me like this.

Part of me wanted the truth to rush out like a fountain, placing the burden on someone who'd know what to do, but another part of me cringed, terrified of opening a door I couldn't close. What if Jewel's parents sent her away? What if Jewel hated me because I told? Mom was a mandated reporter, after all. Fear rose in my gut as I imagined Jewel's intense, angry eyes boring into mine, rejecting me.

I said, "The door's open." My heart pounded in my throat.

The door opened slowly. My mother's head appeared in the crack. "Can we talk?"

I shrugged my shoulders. "It's a free world."

"Watch your smart mouth." She fingered my bed sheets nervously. "Want to tell me what's bothering you? Is it a girl?"

A blush crept up the back of my neck and onto my face. I stayed silent, afraid of betraying Jewel's confidence.

"By the looks of your cheeks, a girl is involved. Your friends teasing you?"

I shrugged, secretly thankful for the direction of her comment. "The usual guy stuff. I've been the last to hold out."

She sat on the bed next to me. "Is it Harvey and Billy?"

I hated when she said their names as though they were serial killers, as though I was guilty by association. "Mom. Leave them out of this."

"You know I don't care for those boys. Remember your birthday party a couple years back?"

I remembered.

Billy and Harvey had found Mom's old Barbie collection, stripped each one naked and assembled them on the basement floor into a wild orgy. We had laughed hysterically—until we heard the footsteps. Dad barged in and gave me the sex talk—again—complete with instructions on proper condom usage. It took me a month to recover.

I pieced things together, and thanks to my feelings for Jewel, those pieces formed a vividly compelling picture. A blush crept up my face.

"Of course I remember," I moaned. I pulled the pillow onto my lap, nervous, feeling twitchy.

"What mischief have they dreamt up?"

27

She'd freak if I mentioned the blood oath. "They're giving me a hard time about a new girl at school."

"Nice of you to make her feel welcome. Does new girl have a name?" Mom tilted her head and squinted.

I didn't want to discuss Jewel at all. "I think her name's Jewel."

Sometimes having a psychologist for a mother sucked.

Mom hesitated. Her mouth opened to talk but she changed her mind. She cleared her throat. "Pretty name. Is she nice?"

I knew Mom well enough to be suspicious. "She's okay."

"Are Billy and Harvey telling you to have sex with her?"

"Mom." I nearly hurled.

My reaction must have been sheer horror because even Mom blushed. "I'm sorry, I shouldn't have brought it up. But I want you to be a gentleman."

"I will. You're so embarrassing."

"Do I need to send your father up to talk about it?"

"No. I like Jewel, that's all." I hoped my shallow lie would encourage Mom to end the awkward conversation.

"Let's keep it that way. I'm proud of you."

My stomach ached with embarrassment and lust welling up inside me.

Mom mussed my hair, calming me down like she'd done since I was a young boy. I struggled between Jewel's confidence and her safety. Peer-pressure raged in me like a rabid animal, animated into a life of its own.

All my choices, incorrigible.

Mom eyed me warily. "Is that it?"

I took a deep breath. "Isn't that enough?"

She smiled, her white teeth glistening in light of my childhood Scooby-Doo puppy lamp that I couldn't seem to let go of. "At your age, I'd say that is plenty. Welcome to the world of girls." She winked.

I wanted to puke all over her nice white blouse.

She glanced over her shoulder with her patented know-it-all smirk.

I slid down onto my back, relieved yet troubled. The quicker I fell asleep, the quicker I got to see Jewel—and her bruises. In all the turmoil, I'd forgotten tomorrow was Saturday.

Chapter 4

I usually loved weekends, the freedom they afforded me, the luxury of a lazy day spent at the beach, Grace Lake, where we swam to cool off between bouts of raising hell with the younger kids—where we collected the toll during the summer months. Only during the daylight hours, though. The night belonged to older and savvier men than us. But that was gonna change—that was before the blood oath.

The only thing better than the beach, was the annual JC's water carnival. The smells, sounds, the overall chaos swirled around me, triggered my memories of Jewel.

I stood at the ticket gate in a light jacket and slightly-worn blue jeans. I shivered, the breeze chilly coming off the lake, ice-out only a month old yet and so the lake still harbored the last vestiges of wintry breath. People came out in droves after a long cold winter of cabin fever.

The attendant strapped a yellow band tightly to my wrist. For the first time in my life, I welcomed my Monday return to school. Lots of bad shit could happen to Jewel in the span of a couple days—lots of bruises. I hoped she'd be at the carnival. But part of me hoped she wouldn't. The gang was here, somewhere out in the wild throng, and it'd be hell to keep everything straight. I still had a lot of thinking to do.

Butterflies tingled my belly.

The carnival smacked of freedom—freedom from the shackles of our families, from the constraints of teachers and their stringent rules. Decadence sprinkled its magic balm over everyone, like all they needed was a reason to loosen their belts, their tongues, their morals. Facades of civility, humility and restraint slipped off us like a prom dress at midnight to reveal our wantonness—our contempt for polite society.

The days after were like a hangover, our lives slipping slowly back into their shells of obedience.

I heard the barkers from near the games. "Step right up and win your girl a prize." The tone of their voices insinuated the carnies would be more than happy to take care of your girl for you.

I imagined one of the greasy carnies getting their filthy hands on Jewel, pawing at her, touching her. A pang of jealousy swept through me and I trembled involuntarily. I hoped Jewel wasn't here. What if Jewel ran away with the carnival? Every year, a cute girl broke a poor sucker's heart by running away with a slippery, fast-talking freak.

What those women saw in loose men, I had no idea.

Live music poured from the beer tent, where most of the people old enough to drink hung out, leaving the carnival itself to the youth. They probably thought it was safer out here but they didn't know. The real danger and excitement was contained in one enthralling ball of chaos, right out here.

The Hurricane ride fired up, blasting *18 And Life*. Fitting. The ride spun, faster and faster, the screams from the passengers louder and more raucous. A volley of screams yanked my attention to the Zipper, which spun upside down, the carnies leering and hoping to collect the change which inevitably would fall from unsuspecting rider's pockets.

But that's not where I was going. Not yet. I slipped around the Hurricane, around back of the rides, where garbage blew around in the breeze and cables ran to power supplies like long slithery snakes. The carnival manager's trailer loomed in front of me, and it didn't take my imagination long to create images of greasy carnies performing despicable acts of carnage. Voices spilled from the trailer so I hastened my pace. Most people didn't use this route, but we did. This was a shortcut to the promised-land—the place I'd meet the gang. A couple carnies were smoking by the port-a-potties, talking quietly. When I walked by they glared at me with solicitous grins, cigarettes hanging off their bottom lips like long white growths.

Everyone knew they'd kill a guy if they got you alone, so I hurried along. I jogged to a narrow gate leading into the game and food area from the backside, where it emptied out of the nether regions into the area right by the Bingo tent. Bingo wasn't meant for old women or little kids. The Bingo den of sin was meant for gamblers. The best part was the carnies who ran this attraction were usually women—women who stirred a puberty-riddled kid's loins.

Yes, our lives were changing.

The gate clicked behind me, and I found myself between two of the portable game wagons. Long shadows loomed here, reminding me of *Dark Shadows* and *The Traveling Vampire Show*. I wasn't supposed to watch scary movies or read horror books—but I did as often as possible.

The shadows moved, shifted in an irregular pattern. A soft moan escaped from the shadows off to my right. Even though I didn't know what the moan meant quite yet—but I would very soon—it stirred something deep inside me, and made my midsection tingle.

For one frightening moment, I looked into those shadows. As my eyes adjusted to the poor lighting, I made out the grinning mouth of a carnie, his teeth half-rotted. His eyes bored into mine like a laser. An evil chortle, like dried cornstalks in a breeze, emanated from his rotten cave of a mouth.

Movement next to him caught my eye and I caught a glimpse of a pasty white breast, one not used to seeing the sun. The nipple stuck out like an eyeball. The rest of her was covered but her soft moan echoed in my mind.

I ran.

The horrible laughter of the carnie followed me as I spilled out into the chaos and welcome brightness of the carnival.

Sweat poured from me despite the chill in the air. The experience, frightening as it was, left me wanting—needing something unexplainable. I breathed hard, briefly contemplating spying back into the shadows. I turned my attention to the Bingo tent instead.

There they were—the gang. My breathing evened out.

The red and white tent stood in the middle of the games and food vendors on a patch of barren earth. Inside, people sat at picnic tables lined up end-to-end, tables adorned with red plastic tablecloths.

Buddy Huge, one of the guys, and yes he's huge, was in the process of stuffing a chili-dog into his big mouth. Chili squirted out the sides and coated his lips with a red sheen. Billy had his back to me, staring at the carnie who tended to the Bingo games.

She had jet-black hair, white pasty skin, and a long skinny face which harbored high cheek-bones, lips plastered with black lipstick, and startling, nearly black, eyes. In her lips, nose, and eyebrows, seven silver rings stuck out like she were a hog being lead to market.

But I was pretty sure Billy wasn't staring at her eyebrows. The top half of her milky white breasts, chopped off right at the nipple line I supposed, pushed over the material of her form-fitting black T-shirt. The shirt read, "The Cake is a Lie." Above the words was a picture of a cake with candles. At the tips of the candles her nipples jutted through the fabric like they might poke Billy in the eye if he didn't watch himself.

Tracey, the only girl in the gang, watched Billy intently, not with jealousy, but interest, like she couldn't quite understand his fascination. A smile played at the corners of her lips as she tilted her head sideways with curiosity, her blonde hair shifting and hanging straight down.

Harvey stood, his full weight leaning on one of the support poles. I hoped the whole tent wouldn't come down. He didn't even glance at me, his attention riveted somewhere out in the middle distance. His eyes were brown, but his pupils were so dilated they appeared black, capturing the light from the carnival, like he was staring into hell. I wondered if he was on drugs or if his pupils naturally opened the size of a dime.

Every few seconds, Harvey's head twitched and his eyes blinked hard, like something unseen slapped him in the face.

It'd been that way since the blood oath—and I didn't want to know why. Harvey scared the shit out of me.

The carnie woman rolled her eyes at Billy before looking in my direction. "Want a card?" she asked, her voice full of boredom. "Two for one tonight." She smirked and it made my heart skip.

"No," Harvey said, suddenly alert. "We got business."

"Hey," Billy squawked. "I ain't done with my Bingo yet. Hold your horses, we got all night."

The carnie shifted her weight, causing her shapely hip to jut out impatiently. She fanned herself with the cards like she might be about to melt. "You want a card or not?"

"You don't care about Bingo," Tracey said with a smirk. "Fact is, you might go blind."

"Shut up," Billy said. He flipped Tracey the bird.

The woman carnie grunted like she'd heard it all before. She fanned herself. I suppose she was used to people drooling over her. It was part of her show. For a moment I let myself imagine her in the shadows, moaning softly. It kinda got me worked up.

I wondered if Billy had told Harvey about what I said—about the gang. I was pretty sure he'd forgotten about it overnight, but you never knew about Billy. Sometimes he didn't remember shit—sometimes he remembered too much.

Harvey was about to say something, when a voice came from behind me. "Harvey, ya little douche," the voice said. "Ma's gonna kick your lily ass for skipping out on dishes. If she don't, I'm gonna because I had to do them for ya."

It was Leonard, Harvey's older brother. Despite the big words, he sounded nervous, like he wanted to rip into Harvey but was playing it cool, biting into him enough to impress his friends.

I turned around.

Leonard stood with his beefy mechanic-sized arms crossed, a friend on each side of him. Leonard had a curious look on his face, not exactly kind, but not too pissed either, like he was feeling Harvey out. Usually, Leonard would walk up and cuff him.

The carnie walked up to Leonard. "You guys wanna play?" she asked. "Two for one." Her voice sounded low and smooth, not at all like when she asked me. I found it exciting somehow.

Leonard smirked. "Sure, we wanna play."

The guys at his side laughed in short breathy gasps. I wasn't sure why, but something odd was playing itself out here. It was cool as all hell. Billy and Tracey watched intently.

Huge still chewed at his hotdog. Harvey stood deadpan, arms crossed over his barrel chest.

One of the other players, a dad with a couple little kids, said, "Let's get this game going. My kids are getting impatient."

Carnie girl glanced at him, rolled her eyes, and brought her attention back to Leonard. I enjoyed the way she stuck her chest out toward him. She was offering herself up to Leonard. My stomach squirmed with anticipation.

Leonard couldn't take his eyes off the area below her neck.

Harvey walked toward Leonard, arms still folded, his lips a thin line of anger. His black eyes danced and his head jerked like it might come off his shoulders.

"Get outta here, Leonard," Harvey said softly—too softly. "Ma will get hers if she tries to punish me for not doing my chores."

Leonard didn't say anything but he didn't back down. His two buddies turned to him, expectant.

"You wanna end up like Mumford?" Harvey asked quietly.

Leonard's eyes narrowed. Like a light flickering on, those eyes turned bigger and the whites became clear. I had no idea who Mumford was, but Leonard did, and it scared him.

"Harvey?" Huge asked. "Mumford, ain't that your dog?"

Harvey didn't bother to answer Huge. He stared at Leonard with those black eyes, his head still twitching away like something in there wanted out.

Backing away, Leonard pointed at Harvey. "Watch yourself, fag." But his heart wasn't in it.

One of his friends asked, "What about the chick? You gonna let Harvey ruin our night?"

Leonard mumbled, "We'll catch her later. I got shit to do."

Carnie girl rolled her eyes and strode back into the tent with long strides of her long skinny legs, to start the next round of Bingo, disappointment dulling her features.

I think we were all wondering what'd happened. Bad shit was happening inside Harvey, but none of us were about to ask him about it. He was obviously ass-capped mad.

"Come on," Harvey said. "I got a job for us. Follow me."

The freak show. It happened after ten o'clock every night the carnival was in town. They didn't let anyone under twenty-one in, which made it more tantalizing to us. We'd never gotten in but Harvey wanted to try.

We knelt out back of the tent and hid behind hay bales. Harvey said someone told him the freaks entered from back here. Crept out of one of the trailers and walked right by this very spot.

I'd heard Dad telling one of his friends he'd seen a three-titted woman. Damned if I didn't want to see her. We all did, except maybe Tracey. I hoped there would be two sets of cleavage—and three pointy nipples.

A scent wafting toward us made my nose wrinkle with disgust, smelling like fresh manure, like someone'd rolled around in it, like dog shit on the bottom of a shoe.

"What's that smell?" Tracey hissed. "Smells like ass."

"Smells like a barn," Huge added. "Maybe them freaks got animals to use in the show."

Billy's eyes widened. "Like one of them shows where the women mate with animals?"

"Screw that," I said. I wasn't sure what he meant but I didn't care.

"No," Harvey said seriously, almost reverently, "that shit happens in Mexico. It's illegal here."

The scent grew stronger, and a man, at least the upper half of him was a man, the lower half was a goat, walked into view. He walked past us, oblivious to our presence, and disappeared into the back of the big canvas tent.

"Was he for real?" Tracey whispered.

Harvey said, "No, a trick."

"Sure smelled real," Billy said. "Do all freak shows smell so bad?"

Another scent wafted to us. This time, at least in comparison to the rotting stench of the last guy, the smell was fresh like cut flowers—intoxicating.

"This is it," Harvey said. "She's coming."

"Who?" Billy asked.

"The three-titted woman," Harvey hissed. "You stupid or what?"

A volley of screams erupted from the Zipper. *Smells Like Teen Spirit* blared from the Hurricane.

A little person with a long beard appeared out of the darkness, a heavy-looking axe on his shoulder, and entered the tent.

The scent grew stronger, as if born on the wind, like sex magic. The thrill of the carnival mixed with the thrill of seeing things no kid should ever see, combined to work us into a frenzy. The figures we'd seen mixed with what I'd experienced in Buck Hill. The blood oath had been our own little freak show. Dizzy and out of control, like a horrible disease that blew on the wind.

"She's coming," Harvey repeated breathlessly, like he was in cardiac arrest.

My stomach hurt with anticipation and guilt. We shouldn't be here. My old man and all our teachers were probably inside.

Everything stilled until a gentle breeze rustled the oak leaves and a figure stepped from the darkness. Her body shone like a diamond, glistening in the moonlight. A goddess. She wore only lace panties, which covered hardly anything, and a small towel around her breasts. She didn't notice us. Surely we weren't the first guys to hide here. Maybe she was intoxicated too. She shimmied away from her towel.

The three-titted woman, my mind screamed.

Harvey stood. "I'm gonna rip that towel right off her and touch her privates." He sounded like a monster, his voice low and guttural. Even in the dark, the silhouette's head ticked up and down.

Billy was breathing hard, and I had no idea what he'd do. Would he follow Harvey and violate this woman? Or would he come to his senses? More importantly, would I?

Tracey said, "Screw you guys." She made to leave, standing up and taking a few tentative steps. She looked over her shoulder like she wanted to say something. Her eyes went from Harvey to the woman.

Huge grunted from somewhere behind me. I wasn't sure if he was scared or aroused. Harvey moved stealthily toward her. Billy made to follow him.

Unbelievably, this was gonna happen. The other day we were naive young men, but all of a sudden, lust overpowered us. We wanted to touch this woman. A poor lady who couldn't make a living any other way because she had three tits.

Harvey confronted her. "Hold it right there," he said. "I got money. We want a private show."

Harvey made me feel creepy, and the urge to do the right thing overtook me. I panicked and stood up, waving my arms wildly. "Look out. Run for the tent."

The goddess looked in my direction with wide white eyes, turned back to Harvey and Billy, and clutched the towel tighter to her body. A slump of her shoulders told me she hated her life. The goddess looked ready to give up, maybe roll over and die.

Luckily, a male voice from behind yelled, "You kids get the hell outta here before I call the cops."

The man who'd shouted came running out of the dark trees. He was gargantuan, with big rippling muscles, way bigger than even Huge or Harvey. Dressed in nothing but tiger's skin, he gave chase. He looked pissed, like he loved the three-titted woman. I understood because I cared for Jewel like that, despite her peculiarities. Maybe Jewel didn't have three tits but she was different—a freak in her own beautiful way.

Harvey and Billy held their ground for a moment before Billy hauled ass, following Huge and Tracey, who'd already took off. Harvey was alone. I thought Harvey would charge the guy, fight him over the three-titted woman. I recalled the blood, the skull from the blood oath, and poor Mumford lying dead in the woods.

"Where the fuck you guys think you're going?" Harvey bellowed after the gang. He looked back toward the tough-man. Thankfully, he didn't have his weapon.

"Get outta here," the tough guy repeated. "You some kinda lil' pervert?"

Harvey twitched, his eyes glowing in the moonlight. Holding ground for another moment, however, Harvey turned and jogged toward the midway. He glanced once over his shoulder, growled like a feral cannibal, his head twitching, and disappeared around the corner of the tent.

I crouched lower behind the hay, too scared to move.

The tough-guy approached the three-titted woman slowly, with a tenderness that belied his massive frame. She turned to him and hugged him, buried her head in his chest— her hero. He took the robe he carried in one hand, opened it, and placed it around her lovely body. She clung to him and sobbed, sad and mournful.

"It's okay," the tough-guy said, "I'm here, baby." He led her back the way they'd come. I found satisfaction there'd be no show tonight. In fact I felt a sharp kinship to these two. As they snuck away, I imagined Jewel and myself.

I snuck away through the dark trees. The shadows didn't seem so bad anymore. They hid me and my shame for witnessing such behavior. The soft moan from the shadows didn't even interest me. I wanted to go home. I wanted Jewel.

Chapter 5

Lockers opening and closing cascaded around me like cymbals. The routine background noise barely fazed me anymore.

That day I noticed it even less.

I opened my own locker, placed my backpack inside. I stood staring like an idiot. Jewel's locker sat exactly ten lockers down from my own. I glanced at it, nervous and excited. Loneliness emanated from it like radiation as it stood empty and alone. My stomach felt like it might bleed. I'd crossed a line with Harvey at the freak show but Jewel somehow made it go away.

I tried hard to remember what time she usually got to school.

I went straight to her home-room. Jewel sometimes sat there, alone. I stuck my head inside, casually, pretending to be hanging out. I quickly scanned the room. Jewel's assigned seat sat empty. Like her locker, loneliness rose from it like heat vapors. My heart sank; I tried to shake it off. I remembered the gym. Sometimes she sat in the bleachers and read. I ran down the stairs as kids poured in the front doors, and I quickly darted through the gym doors.

Jewel looked up from her book, annoyed by the disruption. But her mouth broke into a small smile.

"Hi," I said nonchalantly.

Jewel wrung her hands together and smirked like she knew I'd been searching for her. "Hello," she said slowly. "How was your weekend?"

I shrugged.

"Did you steal anything?" she asked, staring me in the eye as she waited.

"Hell no," I said. Luckily it was the truth but I sure as hell wasn't gonna tell her about the freak show.

"Sit next to me," she said, patting the bench.

My heart beat so fast I almost passed out. Confused, I picked a spot close to her but not so close my leg touched hers, even though I wanted to.

She scooted over until we touched. With both hands, she brushed back her hair.

She wore long sleeves, so her bruises were covered. I was relieved but I didn't like her having to hide

"They're still there, in case you're wondering," Jewel stated blandly.

I looked away for a moment, and bravely turned back to her face. "I know."

A shimmer of tears in her eyes moved me. Jewel took a deep breath. She still offered no explanation for the bruises, but said, "At least I haven't scared you off yet." She reached out and put a hand on my leg, this time square on my thigh.

I feared I might seize up and die, my heart pounding and my stomach aching, but I quickly regained control. I'd been thinking about her so much, I didn't feel strange anymore. I could act normal. "Of course not," I managed.

"You don't know me that good yet," she said, "but time will tell." Jewel squeezed my thigh. "Did you go to the carnival?"

My heart lurched. I nodded feebly.

"Was Harvey there?"

I shrugged, but maintained eye-contact.

To my surprise, she said, "It's okay. I didn't expect you not to go to the carnival. It only comes once a year."

"How come you didn't go?" I asked.

"You didn't ask me," she said, looking me right in the eye, a small smile playing on her lips.

I was mortified. I'd wanted Jewel there with me, but at the same time I didn't.

"It's okay," she said, squeezing my knee. "Mom wouldn't have let me go, anyway. She says the carnival, especially the freak show, is the devil's playground."

Her mother might be right. "I would've liked to have been there with you."

Jewel smiled bigger, a shimmer of moisture coating her eyes. "Would you have taken me on the Ferris Wheel?" she asked.

We knew what happened at the top of the Ferris Wheel. Some of the heat from my groin broke off to rush to my face. I nodded.

With a squeeze of my knee, Jewel leaned over and kissed my cheek. "Thank you, she said. "I can tell you're not lying. Maybe next year."

I didn't trust myself to speak.

Jewel looked at me seriously. "You took a stand, didn't you?"

"What?" I asked.

"At the carnival," she stated, "against Harvey."

"How did you..?"

"How did I know?" she asked. "Sometimes I just know. I'm sensitive about things like this." She glanced at her arms.

I shrugged, not knowing, as usual, what to say.

"It's okay," she said. "You don't have to tell me. I'm proud of you. It makes me want to be with you more."

Be with me?

She smiled, leaned over and kissed my cheek again. "I enjoy your silence most, Jason," she said. "No wasted words. Sometimes words aren't necessary. They get in the way."

I smiled.

Jewel edged closer to me, her whole side wedged against mine. Her left breast mashed against my ribs.

"You wanna hang out at lunch time?" I asked.

With a sad face, she said, "I'd like to but I have a— appointment over lunch. Maybe tomorrow?"

The bell rang.

With a quick kiss, this time to my chin, Jewel jumped up. "If I'm late again, I'll probably get expelled." She glanced at her arms. "See you after school?"

Hell yes, I'd see her.

"Good," she said with a smile. "You make my brain tingle something fierce." She flew out the gym door and disappeared.

I composed myself before heading to class. I felt happy, content, maybe even thrilled.

At lunch, I wandered about the halls of our school in a daze. I stayed inside, because I didn't wanna run into Harvey but it was also easier to think about Jewel while I was alone. Encapsulated by thoughts of her, I fathomed no one else.

When a hand touched my shoulder, every instinct in my body needed it to be her. I turned, leaning into it, drawing near enough to be close to her and see those blue eyes.

Billy backed away, his own eyes wild. "Dude, you going gay or what?"

I backed away as quick, mortified. "I thought you were someone else."

Billy slid his index finger through the hole made by his left hand. "You thought I was Jewel," he said, laughing.

"Shut up before I punch you in the goddamn mouth." Friendship only went so far.

"You and what army?" he asked. Uncertainty crept over him. Harvey usually fought his battles for him.

I took advantage of his hesitation and shoved him, hard. I was still pissed from the night before. He and Harvey would've groped that poor woman.

Billy wasn't a fighter, especially without Harvey around, so he attempted to smooth things. "Whoa, Jason, okay man, calm down," he said. "I'm teasing."

"Sorry, I'm a little edgy."

"Why?"

"I don't know," I said. "What do you care? You said I didn't need you no more. You didn't even talk to me at the carnival."

Billy looked away, indicating he was lying. "I was fooling," he said. "Fuck the carnival. We're boys—for always."

I wondered about his angle but I ignored it for the moment. "Let's put it behind us."

"No problem," he said, "don't sweat it." Billy seemed grateful for the reprieve. His eyes widened like he'd remembered something. "Harvey wants us all outside," he said. "He has something for all of us."

The pit of my stomach felt empty. Harvey, the last person I wanted to see. I understood why Billy looked guilty. "What kind of job is it?"

Billy shrugged. "Probably bullshit, head across the street, take cards from the little kids or something."

His eyes faltered with another lie. I frowned but went along to see. I needed something to keep my mind off Jewel, anyway, and since she wouldn't be back to school until after lunch, she couldn't hate me for hanging out with Harvey. Besides, no way was I gonna do anything stupid.

Billy and I strutted across the black asphalt with purpose, past the picnic tables where the high-school kids were meant to hang, across the narrow street, all the way to the playground where the little kids played and eyed us warily. I'd always been convinced we were the good guys but Jewel made me question my opinion. I wondered what Mom would have to say about the whole matter.

I was sure she'd hate it, also.

Even though it was early, the heat from the sun already reflected off from the black asphalt. Billy's shirt, laden with pit rings, made him look slovenly.

I scanned the crowd and saw Harvey, most of our gang already gathered around him as if worshipping a god. They quit speaking as Billy and I approached. Billy drifted away from me to stand by Harvey. My stomach turned; my instincts told me to run. They had quit speaking too fast, and besides, Billy almost never left my side. *Freak show.*

For the first time, I felt alone. Betrayed.

Harvey twirled his finger over his head, signaling a private discussion. My stomach lurched.

Harvey, notorious for his private discussions, stood with hands on his hips. He called these discussions the "goat in the middle." Harvey, the sole bearer of responsibility for the gang's discipline, was a firm and unforgiving practitioner. It'd always kept most of us under his thumb, out of fear—fear of taking a beating. Fear of the blood oath.

Small flames danced over the surface of the tar, an optical illusion.

Harvey grinned one last time before he turned around and knelt in front of a mound of—something. The mound was on fire, also. I didn't need to get too close before I smelled it, the burning flesh. Harvey'd scooped together a big pile of earthworms from the asphalt, piled them, and set them ablaze.

The gang remained in the circle, looking over Harvey's shoulder. Tracey frowned like she bit into something sour. Billy's eyes were wide with amazement. Huge was harder to read, arms crossed, features non-committal, like he didn't care.

How did he do that? Do worms burn? I glanced at the empty Mountain Dew can next to the flaming pile. He'd poured gas brought from home. Poor Mumford. What kind of end had he met? I should go home and tell Mom but we liked to solve our own problems. We knew Harvey was going off the deep end but I refused to show my fear.

He was bad—evil. The poor worms writhed in pain, struggling to find relief, wishing they'd stayed in the wet ground. If their voices were audible, those poor bastards would've been screaming. The earthworms were bad. The act made me feel sick but it wasn't the worst part. The worst part was when Harvey stood up and turned back around. He knew I'd seen it all. His eyes reflected death, black holes in his head. Harvey's pupils were so dilated they covered even the color of his eyes, like at the carnival, but worse, like he was enjoying himself—getting off somehow.

Harvey gazed with no expression, like he didn't even see me. He drooled wet strings from his mouth like Novocain was injected in there. He never said a word.

Young men don't understand about insanity. I should have walked away from the gang entirely, right there.

The other members looked from me to Harvey. They considered me with a solemn respect—I was one of their own, after all. Harvey grinned, and on his command, they surrounded me. The goat in the middle this time, I would find out what it was like on this side of the fence. My heart beat so fast it felt like it might explode. The worms had been meant as intimidation, but I was damned if I'd show any reservations.

Harvey strutted inside the circle next to me like a bull peacock. Sweat glistened on his brow from the flames. His pits were stained too and I smelled his rich hormonal stench.

You need deodorant boy. I grinned, which infuriated Harvey.

"What you grinning about, Jason?" he demanded. "You wanna get your ass kicked? Wanna end up like them bastards?" He pointed at the still-smoldering pile of crispy bodies.

I refused to show fear. Among the elite, even if out of favor at the moment, I had a reputation to uphold. So, I made a small waving gesture with my right hand, a clear indication of my ambivalence.

Harvey frowned, his small sallow eyes glowering. "I'm not sure I appreciate your attitude, Jason," he said. "I for sure didn't last night."

I nearly laughed at his attempt to sound sophisticated. Still, I didn't want a confrontation. "Let's not fight, man. We're all boys, huh? I'm sorry about last night, about the three-titted woman." But I wasn't—not in the least.

Harvey straightened his beefy shoulders, emboldened by my apparent lack of courage. He glanced at the other kids; they knew and all smiled. Even Billy smirked with a nervous, twitching grin. He didn't appear as sure of my intentions as Harvey—he knew me better. Tracey watched me intently, no smile, curious, as if wondering what would play out.

Harvey raised his head and bumped my chest with his. I coughed at his fetid breath and the feral stink of his body. He said, "I think you're down to two choices, Jason."

Harvey's voice reminded me of a snake. Even though he wasn't the sharpest tool in the shed, he could be dangerous, especially if he felt his control start to slip away.

I chose my response carefully. "Okay, what are they?"

He eyed me with a suspicious stare. He let out a small grunt, as if his brain worked overtime to figure out if I was serious or being a smart-ass. Then Harvey grinned like a boy who'd won a sparring match. "I like your cooperation," he said smoothly. "You aren't pussy-whipped like Billy here thinks."

I shot a glare at Billy. He shuffled to his right, placing Harvey back in between us.

Harvey smiled. He knew he'd pissed me off.

I stayed silent.

"It's simple, buddy. Your loyalty to the gang has come into question. You can make this all go away by proving yourself. Walk over to those kids and demand our toll. Go collect." He pointed at a group of little kids playing marbles in the sand. "Everyone's entitled to a letdown occasionally. Especially you, since your Mom's a shrink. Go make it right."

I already knew what the other option was, but I stalled. "And if I won't?"

Harvey grinned big and smacked his fist into his palm. He pointed to the worms. "We're gonna kick your ass and take ya down to Buck Hill." I didn't like the implication.

He moved closer to me to prove his point, obvious he expected the rest of the gang to do the same. They didn't break the circle but they didn't get any closer either.

One on one, I wasn't scared of Harvey. But the whole gang together—an entirely different matter. I considered my two options: fight or collect the marbles. I searched everywhere for Jewel.

Harvey pumped another fist into his palm.

I let out my breath and shook my head, frustrated. What would one more time hurt, right? I pushed two of the members of the gang out of the way—they nearly fell over. I headed toward the second graders and hated myself as I walked.

Billy said, "I told you, see, he ain't pussy-whipped."

I glared at Billy.

He shut his mouth.

I kicked rocks ahead of me as I walked down the road to hell. Heat radiated from the asphalt up through my shoes. The kids glanced nervously as I got closer. They tried to ignore me but they couldn't. They knew the drill. We stole from them, we protected them, and they lived with it. If they couldn't live with it, they got their asses kicked too.

I made sure Jewel hadn't made it to school. The last thing I wanted was for her to see me. Not seeing her, I approached the kids. I spoke softly. "Hey, guys."

One of the younger boys looked up nervously. He said, "Um, hey, Jason."

I cleared my throat and held out my hand. The boys handed me two marbles. None of them made eye contact. They knew they were being extorted but they didn't have a choice.

After collecting, I walked back to the group. I sauntered and played it cool, not wanting to rush. Harvey stood with a smile on his grubby mug and his hand out.

"Give 'em, Jason," Harvey demanded. "You did real good, buddy, but you need to give 'em to me."

Harvey twitched in anticipation of the reaping. His pupils were huge in a weird brutal way. His chest heaved with emotional exertion.

Worms, blood oath, a three-titted woman . . . Mumford.

I handed all but two to Harvey. This wasn't the way it worked but I did it anyway.

Harvey accepted the marbles like they were manna from god, reverently holding them in the palm of his hands, his glossy large-pupiled pig eyes ogling them like they were a naked woman or something. Maybe they were his own dark magic. His head twitched like a Mexican jumping bean. But eventually, he shifted his stare to the pair in my hand like he wasn't sure what to do about them. His eyes cleared. "Okay, keep 'em. I made you prove yourself and you came through. Keep 'em."

It wasn't what I'd expected. I tossed the marbles in my hand as I pondered what to do. I took Easy Road. "Thanks, Harvey."

It's funny; the impact two little words can have on a man's life.

The group let out a collective sigh of relief. Maybe all could be normal.

I turned to look at the school parking lot once more, just in time to see the door of a rusty Chevette with black tinted windows open. Jewel stepped out—she glared directly at me.

Chapter 6

Our schools, bordered on three sides by a thirty-acre grove, gave a rural impression despite being in town. The grove, a tangle of dying Jack Pine—turned red due to the budworm demise—and scrub oak was off limits, technically. But I only needed to wait until the playground attendant, damn near blind, turned her back. No one cared, one way or the other, what the seniors did anyway.

Within the most tangled section of overgrowth is where we built our fort back when we were little kids, made of dead Jack Pine branches. The long-dead branches on the roof did a great job of keeping the snow and rain out, so you could sit on the floor without getting too muddy. Most of the gang had forgotten about the fort but not me. I took great pride in it. Times changed. We used to build a new one every fall. Anyway, I was confident I would have it to myself. And I did.

The fort was the only place I could escape Jewel, for a little while anyway. But I would eventually have to face her if I wanted to mend things. My stomach hurt, ashamed of myself. Jewel witnessing my actions made the situation unbearable. I didn't understand the feelings ripping at me but I'd done serious damage to my relationship with her.

Pine needles crunched beneath my feet. Quiet, the din from the playground muted by the tall pines and thick Aspen stands, the somber woods matched my mood. I always needed to listen closely for the school bell; every year someone got detention for being tardy. A red squirrel scavenged from the hodgepodge of trash we left in the fort. It scurried away as I approached and chattered at me from the safety of the heights.

I bent down and duck-walked through the crude opening we used as a door. I sat on one of the seven rusty lawn chairs, scavenged so many years ago. I put my head in my hands. The bell would ring in a few minutes but I needed the time to think. The worst part was my next class was American Lit— and Jewel would be there. Last night I fantasized about passing her a note in class, but my actions on the playground halted the romance. I could apologize but would she believe I was sincere? She'd given me fair warning and I blew it, taking Easy Road.

"Thanks, Harvey."

The words I'd used on the playground rang in my head.

The sounds of footfalls brought me out of my doldrums. Someone else had the same idea about visiting the fort. My heart skipped a beat. Could it be Jewel? I closed my eyes, tried to picture her walking through the grove, and her red hair as it dangled over her sunken blue eyes. I couldn't quite conjure her image.

Even with all the time I spent thinking about her the past twenty-four hours, I never considered telling Jewel about the fort. It seemed inappropriate and taboo. There was something so temporary about Jewel—like she might be whisked away at any moment like a mist, like a daydream. I instinctively knew that anything precarious enough to raise my fears had no business in the fort—my safe place. Maybe Jewel's translucence of spirit reminded us all next year didn't exist, not at this school. Next year, we were off to college—or God knew where. Anyway, it'd be a new set of problems for all of us. None of us wanted to think of it. Maybe I feared what she harbored in her soul might be contagious—a slow-burning disease eating one's life a little more each day. I shook it off, knowing I could help resurrect her.

The footsteps grew closer. Whoever made them walked directly for the fort, and knew their way. I held my breath. I wanted it to be Jewel, but anybody would be better than Harvey. Rugged leather hiking boots told me it wasn't either of them. Tracey ducked and crawled into the fort. She plopped into the chair and frowned.

Tracey wasn't mean, but she was blunt, and one of the most complete tomboys I ever knew. She kept her blonde hair long but messy, and sometimes even stole her old man's chew tin. Tracey could collect the toll as good as, or better than, any of us and therefore quickly became one of Harvey's favorites. Equally good at holding up the gang's pledge of protection, no one crossed Tracey. She was too tough and fair.

She glowered with her dark brown eyes, almost black. "What?" I asked uncomfortably.

Tracey smirked and spat chew juice on the floor. "You need to talk?"

Tracey didn't miss much.

"Do I look bad?" I asked.

Tracey leaned back in her chair and crossed her legs, much as Mom did when about to break out her psychologists' bag of tricks. "Dude, you look like you lost your best friend," she said, "and like a warmed over lump of shit."

The truth—I didn't have a best friend, besides Billy. But nobody knew. For the first time, I understood most of my time with the gang came at the expense of others. We formed purposeful relationships, means to an end. We worked toward a common goal that never reached the level of best friends. Perhaps Jewel could be different *IF*.

It remained a big IF, a gigantic cross to bear.

I answered, "I'm tired of all the taking. Next year we go off into a different world, right? If we act like this we'll get our asses kicked—arrested probably." I hoped my answer placated her.

Tracey's scowl deepened. She coughed and spat a wad of fibrous juice onto the floor. She spat again and a Skoal Bandit followed suit. She dug in her pocket for another. Tracey chewed Skoal like I ate candy. "You're so full of shit. You aren't worried about next year. You're pissed because the chick saw you collect the toll."

I eyeballed her with a suspicious glare. Was she here for me or did she represent the gang? "That too, I guess."

"I ain't guessing shit. My big brother looked like this when he met his first serious girl."

I stammered, "Jewel isn't my girl."

Tracey waved her hand. "You're eighteen years old. Stop the bullshit. You like her, maybe wanna kiss her. Maybe more than kiss."

"No, I—"

She waved me off and kicked a clump of pine needles. "You can lie to Harvey, he's stupid. But don't lie to me. I don't give a shit. If you like the girl, you should hang with her. Like you said, this gang'll be together for another month and a half, and we're done. Fuck Harvey. He changed for the worse. Last night at the carnival was the last straw for me."

"I think Harvey might be going nuts," I said, "maybe ass-capped mad."

"This gang shit is going to his head, like he thinks we're a big deal or something," she said. "Last week he pulled a knife on a little kid to collect toll. The poor little shit pissed himself."

I shook my head. I hadn't heard the rumor yet but I wasn't surprised. "Oh, man, he's gonna get us sent down the river. I should've stood up to him. Someone has to or we're heading for some bad shit. Jewel's pissed, and I blew it with her today."

"Hey," Tracey said, "wanna hear something else real fucked up? I guess Harvey's sister went missing last night. They're saying she might've run off with a carnie."

"Who said that?" I asked. Harvey cowing Leonard, the threats to their mother, the worms, and poor old Mumford—and all the other bad shit, too, came flooding back to me.

"Huge heard it from Leonard, I guess," she answered. "You think she ran off with a carnie?"

Fuck no, I didn't think that. I didn't have to answer her, though.

"Me either," Tracey said, her eyes never leaving mine. "I think Harvey did something to her. Huge said they found her purse in the tall-grass next to Buck Hill."

Harvey was going to hell in a hand basket. If we didn't do something about it, he was gonna take us with him. "Maybe she'll turn up, you know, if she did run off."

Tracey agreed without conviction. "Maybe she's off getting knocked up."

I wanted to change the subject—bad. "I should've stood up to him."

Tracey shrugged. "I was disappointed. If anyone is ever gonna cross Harvey, it should be you. We'd all follow your lead."

"Now you tell me," I moaned.

"Never too late," Tracey said. She slugged me in the shoulder. "If you like Jewel, go patch it up. Stop pouting like a baby."

We laughed.

I felt much better. The bell rang and we headed to class. I hoped Harvey wouldn't continue being a problem.

My seat resided two forward and one row over from where Jewel sat, making it difficult to make eye contact with her. I got into class late and she was already seated. Turned around in my seat, I smiled at her.

She ignored me completely, feigning ambivalence, but obviously angry.

She read from a novel, Susan Cooper's *Dark Is Rising*. Gauze on her forearms held in place by medical tape. My heart sank to see her hurt; I wanted to help her, to make her life okay. I felt the butterflies seeking an exit from my belly—my insides hurt. Not knowing what to do, I took my seat.

The teacher, Mrs. Melchen, told us to get our American Lit books out. The class came alive with the shuffling of books. I took the opportunity to rip a piece of paper out of my notebook, knowing the sound would be camouflaged. Mrs. Melchen, seasoned well enough to recognize notepaper when she heard it, could be a bitch.

At the time, she'd been in the habit of intercepting notes being passed. The week before, a girl had been forced to hand over a note passed to her by the most nerdish kid in our class. The note, a complete profession of his love, got read in front of the class.

The girl didn't come to school the next day.

I scribbled on the paper I'd torn out, covering what I'd already written with my notebook. I didn't consider myself a writer of fine prose, but I held my own. I kept it brief.

Justin Holley

Jewel,

I've been thinking about you a lot. I was sad when you saw me take toll. I made a mistake. I won't be taking the toll from anybody no more. Please still hang with me. Do you like me?   Yes   No

I like you. A lot. Jason

I glanced at Mrs. Melchen to see if she was watching.

One of my classmates, who had a question, distracted her, so I considered myself safe.

I folded the note like a football and tossed it with a gentle motion. The note plopped on top of Jewel's open book. Jewel, not even blinking, took the note and slid it inside a folder. She resumed reading. Devastated, my heart sank. I knew she hated me.

I sat quiet for a moment, my heart thumping in my chest, my ears ringing and hot with my emotions. I chanced another look at her and she leaned the opposite direction. Maybe my immature paranoia was rearing its head, but it felt real. I whispered her name.

Jewel flinched, a slight reaction. She tried hard—too hard—to ignore me.

"Jewel," I whispered louder.

Students behind me started whispering her name also, either to help or mock. Either way, it caused far too much confusion and noise.

"Jason," Mrs. Melchen said. I cringed and turned with a slow motion toward the front of the room. She had her hand on her hips. I hoped she hadn't seen the note. "Could you stop chattering, please? I'm helping a student."

"Yes, ma'am," I replied.

She watched me. A kid behind me snickered.

Mrs. Melchen stood up straight, and the snickering stopped. "Maybe I need to send someone to see the principal."

Shit.

Jewel raised her hand and spoke with a silken voice. "It's not Jason's fault," she said. "He was returning the notebook I let him borrow. I ignored him because I was reading." She held up her notebook.

Mrs. Melchen resembled a confused dog. "Thank you, Jewel. Sorry if I was too abrupt, Jason."

My smile felt like it might split my face in half.

Mrs. Melchen turned back to the student at her desk.

Jewel rolled her eyes and continued reading.

But I knew she cared.

As soon as the bell rang, Jewel scooped up her books and headed for the door. My anxiety ran on overtime. I hollered for her.

Jewel kept walking and I ran to touch her shoulder.

Jewel whirled around so quick it scared me. Her eyes were fierce. "Don't ever touch me unless I ask you to, understand?"

I put my hands up. "I'm sorry. I wanna talk to you."

Jewel's voice came out raspy. "I figured you'd get it when I didn't move my lips."

"What do you mean? Get what?" I asked.

Jewel rolled her eyes. "I don't wish to speak to you."

I was confused. "But you lied to Mrs. Melchen for me."

"I would have lied for anyone." She walked away.

My heart sank. I struggled through the last two agonizing hours of the day and went straight home, dejected.

Chapter 7

The rain started as I got home. The noise it made off the tin roof of my tree fort sounded like a set of cymbals. I liked the noise because it enhanced my depression and drowned out the world. I pretended I was the last boy on earth. If Jewel could be the last girl, I might have a chance. I had to stop thinking about it because it served to depress me further.

I reread, probably for the hundredth time, one of my Colossus comics. It was my favorite, especially today. Everything comes with a price and The Colossus, at the end, watches his girl sail away with another man, a mortal, crushing all joy of being a super-hero. He saved her, but she would never know it.

The Colossus and I cried together.

My mood reached dangerous proportions of bad. Two days before, I'd thought girls—with the exception of Tracey—

were a necessary evil. The carnie girls excited me but they didn't count.

I let out my breath, the tinny taste of self-induced rejection bitter in my mouth.

I considered speaking with Mom about Jewel.

I made up my mind—having a psychologist for a mother needed to pay off for once.

The rungs of the tree fort ladder felt slimy from the rain so I held on tighter than usual. The rain pelted me as I ran for the house, but also obscured the noise I made sliding the deck-door open. Entering, I slid the door shut quietly and wiped my feet.

It was more silent than normal in my house, like someone tried extra hard to be quiet. Not even the television could be heard, unusual. The quietness made me whisper. "Mom?"

"Oh, you're kidding me, honey, poor girl. Does Jason know?" Dad spoke in a hushed tone.

My mom let out her breath. "No—no he doesn't, and to be honest, I'm not sure what to do."

"You have to tell him, don't you?" Dad sounded concerned.

Mom paused. "I'm not sure. Confidentiality is tricky."

"But he likes her. He's going to ask questions. What if he asks her about the bruises and cuts?"

Tiny needles of dread poked at my stomach. They were speaking about Jewel. I crept closer to their bedroom door.

Mom spoke anxiously. "She can explain what she wants."

"She's not going to tell him the truth. She's hitting and cutting herself, why would she tell him about that?"

My blood froze. I wanted to run in there and make them tell me everything, but I resisted my urge and edged nearer the door.

"She wouldn't, I don't think," she said. "Jewel doesn't even believe it's self-induced. But if she does, Jason's going to have a lot of questions anyway."

"What's her mom like, for God sake?" Dad sounded skeptical of her parenting skills.

"Lots of repressed emotion," she said. "She hardly spoke at all. She said Jewel needed help, and she was convinced Jewel was hurting herself. She needs help as bad as Jewel does, doesn't even keep herself clean. I smelled her from across the room."

Dad sighed. "Must be rough losing your dad and husband, especially after having a fight before. You think Jewel blames herself?"

Mom hesitated. "Probably, why else would she do this? Guilt is a very powerful motivator, and it sounds like she and her dad shouted the day he died. A teen might believe the fight played a part in his death. She claims she wakes up with the bruises and cuts, but that's not possible. She could be repressing the memories, but I don't know yet."

"Maybe until you do, it would be better not to tell Jason," he said. "Maybe whatever answers Jewel gives him will have to be sufficient."

I'd heard enough. I stepped around the corner and into their room, making the decision for them. "Not tell Jason what?"

I wept immediately.

Mom started, paused. "I'm sorry, you weren't supposed to hear that."

"But I did," I said. "When were you going to tell me she was your client?" My own guilt flowed freely. It threatened to wash my soul away with it. Jewel needed a friend, and I'd let her down.

Mom crossed the room and hugged me. "You know it was a secret."

I wiped my eyes. "I know," I said. "It sucks. I didn't know she was hurting herself. Why would she do that?" A horrible unbidden thought about Harvey surfaced. People *could* do terrible things—to themselves or otherwise.

"Sometimes bad things happen to people," Mom said. "Everyone reacts differently. Jewel's having a hard time right now."

I buried my face in Mom's shoulder. "Are you sure Jewel is hurting herself?" I asked.

Mom sighed, a deep mournful note. "We don't know for sure because she can't remember. Sometimes when people face horrible events, their brain blocks out the memories to save their mental health."

I'd been listening to her mental health psycho-babble for eighteen years but now I understood. "Can I talk to her about it? I don't want her to hurt herself anymore."

Mom hugged me. "Only if she brings it up first," she answered. "Otherwise, be her friend. She needs friendship more than anything. She lost her dad recently."

I teared up, and sadness pulled my gaze away.

Dad hugged me gently, sharing the moment with me.

I sniffed and wiped my nose on my shirt. "I'll do my best," I said. "I like her."

Mom hugged me too. "You're a strong young man. She needs your strength, but remember to keep her confidentiality."

"May I go to my room?" I asked.

"What about supper?" Dad asked, as expected.

"I'm not hungry."

Mom smiled. "Go ahead. I'm sure you have a lot to think about."

Closing my bedroom door, I whispered, "Jewel, please let me help you." I curled up on my side and extended my arm, pretending I held Jewel and protected her. I prayed for the first time in my life. "God, please watch over Jewel and keep her safe"

I awoke to the rain rapping my window as if hell bent on entrance. I opened one eye, blinked hard, discarding the sleep. A clap of thunder made me jump—loud as hell. Maybe the electricity had gone out. It made my room dank, like the moisture somehow seeped inside. My closet door stood open. Odd. I always closed it when I went to bed. The color of my carpet darkened somehow, like everything else. I chalked it up to the poor lighting.

My mouth pasty from worry, I wanted to get a drink.

I swung my legs off the bed and walked to my desk, one of the folding kinds with the wooden slats. I kept a package of sunflower seeds in there, which would help with my thirst. The desk, locked as always, looked normal. But the key— which I always kept in the lock—was gone. I bent over to search the floor, but the darkness made it too hard to see. The corner of my room darkened too, perhaps darker than normal.

I didn't usually wake up in the middle of the night.

Suddenly, a flash of lightening illuminated the corner like daytime. I jumped back onto my bed, startled. Someone stood in the corner. When the flash dissipated, so did the apparition, back into the darkness.

"Wh—who is it?" My little brother? But the figure stood too tall. No one answered. I repeated myself. "Who are you?" Goose bumps formed on my arms even though my room felt hot, rife with the summer air. I thought of Harvey and about vomited, pains of terror shooting through my shoulders. When nothing happened, I assumed I'd imagined the whole thing.

A flicker of movement in the corner made my heart lurch. A figure stepped out of the shadows. White bandages. A cold breath of air reached out to me, enveloped me like a glove. I shivered.

"Hi, Jason," she said.

My breathing stopped. How the hell did she get into my house? I was exhilarated and terrified all at the same time. I managed, "Hi . . . Jewel. How did you get in here?"

Jewel smiled. A friendlier smile than I remembered her having. "Don't be scared," she whispered. Her voice had a distant, echo-like quality. "I thought you liked me."

"I—I do like you," I said. "It's the middle of the night. How did you get here?"

She smiled. "Don't worry, Jason. Hold me." She crossed the room with a steady, easy saunter, and held out her gauzed arms to me.

I gently touched the coarse gauze, wanting to soothe her. A warming sensation spread in my stomach. "Does it hurt?"

She sat on my lap and wrapped her arms around my neck. "Not anymore," she said. "I'm here with you."

I returned her gentle embrace, and we rocked back and forth with a slight motion. I felt her in my lap, solid and real. My penis grew. Scared Jewel would feel it pressing against her, I shrunk away slightly. But it felt so good. I tried to adjust myself, to hide the lump in my boxers. At least I thought I put boxers on—perhaps I forgot. I stared at my white underwear visible beneath Jewel's hind end. I turned red and flushed in the dark room, both from embarrassment and my arousal

Jewel rocked in my lap. "Keep me safe," she whispered. "I only feel safe when I'm with you, now that Daddy's gone." She held me close and tight.

I breathed heavily, enjoying the unbearably pleasure like nothing I'd ever felt. "I wanna help you but maybe you could let go for a minute so we can talk?"

Jewel squeezed me tighter. "Don't you like me hugging you?"

"Of course I do, it's—"

Jewel stopped rocking.

I didn't want her to stop.

"It feels *soooo* good? Is that it?" The emphasis on "so" drove me wild.

"Yes," I whispered. "*Toooo* good."

Jewel smiled. "Good, I wanted it to." She rocked back and forth even harder.

I held Jewel tight as I thrust my hips, lost in pleasure.

I woke up, confused and sweaty, and quickly checked myself.

Disappointed Jewel wasn't with me, I was relieved not to explain this mess.

I stripped out of my boxers and stuffed them under the bed. The event left me confused, but the one thing I did know—I loved Jewel. I'd die for her.

Chapter 8

I rode my bike to school in order to arrive early. My dad said he'd buy me a car when I went to college, but not before. The attendant for the little kids gawked with a suspicious furl of the brow; she wasn't used to me getting to school so early, under the earliest time allowed. She let me pass, anyway. Good, because no way was I going to let Jewel get there before me.

I stood at my locker and rode a wave of newfound urgency. I had rehearsed what I would say to her, careful not to blurt out Mom thought Jewel hurt herself. I decided to play it by ear. Impromptu speeches could be dangerous, and I was inept at spurring dialogue on the spot. But I didn't know what else to do.

My locker door rattled as I hung my mirror on it. I checked my hair for the third time, having applied a bit of gel—usually something saved for weddings or school pictures.

I busied myself and calmed my nerves by smoothing out the rogue hairs. The errant hair made me think of my boner from the previous night. I chuckled.

"You are pretty funny looking. I'd laugh too." The voice came from behind me.

I whirled around, startled. I bumped my locker door, and the mirror unloosed from its moorings. It shattered on the ground. Shards like ice crystals cascaded around my feet.

"Seven years' bad luck, Jason. A shame." Her voice rang cold.

I glanced from her, to the broken mirror, and back to her. I covered my midsection with my hands. "Jewel, you're in early."

She stared at my hands, ignoring the gesture. "I need to get my homework. I've missed so many days." Her voice wasn't any warmer.

Thick black bruises encircled her forearms, a line of cuts etching away at the blackened skin. I wished she'd kept the gauze on.

Jewel broke my trance. "Didn't your mom teach you not to stare?"

Her mentioning Mom unnerved me. I wondered if she knew. "I'm sorry, it's . . ."

"It's hard to ignore something so ugly." Her eyes defied me to disagree.

"No, not at all," I said. "You're beautiful," I blurted.

Jewel's eyes softened. "I didn't mean me personally," she said. "I meant the cuts were ugly. But thank you."

I felt the familiar heat and knew I blushed.

Jewel smiled briefly. "You can be nice when you want to be." She walked away.

I ran after her. "Jewel, wait up. I *am* nice."

Jewel stopped and spoke turning around. "Do you suppose if I asked the little kids from the playground, they'd say you're nice?"

My stomach ached. I didn't want to tell her the truth. But she already knew the truth. "Oh no, they would say I take advantage of them, along with the rest of the gang."

Jewel whipped around, her eyes flashing. "I don't care about the rest of the gang. I care about you." Her eyes softened.

I wasn't sure if she meant she actually cared about me, or if she didn't like me including the rest of the gang by way of an excuse. I flushed anyway. "I'm done with the gang. I swear I am."

Jewel walked away. "Where have I heard that before?"

"I mean it this time." My voice sounded strained.

Jewel turned around with a curious expression. "People go back on what they say all the time. What I'm wondering, is why you even care what I think?"

I had no idea how to answer her question without sounding mushy. "I do care . . . a lot. I—" My mouth hung open as more words wouldn't come.

Jewel shook her head. "Obviously you care. Why? Why do you care? Because I'm cut up and bruised? Are you going to be my white knight, Jason?" Her voice dripped with venom.

I glanced at her bruises and back at her eyes, which flashed with a ferocious light. Her pupils danced like shadows—like they were alive. "You're all I can think about." It had slipped out, but it was out nonetheless. The elephant sat huge in the room. I put my hand over my mouth, as if in shock of what I did.

Jewel was speechless—an answer she didn't expect. She trembled slightly and frowned. A tear escaped one lonely eye, making its way slowly down her cheek like a snake. "You think about me? Why?" Her voice sounded distant.

I started to speak a couple times, and changed my mind twice. "I don't know," I said honestly. "It makes me feel good to think of you."

"You took a long time to answer me. Do you care about me?" Her quiet voice sounded breathy, like someone taken completely by surprise. Her face contorted into the curious look I'd grown familiar with.

"I care about you a lot." The last word trailed off in a squeak.

She shook her head. "No," she whispered. "Nobody cares about me. I'm a loser." Jewel ran up the stairs toward homeroom.

The stairway extended longer than normal. Mud from Jewel's shoes had tarnished the otherwise spotless steps; mud from a driveway I hadn't even seen yet. Morris, our gangster janitor, would scowl at the work it created.

The dirt was the least of my worries.

The image of those bruises and cuts kept me moving forward, despite being scared as hell. I wasn't sure exactly what scared me more, rejection or the truth behind Jewel's scars. My words always failed me at the most inopportune times. I climbed the steps slowly, finding those words—the right ones.

The trail of mud, scattered about like tiny pieces of rat food, led into our homeroom. I didn't have a clue if Jewel wanted me around or not, but I was committed to seeing this through—wherever it led me. Upon entering the room, much like entering a black tunnel barely big enough for me to get myself into, it swallowed me. Once inside, I couldn't turn back. My stomach churned and bile burned my esophagus. I took a deep breath to suppress my anxiety.

Jewel, hidden from view as I entered the homeroom, sobbed from her hiding place. Her sobs resonated and floated around the room as if produced from no one spot in particular, disembodied and vague. I walked toward the spot they'd be coming from.

I approached the reading nook where Mrs. Melchen used to read to us when we were younger. A former lifetime of goofing off while listening to stories.

The sobs grew louder as I entered the nook. Jewel sat in the oversized beanbag chair, her tears dripping on a sheet of drawing paper she held on her lap. Her tear-reddened eyes searched me for sincerity, seeming to invite me if I was sure I wanted to be a part of her difficult life, perhaps daring me. The beanbag chair shifted under my weight as I sat next to her.

"Hi," I muttered, unsure what else to say.

Jewel sniffed and wiped the tears from her eyes.

I imagined myself doing it for her. Maybe I should have.

"Hi," she sobbed. "Sorry I'm such a mess." She wiped her face.

This time I reached over and caught one of her tears with my index finger, before it could drip off her chin. "What's wrong?" I asked, blunt and to the point. I mentally gave myself a swift kick to the ass.

She smiled briefly. "It's nice to have someone care— people don't seem to care about me anymore." She cried.

Her dad died recently but I also promised Mom I wouldn't bring it up. I used one of Mom's tricks and stayed silent, determined not to stick my foot in my mouth.

Jewel pulled a tissue from her back pocket and wiped her eyes. She needed the tissues a lot lately.

Jewel continued, "I had to move from my old school, but I didn't have friends there either."

She aroused my morbid curiosity. "Why?"

Another tear trickled down her cheek. "I guess I've been acting weird since Dad died. My patience is low. I got in fights at my old school, and everyone thought a change of scenery would help. It didn't." She sobbed.

I tried not to let on I already knew about her dad. "I'm sorry about your dad." I shook my head, frustrated with my lack of words.

"Don't feel bad. You're here with me. Nothing you say can bring Dad back."

Her kindness made my heart swell.

I reached out with my hand and touched her shoulder. Jewel brought her hand up and touched mine. Only a brief contact, but I felt the electricity, the spark of life.

Jewel smiled, weak, but a smile nonetheless. "I don't normally allow people to touch me. Maybe you're special."

I took my hand away, not knowing what else to do. I felt scared and tentative. My nerves caused me to blurt out another stupid observation. "Someone has been." I pointed at her bruises and I immediately felt the bile rise in my guts. *Stupid, stupid, stupid.*

Jewel's attention ranged elsewhere. She whispered, "I fell off the front porch at home."

I let the lie go. Jewel already knew I thought her answer was bullshit. Her shoulders slumped, and she brought her hands together, wringing them slowly.

Jewel changed the subject. "Want to see what I've been drawing?"

As bad as I wanted to get to the bottom of what plagued her, pushing Jewel would only serve in her pushing back—and perhaps pushing me away. "Sure, I'd love to see it."

The word love made both of us blush.

Jewel shifted toward me to show me the drawing she had on her lap. Three horizontal lines filled the paper, breaking the paper into three vertical sections. Several steps and ladders connected the sections—or each floor, as I was to find out.

"It's good," I said. "But what is it?"

Jewel giggled through her tears. "A dungeon." Her eyes searched mine for approval.

I didn't let her down.

I smiled. "A dungeon? Like a torture chamber dungeon?" Malicious-looking devices lay scattered about the floor.

"See all my torture devices?" She giggled.

I wondered if drawing horrible things was how she dealt with her own issues.

Jewel continued, "Here is where the person comes in." The entrance resembled a submarine door. "They climb down these stairs and have to avoid the acid pit."

Bones had collected at the bottom of the pit. Apparently, not everyone who entered Jewel's dungeon made it out alive. I tried hard not to appear weirded out by it.

"What's that thing?" I asked.

Jewel's eyes radiated light and enthusiasm. "It's one of my favorites, a brain burner. If you step on its sensor tile, the floor lifts you up into the oven and it cooks your brain . . . and your head, I suppose."

Never in my life had I seen anything so cool from a girl. I liked her even more. "What's that?" I pointed to a device, a big box dangling from a chain attached to the ceiling, toward the top of the page. Someone lay squished underneath it, their guts hanging out like greasy snakes.

Jewel sobbed.

"What is it?" I asked. "I'm sorry"

She turned back and smiled a small, sad smile. "Don't apologize. It's not your fault. It's mine."

"You can tell me anything," I said. "I won't repeat it."

Jewel searched my eyes. She must have decided I told the truth. "Big cement brick." She pointed at it like it was her nemesis.

"Who's under it?" To this day, I don't know what prompted me to ask.

Jewel's unblinking eyes stabbed mine.

I recoiled, knowing a life changing event may be hanging in the balance.

Jewel didn't seem to notice.

She whispered through clenched teeth, "My daddy." She stated this so blandly, I thought she bit her tongue and swallowed a mouthful of blood. She trembled as her tears renewed.

"Is—is he dead?" I asked. Of course he was. What a stupid question.

"He's dead," she agreed. "His guts were squished out." Jewel deadpanned.

"I mean, is—is this how he died?"

Jewel nodded almost imperceptibly. "It might as well be."

Horrified, I said, "You drew him dead in your dungeon, but it's not your fault."

She shook her head. "I argued with him the day he died, made him mad. He never was good when he was mad."

"Look," I pleaded, "I'm sorry about your dad, but don't you think...I mean, did he have a heart attack?" At our age everyone died of a heart attack. But I was about to learn different—big time.

Jewel frowned and spouted her answer as if in a trance. "No, his whole face was crushed at work, crushed until his skull and face bones shattered...crushed."

She continued saying, "crushed" as if in a trance and I wanted to snap her out of it. "Enough. I want to believe"

Jewel snapped. "You want to believe what? I'm his innocent little darling and I'm not to blame for what happened?"

My stomach turned, unable to imagine losing Dad. How could she talk about it so coldly? "You didn't do it to him. It's not your fault. People die, you know?" I was sliding into concepts with which I possessed little experience. I wished Mom were there to talk sense into Jewel.

"He didn't just die. He fell underneath his own steamroller because he wasn't paying attention, because I upset him."

I shook my head. "No," I said, "it's not your fault."

She put her arms up in front of my face. "These bruises and cuts say I am, Jason. I am."

"No," I squeaked. "You don't need to do this to yourself." I wasn't sure if I meant the bruises or the emotional beating she bestowed upon herself—either way. I also knew I may have said too much.

"No, not to myself," she whispered.

I let out a breath, glad she didn't call me out for thinking she hurt herself. Confusion still wrestled with my brain. "What do you mean—who else?"

Before Jewel could answer, a swarm of students entered the room. We wiped at our eyes—like kindred spirits. Was I making her brain tingle?

Jewel spoke as she got up. "I'll tell you more at lunch. Can I trust you?"

"Of course you can." I hugged her, brief but urgent.

Jewel tightened her body at first. She relaxed, allowing the embrace. Her long skinny arms slipped over my shoulders for a moment but she backed away abruptly. "See you at lunch," she whispered, and went to find her seat.

I reluctantly left the room and headed for social studies.

* * *

The secondhand ticked off during the last ten minutes of Calculus, my last before the lunch break. The longest ten minutes of my life. My stomach hurt and my breath was shallow. I wanted badly to help Jewel.

But maybe I couldn't. Either way, I absolutely needed to know what went on in Jewel's head—and about her bruises. Obviously, there was something Mom knew nothing about.

Or maybe she did—maybe I remained the only one to not know anything.

The bell rang and I damn near jumped from my skin. I scooped up my books, already organized and ready to go, the most organized I'd ever been. Perhaps Jewel was good for me. I smiled to myself. I remembered, Jewel needed me and I sprinted to my locker. I hoped she would be at hers, but she wasn't. I hustled to the cafeteria wishing we had set a specific place to meet. My stomach rumbled.

I glanced around, trying to look inconspicuous. Jewel wasn't in the lunch-line or at any of the cafeteria tables. A cold hand grabbed my arm.

"Jewel . . ." I started. It wasn't Jewel, and by the expression on her face, she had bad news.

Tracey, her face a mask of concern, blurted, "Jason, you have to get to the old fort. Jewel stood up to Harvey. He was stealing a kid's marbles, and hitting him too. He has her at the fort."

Rage enveloped me. The son-of-a-bitch crossed the line. If he even touched a hair on her beautiful head, he'd pay— screw the blood oath. I had no idea if Tracey followed me or not and I didn't care, Harvey was about to die. "If she even has a scratch, Harvey, a scratch, I swear I will kill you," I screamed.

I sprinted across the asphalt. Tracey plodded along somewhere behind me, watching my back. I hit the woods running fast, knowing the way by heart. Jewel started screaming.

"Get off me."

The frustrated and fearful tone of her voice raised my hackles and broke my heart.

Harvey mumbled gibberish, his baritone voice too low to hear. His voice reminded me of a pig rutting.

I rounded the corner of the trail and the fort came into sight. The rest of the gang stood or crouched outside, peeking in. Harvey and Jewel were inside—and she screamed.

"Please stop. You're hurting me." Her voice, firm yet sorrowful, broke my heart.

This time I heard Harvey. "Someone already beat me to it, Jewel. What's a little more?" His thick voice dripped with arousal.

I balled my fists in anger. How could the gang stand around and watch this, like the mauling of an innocent girl somehow made for good entertainment? It was beyond my comprehension and I snapped. Nothing could've stopped me—nothing.

Billy turned around as I ran up. "Back off, Jason; Harvey's mad," he said. "He'll kick your ass if you interrupt him, says he's gonna touch her in the privates like he was gonna do to the three-titted woman." Billy grinned, his toothy gap-bite flashing between his chapped lips. He enjoyed this way too much.

My anger damn near blinded me, everything and everyone one big blur. I did have the presence of mind to want Billy's stupid mouth shut. About to punch him—punch the fucker hard for watching Jewel be attacked—a hand flew past me, grabbing Billy by the shirt.

"Help Jewel, I have this trash." Tracey deposited a haymaker into Billy's mouth. Billy fell on his ass, blood covering his buck teeth. I slipped inside the fort.

Harvey's bare back shined with sweat. His flabby love handles dangled like quivering gelatin. He plopped on Jewel's midsection, only her skinny pale legs visible, trailing out behind him.

"You like me touching your stomach? Maybe this'll teach you to interrupt me when I'm doing business."

Jewel screamed. "Leave me alone."

Harvey laughed. He sounded disturbed and cruel. His head twitched as he spoke. "Maybe it won't be so bad," Harvey said. "Jason's boring. I might be better." He sounded like he believed what he said.

"I'd never let you touch me"—she struggled to catch her breath as Harvey's weight bared down on her—"you filthy piece of trash."

Harvey slapped her. "I'm gonna touch you somewhere better." Harvey grasped at Jewel's pants, and Jewel screamed.

I threw my hatred and the entire force of my body into Harvey's greasy back. The momentum carried me and Harvey off Jewel and onto the earthen floor.

Harvey grunted like a pig.

Jewel rolled out of the way. "I'm fine, don't worry about me," she said. Relief etched her face and gave me strength.

Harvey had picked himself up, his side and back smeared with pine-needle riddled mud, like corn stuck in feces. His sweat turned the muddy mess even mushier. Breathing heavy, he actually snarled, like a cross between a pig and a dog. His head twitched constantly and his eyes were black as pitch, like they had no irises at all. "You're gonna pay, pussy boy. Lots of places to hide your body out here."

I didn't think he'd kill me, not right here in front of everybody, but who knew? He probably killed Mumford—maybe even his sister. No telling what Harvey was capable of.

Harvey looked out where the gang stood slack jawed, trying to garner support.

The gang, most with looks of shock on their faces, stood there, knowing he'd gone too far.

Harvey gasped for air, as though he crossed the finish line at a marathon. "Come on, you pussy fuckers, get him."

No one moved—not even to blink.

Harvey sneered. "No more loyalty? You're all gonna break the oath? I'll get each and every last one of you fuckers. And Jason, you're going down first."

Harvey rushed me.

I planted my back foot and met him head-on. He was built like a bull. His weight forced me backward toward the door. I twisted my arms and we fell to the floor with a heavy thud. I fell on my ribs and something popped. I didn't care. I rolled out of the way, and Harvey landed where I'd been. His intent, to knock the wind out of me, failed—I was quicker than him by a long ways. I got up, quick and lithe, and deposited a kick to Harvey's huge head. His head barely moved, but a trickle of blood formed in his nostril. I'd hurt the son-of-a-bitch.

Harvey grunted and got to his feet. He wiped his bloody nose with the back of his hand. "You pussy-whipped mother fucker, I'll kill you. Then I'm gonna touch your little girlfriend all over her sexy body." He rushed me.

I whirled and grabbed the aluminum baseball bat by the door, a tool we used to use to break up dead pine branches.

Using his bull-like style, Harvey hurtled forward like a corpulent missile. His jiggly stomach preceded him by twelve inches.

I remember thinking his fat ass needed a bra, a stupid thing to think when my life hung in the balance. But, the thing I needed to keep focused.

His scent, animal and musky, his arousal interfered with, Harvey grunted as he charged. I waited for the right moment.

Harvey reached out his hands to grapple, and I swung—hard. The bat came around like a silver blur and caught Harvey, the swine-man, right in the bridge of the nose. His face gave way and it felt great, satisfying.

Harvey squealed and fell to the floor, his face buried in his hands.

I rolled the bastard over, about to finish the job. Blood spurt everywhere. Harvey's nose, obviously broken, sat off to one side of his face. Three of Harvey's teeth lay on the ground, the rest of his mouth reduced to a bloody orifice. His lips already were swelled beyond recognition.

Harvey moaned like a zombie on *Night of the Living Dead.*

Someone grabbed my hand. My adrenaline, still pumping hard, bore fruit to my first instinct which urged me to fight. I assumed it was Billy and I put my arm back to punch.

"Jason, it's me."

I dropped my arm and hugged her. My bruised rib hurt like hell but I didn't care.

"C'mon, we have to get out of here. The others went to get a teacher."

Harvey lay with his eyes closed, moaning like he might die.

Fear gripped me. What if he was dying? I regretted hitting him that hard but he deserved it. Jewel lead me out of the fort and down the path. The feel of her hand in mine was like a morphine drip.

Tracey ran up to us. "Don't worry, I'll tell everyone the truth. You're a hero, bro."

I did my best to smile back, but my rib hurt too badly. Jewel pulled me down the trail. I wasn't sure where she was taking me.

Tracey yelled from behind, "Don't worry about Billy. He's seen the light." I smiled as Jewel dragged me down the trail.

I feared it would be my last smile for a while.

Chapter 9

Fear develops from the inside out. Believe me, I know.

The lights from the ambulance outside reflected like a macabre dance off the ceiling of the principal's office, taunting me. They carried Harvey from the fort to the ambulance, his entire face wrapped up in gauze like a mummy, slits left open only for his baleful eyes and broken mouth. I busted his nose and smashed out his teeth, but his whole face?

What had I done?

I shook with fear, but in the pit of my stomach, a small flame of vindication leaped like a sprig of hope, a warming flame. I saved the girl I cared about so much; she'd been through enough.

No more.

They separated us immediately, Jewel and me. I supposed they wanted to see if our stories jived, like on McCloud. She sat in the next room, interrogated by Principal Hammond, but she felt miles away. Hammond's angry voice in full crescendo when Jewel told him things he didn't wanna hear. The word police muttered through the door made my heart stop for a moment, icy tendrils poking at my skin.

Oh, shit.

Calling Mom was bad enough. On the way and not happy about it, I would pay the price. But the police—was I to go to jail, too? I took a deep breath and threw my shoulders back, stifling a sob forming in my throat. After all, Harvey, the one to attack Jewel, he's the guilty one—a monster. I only defended her and her honor, a damn hero. I prayed to God Mom and the police saw it the same way. I thought about Mumford, the three-titted-woman, the worms. My skin crawled.

Then I winced, my ribs hurting. I adjusted my position and recalled the time Dad had gotten thrown in jail.

I was seven, and people underestimated my ability to pay attention—wrong. Mom finished grad school and passed her licensing exam. I remember—as a family—we made a production out of hanging both the diploma and the license on her office wall. Mom pranced around like a little girl. Dad strangely distracted, distant.

My father, in terrible need of adult fun, had been on the pout. Perhaps he took the situation further than even he anticipated, the night somehow turning into more of something about him and less about Mom's accomplishments. Maybe my father finally put his foot down—a piece of paper didn't make someone the boss.

Perhaps that's what pissed her off the most.

The babysitter needed to spend the night. I remember thinking how weird it was to have two female authority figures at home, at one time, a lot of damn estrogen. It surprised me when I got the opportunity to overhear Mom's conversation.

Caught up in the excitement of the moment, I snuck from my room. Both women assumed I would stay put, powerless against their will—a bad assumption.

I peered in through a crack in the partially opened door to the kitchen. Both Erica—my sitter—and Mom sat at the breakfast nook table, legs crossed identically, both sipping on cups of coffee. They both wagged their heads in conspiring nods, Erica obviously kissing Mom's ass and lending emotional support. The sight concerned me. What heinous act had my father committed to unleash the wrath of both women? I listened with as much intent as the concern for my own safety would allow.

"My goodness, Mr. Hylden did that?"

Erica chose her words carefully, caught up in the power of an adult situation, yet not wishing to overstep her place. She must have got it right.

Mom leaned toward her. "Yes, Erica, I'm ashamed to admit it even, but he did. He must have had too much to drink."

"You mean all this other guy did was come and congratulate you on getting your degree?" Erica's voice sounded incredulous.

It pissed me off, as if she knew anything about anything. Erica wasn't much older than me.

"It's a little more complicated, Erica." She leaned in even further, as if what she had to say, so horrific she didn't even want the fly on the wall to overhear, might stop the world.

I crowded in closer to the door.

"Jesse is a colleague. We've spent a lot of time studying together over the last three years. I thought Michael would be comfortable with him by now."

Or maybe his resentment took that long to build.

Erica covered her mouth, like girls were prone to when they wanted someone to think they were appalled by something. "So Mr. Hylden punched Jesse, right there at the table?"

Mom paused, perhaps regretting sharing such personal information. But, already in deep anyway, she continued, "No, it happened in the men's bathroom, actually. Apparently, Michael was peeing when Jesse came in. Jesse asked him if he'd heard about the weeklong seminar in Boston. It's tradition in our school. The year after graduation, our department chair takes all the new grads. It's a celebration, our first real conference as peers rather than students."

Erica possessed no idea of what Mom talked about. She wasn't the brightest bulb on the tree, the sharpest tool in the shed, pick your analogy. So furious with Mom, with her wanting to disappear for yet another week when she already subjected my father to three years of, basically, single parenting, I slid sideways, almost losing my balance and spilling into the kitchen.

Mom donned a sad look. "It's cool. He should have understood."

I cringed. I wished Erica would go home and stay out of our business. Bile rose in my gut.

Mom said, "Michael didn't think it was cool. He asked Jesse if he'd be going. Of course, Jesse said he'd be. They all would. Michael hadn't heard it from me yet, so I guess he got a little shook up."

Erica shook her head with a dramatic swing of her pigtails.

I'd heard enough. I erupted before even thinking about it. My old man's genes were flowing through me like wind through a sail. "A little shook up? Maybe he'd like to have the mother of his children around once in a while."

I was always smart for my age, even if immature—a lot smarter than Erica anyway, three years older than me. The expression on her face indicated she had no idea what I was talking about, or maybe shocked I flew into the kitchen so quickly, screaming. Either way, she sat there with a stupid, confused look on her face. Mom on the other hand, knew perfectly well what I spoke about. It'd been discussed before, but she didn't know I overheard.

It's funny how heating ducts carry sound.

Mom's eyes flashed an angry defiant glare. She soon blinked, as if she managed a change of heart. When her eyes opened, they were softer, from anger to mommy love. She remained silent.

I stood there with my hands on my hips, a miniature statue of my father.

Erica stood up. "Jason, you should be in bed. This isn't for little kid ears."

I lost my mind. "If I'm a little kid, you're a mental midget, Erica. This is my family, my business, and if you don't like it, get out."

My vocabulary, already quite developed, even at seven, overwhelmed her. So Erica could only stammer, out-dueled by someone three years younger. Proud of myself, defending Dad, my smile beamed. Erica sat back down with a plop into the kitchen chair, the estrogen in the room definitely waning.

The phone rang, and my mother said, "We'll speak about this"

Mom glared at it like it was a personal insult. "Hello?"

A male voice on the other end. I yelled, "Dad? Are you okay?"

Mom faced the other way. "No, he isn't home yet. No, don't come over."

I completely understood my old man's frustration. "Leave Mom alone, you hot-shot psychology asshole."

Mom covered the receiver and glared. She put the phone back to her mouth. "Look, Jesse, I have to go. Maybe you shouldn't call anymore, not for a while anyway. You seem to rile up my family." She smirked, her eyes glistening.

I smirked back, knowing I scored a big win for the home team.

"Goodbye, Jesse. Have fun at the conference." She hung the receiver up with a gentle push.

Erica glowered at me with a scared look. At least she kept her mouth shut, which must have been hard for her.

Mom considered me with her big brown eyes. "Let's not make a habit out of speaking rudely, okay? I'll be around more often."

I smiled. I wouldn't be punished this time because I'd done something just and good. "Okay, I won't. Thanks."

My parents smoothed things over. Jesse didn't press charges and my parents found a more useful form of communication. They still argued occasionally—who didn't?— But they were always healthy arguments. He learned to live with her professional relationships and she learned to not let them get in the way of their family.

Problem solved.

As I sat in the principal's office, I wondered if Dad would have stuck up for Jewel like I did. I wondered if Jesse, like Harvey, would have understood any other form of communication. Something inside told me a good beating was all either of their minds could wrap itself around, shaking loose the innate need to take what wasn't theirs to take.

Footsteps clomped outside the door to the office, and it swung open. My eyes widened with anticipation, relieved beyond all measure it wasn't the police. Mom spilled in, her purse slipping off her shoulder as she entered.

The secretary looked up from whatever she was doing. "Yes, may I help you?"

I grinned without being sure why.

Mom righted her purse and ran a hand through her brown hair. She glanced at me with a brief stare, erasing my smile. She addressed the secretary. "I'm here to see my son. He's in some trouble, I understand?"

The secretary stood. "Mrs. Hylden, Principal Hammond will be right with you. He's speaking with one of the other students involved."

"There's an ambulance here. Is everyone okay?" Mom's concern gleamed in her wide eyes.

The secretary frowned. "No, everyone's not okay. Jason here struck another student with an aluminum bat."

Mom, calmer than I expected she would be, said, "I see. So he struck another kid for no good reason? He wasn't defending himself or anyone else?"

The secretary shrugged. "You'll have to speak with Principal Hammond. He has the details, though it's never okay to hit."

"No, of course not. But I would hate to see Jason take all the blame if he didn't initiate the incident."

I jumped in and immediately wished I would have kept my mouth closed. "What if I had to pull Harvey the heifer off Jewel because he was trying to hump her?"

The secretary sucked in a lungful of air. Usually she looked like the living dead—but that moment she came to life.

Mom turned to me. "Are you saying Harvey Kuchenbecker was trying to rape Jewel? Because if you are…"

Hearing the word rape made me cringe. You hear it on the five o'clock news, not in your own principal's office. I said, "He had his shirt off and he was rubbing her stomach and pulling her pants and saying he was going to touch her private parts."

The secretary inhaled sharply.

Mom stayed silent. Jewel, her client after all, needed her help. She addressed the secretary. "Look, ma'am, I know there are a lot of things to sort out here, but I think it's best if Jason is gone when Principal Hammond finishes speaking with Jewel."

The secretary furrowed her brow, shaking her head sadly. "Principal Hammond gave strict orders to keep Jason here. He needs to decide if the police will be called."

Mom's eyes flashed. "Unless my son is under arrest, which I find highly unlikely, no one will tell me when I can and can't take my son home. If he needs to speak with us, the principal can reach me at home to set up an appointment."

The secretary squinted, her eyes reduced to slits. She clucked her tongue like she pondered a grand topic involving the human condition. When she spoke, it was with less conviction. Maybe she knew from personal experience how tricky these situations could be. "I'm not sure what your problem is with meeting now, but I'm sure you have your reasons. At least let me tell Principal Hammond. Perhaps something can be arranged."

Mom silently consented.

The secretary turned and went through a door behind her. She muttered something to Principal Hammond. Jewel spoke, her deep rich voice laced with anxiety. It could've been my imagination, but I thought she mentioned my name. I wanted more than anything to go comfort her. I would, the first chance I got.

Mom turned to me. "I need you to go wait in the car. I'll be out in a moment."

I didn't want to leave Jewel. "Why? I want to talk to Jewel."

She patted my head and smiled a quick empathic smile. "You know why. Jewel is my patient and she deserves to speak with me about this on her terms, not because you are her friend and I happen to be your mother."

"But I saved her, I care about her. I want to help her." I was out of line but I had to try—for Jewel.

Mom gave me a curt smile. "You can speak with Jewel at school tomorrow, but let me speak to her now."

"Why? Because you're a psychologist and you know better?"

To Mom's credit, she kept her cool. "Is this a contest to see who can help Jewel the most?"

I grinned.

She continued, "Look, I know you care about Jewel. What you did was noble. A bit extreme perhaps, but noble.

But I have a professional obligation here to speak with her. It's not even so much I think she needs my counseling . . . but please understand, Jason. Think how confused she's going to be when she finds out you're my son and she has been speaking to us about the same highly sensitive issue. It might diminish her trust in both of us. I think I should speak to her about it. If she wants, she can speak to you, as a friend."

She was right. The last thing I wanted was Jewel distrusting me. Probably best to get everything out in the open and let Jewel decide what to do next. Tears welled up in my eyes. I said, "Okay, mom, I'll go wait in the car. Please, when you tell Jewel you're Mom, tell her I do like her."

Mom wiped a tear from her eye also. She bent down and gave me a hug. "I certainly will."

I started to walk away, but she continued, "If you need someone to talk to, will you come to me, as your mother?" She searched my eyes.

"Of course. You can't shrink me anyway."

We laughed in sync.

I walked for the car, head down, deep in thought. I approached the parking lot, where a rusty Chevette pulled up to the curb. Jewel's mom. I slowed my pace, loitered, wanting to see the woman who gave birth to the girl I loved. I knelt down, pretending my shoe needed tying.

The tinted windows skewed my view. I wondered if the tint was original or a recent development. The door opened and an apparition stepped out. I shuddered. If Mom represented God, Satan entered stage left.

I didn't believe this thing took care of Jewel.

I remembered what Jewel said, the thing she didn't have time to explain, but was going to at lunch—before Harvey got a hold of her. "No, not me"

I shuddered.

It wasn't the long unkempt, dirty hair covering her face and eyes bothering me. Her gait—the ambling sway with which she moved herself, like someone twice her age, a zombie—ate at me like a grub in my grey matter. No life existed in her. As she neared me, her stench assaulted my nose. It wasn't exactly like the dead dog Billy and I found in the ditch, bloated and full of bugs. It was akin to the soupy cabbage smell people get when they haven't bathed in a long time. I held my breath as she limped by me.

She wore gray sweat pants two sizes too large for her frame. Over her top, a silk moo-moo sagged, stained with rusty splotches of God-knows-what, didn't belong on even a vagabond.

Impossible to tell what figure lay beneath it all. She wore black dress shoes with bows in front. I was young but I knew normal people didn't go out in public dressed like a homeless person.

My first impression—bag lady. I'd seen one once when we were on vacation in Minneapolis. We walked the skywalk system from our parking ramp to the Target Center. The Timberwolves, the local NBA team, on the verge of winning its first playoff series ever, played. Panhandlers were earning their handouts by playing instruments. But a haggard woman who begged and did little else to earn the money she sought, approached us. Her dish remained empty but the musicians did quite well. Dad tried to explain the difference between Republicans and Democrats but it was lost on me.

Jewel's mom, by appearance, reminded me of that woman.

My impression of Jewel's mom was she didn't want any help. Or maybe she couldn't even help herself and so she didn't give a fuck anymore. If this is what happened when you lost a husband, I sure as hell hoped Dad lived a whole lot longer.

She turned with a quick motion. Her hair flowed wildly because of her rapid change in direction. Her eyes, which avoided my attention before, glared with an intensity I never knew the woman capable of, where all the life in her body lived. The rest of her could be dead but not those blue eyes that were more alive than the rest of her put together. I recognized them.

I knew where Jewel got hers.

She glared, daring me to mock her.

I wasn't about to do any such thing, nothing in fact except tie my shoe. I wilted under her gaze and felt guilty for gawking. I wanted to introduce myself but I was frightened. Did she know who I was? Did Jewel point me out? Tell her what a jerk I was for taking the kid's marbles?

"I spy, with my little eye, a good young man." Her voice rasped low and serious like gravel.

"Wh—what?" I stammered, not understanding.

She closed her eyes slightly, as if tired. "The principal told me someone attacked my Jewel. Someone else saved her, and put a beating on the boy who would have defiled my little girl. You look like a good boy."

How had she known I was the one? "I—yes, I rescued Jewel. I had to." I was powerless to stop my stammering.

The woman regarded me with a cautious gaze. "Ain't nobody got to help anybody else. But you did."

The woman didn't ask why, but it was implied. The last thing I wanted to talk about with Jewel's mom were my feelings for Jewel. "Nobody should have to be treated like an animal," I said.

"Nobody should endure being rutted on by a squealing little piggy." Her eyes flashed.

Her bluntness made me cringe but I stood my ground, my pulse increasing with every passing moment. I lost my voice.

"The bastard wanted to stick his fat hog in her, have his way. That's the way boys are. Do you wanna rut with my daughter too? Did ya save her for yourself?"

Appalled by guilt for dreaming and thinking about Jewel, I said, "No, I mean, yes, I like Jewel. But I wouldn't—" I wrestled with my words, failing miserably.

She scrutinized me. "You want to ride her like a horse, satisfy your carnal urges, fill her with your foul fluids."

My breathing came in gasps. An image of my stained underwear, my dream, flashed as if this woman had conjured it from my subconscious like a witch. I blushed in shame. *I can take better care of Jewel than you can.* But my tongue couldn't defend me.

Maybe there was no defense.

"Don't even bother with excuses boy. Maybe you did save her—good for you. But it don't make what I said any less the truth."

As quickly as she came, the horrid looking woman, the birth mother of the girl I adored, the girl I loved, turned and walked for the door to the school, her shoes clacking on the broken tar.

I supposed she'd seen the answer she wanted in my eyes, or she didn't care anymore. I wasn't sure which. I wasn't sure of much of anything.

I walked briskly for Mom's car. I hoped like hell she'd know how to deal with this crazy woman.

As I sat in the car, a memory nagged at me, something familiar, dislodged from my subconscious by Jewel's mother. Jewel's mom reminded me of another character from my life, as blunt as she. I never understood exactly what happened, or how it affected me, until the memory flooded me:

I sat on top of the metal slide, afraid to come down. The woman's children wanted a turn, but frozen with fear, I wanted to disappear.

It was a simple problem. Come down the slide, right? But to a shy seven year old? A lot happened when I was seven. Upon reaching the top of the slide, the metal foot stand caught the top of my pants, popping my pant snap. To my horror, the snap broke in my hands. Stuck with my pants hanging wide open, fear froze me to the top of the slide.

I didn't want to slide down with my underwear showing. Still I hesitated. The other kids became increasingly more agitated.

Their mother, putting down her horror novel, *Salem's Lot* as I recall, unstuck her fat ass from the swing where she'd been sitting and sauntered over to see what caused her brood to squawk. She didn't look pleased.

I perched at the top of the slide, frozen.

The woman, frown lines cutting her face into pieces, said, "Get your little ass down the slide, boy. Other kids need a turn."

"I—can't. I—"

As she shook her head, her greasy hair swung back and forth like an old mop head as her beady pig eyes bored into me. "You scared or what? Go down the fucking slide."

My breath came harder.

She sighed. "You best get down or I'll let my oldest whoop your ass good."

I cried. Desperate, I pointed at my pants.

She leaned forward. "Come down here and I'll fix them pants."

Maybe she was being sincere but I wasn't chancing it. I stayed atop the slide, momentarily out of the foul-mouthed woman's reach.

"Not gonna come down, huh? You think I'm a pervert who wants your little willy in there? Your little wiener couldn't please a woman like me. I need a real man, with a great big Johnson to drive." The woman cackled.

I didn't understand exactly her meaning but it wasn't good. I ran for home.

I didn't return to that park for a long time.

But I would give anything to go there with Jewel.

Chapter 10

I sat in my room, waiting for my parents. I spent most of the ride home staring out the passenger window, not actually seeing much of anything, Mom also deep in thought, trying to divine answers out of this whole mess. I wanted to ask her about Jewel and her mom. I wanted to know how Jewel reacted to my Mom being her therapist. But I waited, confidentiality rearing its ugly head.

I skipped supper again but no one yelled at me. I guess they understood. My stomach gurgled with anxiety. What the hell took them so long? I was about to go and drag Mom upstairs when footsteps sounded from the hallway.

My door swung open and Dad stepped through the doorway. His smile put me at ease as he sat on my bed next to me.

He took a deep breath. "Mom said you had an altercation at school today."

I nodded.

"Are you okay? Are you hurt at all?"

I shrugged. "My ribs hurt." Tears welled up.

"Bruised would be my guess. I'll get Ibuprofen." He let out another breath. "Mom said it was over a girl, this Jewel."

I looked Dad in the eyes. "I fought Harvey; he was on top of her, he was gonna, you know . . ."

"You did a good deed today. You did what you had to do, to protect someone you care about." A tear slipped out of his eye.

My tears spilled also. "I couldn't let him."

"I know, son. I wouldn't have let him either. I wanted to make sure you didn't do it because of what I did. I didn't teach you this way." My father's shoulders heaved.

"You and mom have taught me right from wrong. It has nothing to do with you. Jewel needed my help so I helped her."

Dad hugged me, burying my face into his neck. "I know, you're a good young man. I don't care what the principal says, you did fine. Harvey deserved what he got."

I cried into his shoulder. "Thanks—thanks for understanding."

Standing up, he said, "Anytime. Anything else we need to talk about? Girls or anything?"

We grinned in unison. "No, Dad."

"I'll send your mom up. She needs to speak with you about Jewel. If you ever need to talk..."

I smiled. "I will." He left the room.

Their whispers from the bottom of the steps wafted up. Mom's lighter footfalls, much more graceful than Dad's, came up the stairway.

I shivered with anticipation.

She knocked before entering. I worried she'd discover my dirty boxers but I had bigger issues to worry about.

"Your father tells me you established your behavior isn't a learned trait." She looked stern.

"What I did has nothing to do with Dad. I did it for Jewel."

"Do you foresee having to fight? Be honest." She searched my eyes for the truth.

"No," I said, not sure if it was the truth or not. "I want Jewel to feel safe and not to be...you know." I remembered her bruises and quickly added, "At school anyway." I didn't want Mom thinking I would delve into her home life. That was Mom's job.

She never took her therapist's eyes off me. "As reluctant as I am to say this, I understand why you fought. I hope I never need to understand again."

"Mom, I'm sorry. I—"

She grabbed me with fierce passion, like only a mother can. She buried my head in her shoulder, much harder than Dad did. "I want you to exhaust all means of peace before you fight."

"I know," I whispered. "I promise."

"Good. Principal Hammond let me decide your punishment. He sees no need to suspend you, under the circumstances."

I let out my breath. "Thank you."

"No problem. We have other business. Do you feel you are mature enough to handle some fairly adult things?"

My heart about stopped and my breath caught. I was an adult, technically. I was ready. "About Jewel?"

She smiled. "We had a nice talk. She's quite fond of you, despite you running with a crowd that steals marbles and cards from little kids."

"She told you? I told her, I'm done with them."

"My son the extortionist." She smirked. "Jewel said Harvey is the leader. True?"

"Yes," I whispered. I never thought this topic would come up. "It's falling apart though, we only have another month."

She sighed. "I always knew Harvey was trouble. He's the least of my worries right now but knock it off. He can only lead to trouble."

"It's not like we didn't give them anything in return. We kept them safe, like what I did for Jewel."

Her eyes pierced mine. "It is nothing like what you did for Jewel. What you guys are doing is called extortion, and in the real world, people go to jail for that."

"I'm done with the gang anyway."

Mom softened. "Despite her peculiarities, Jewel has a good head on her shoulders, and she's a positive influence over you."

I grinned. "She is. I don't like to disappoint her."

"Good. But it seems we have a peculiar problem. Your friend is also my client."

My blood froze. "I can't be friends with her anymore?"

"It's complicated but we need to move forward carefully."

"What does Jewel think?" I held my breath.

"She was shocked. You must admit this is a big coincidence, given the circumstances."

"I was friends with her way before I knew you were her therapist." I cried tears of frustration—and perhaps love.

"Hold on. I said she was a bit taken aback at first. But she came around. We had a nice talk about it. I think we can continue with me as her therapist and you as her friend. As long as..."

"As long as what?"

"As long as we don't break..."

"Confidentiality."

"Yes, correct, confidentiality. If she chooses to share what she and I discuss, it's her choice. You cannot, under any circumstances, pry it out of her."

"Okay," I said. "I promise; I won't."

"Good. There's my part also. I promise not to ask you to divulge what she and you discuss, none of my business, fair is fair."

I should have been ecstatic. "Wh—what if she tells me something bad? Like, what if she talks about the bruises?"

She hugged me. "You can always choose to talk to me. Use your best judgment."

My best judgment is what bothered me. How was I supposed to know? The curse of being a therapist's kid, I guess. "Did Jewel's mother pick her up? She was in the parking lot."

"Yes, she was waiting when Jewel and I finished talking."

"She's weird, I mean real weird."

"Weird is one way to say it. I can't break confidentiality but she's working through resentment regarding the death of Jewel's dad."

Jewel blamed herself. I wondered how her mom felt. "Well, she"—I grasped for the words but let them go and dealt with Jewel's harmless mom head-on—"she's weird and stinky."

Mom punched me in the arm. "You're mean." She grinned. "But she is a stinky one. I'm glad, for your sake, Jewel has better hygiene habits."

I laughed. "Me, too. Thanks, Mom."

"No problem. Use your head, but don't trap your heart." She closed my door on her way out.

My heart thumped. Mom told me to hang out with Jewel. Better yet, Jewel wanted to hang out with me. I was thrilled for school.

I woke up, sweating. I lay on my bed not moving, remembering the night before too clearly. After assuring myself I wasn't dreaming, I sat up.

The corner of my room, the one my "dream Jewel" had stepped out of appeared normal this time. My closet door remained closed, as I left it before bed. I found myself having mixed emotions about this, part of me wanting her to return.

Guilt flowed through me.

My laptop lay booted up on my desk. I hopped out of bed and sat at the desk, my computer screen nearly blinding me until my eyes adjusted. I checked my social media pages. No new private messages, not unusual. Nothing important on my timeline. Not too many eighteen-year-old boys left messages on the social network.

But girls, on the other hand, did.

My heart beat faster as I searched for Jewel's profile. I didn't know her last name—shocking, after everything that had happened. I hit enter anyway.

The computer spit out seventeen Jewels.

Toward the bottom of the last page, I nearly choked. Jewel Wylander from northern Minnesota.

I clicked on the profile picture.

My Jewel's timeline popped up. Modest, no fancy wallpaper. One forlorn picture of her adorned the page. She barely made eye contact with whoever took the photo. Her body language made her look pensive. Her red hair hung over her eyes as usual. She rested her head on her left hand, elbow planted on her desk.

She wore the same clothes she'd worn to school. The same necklace, the one with the cross and butterfly, one she rarely wore.

The photo had to be taken this very day. The new bruises made me hyperventilate.

I scrolled down to her friends, desperate. My blood went cold. There were only two friends. One was Brian Keene, the horror author—the other, her dad in his coffin.

She'd created a Facebook account for her dead father.

I couldn't bring myself to click on his profile link, no telling what I'd find, something gross no doubt.

By the looks of him, I couldn't believe they allowed an open casket. He was paper thin with most of his insides obviously missing. His eyes were closed, quarters placed above the eye lids—they shined like diamonds.

I wondered if eyes still resided under those lids and if they were blue. I creeped myself out as a result.

I scrolled furiously to the top to see her last log in date. Today—she'd logged on to look at the picture today. What else could she have been looking at? There was nothing else to see except Keene's mug-shot. I smacked my forehead. Of course she looked at it today, the picture of her being from today as well, along with the extra bruises.

I considered telling Mom but I didn't want to wake her. Mom told me what I shared was my business.

I wish I would have—I do. It could have staved off what would come next.

I didn't send Jewel a friendship request because she'd deem the act intrusive. Obviously a very private matter. I didn't want to push it even though Jewel listed it on a public setting.

I often wonder if maybe she wanted me to find it.

I decided to wait for the next day to ask about the profile.

The next day took an eternity to come.

Chapter 11

Jittery, I fidgeted about my locker waiting for Jewel. I wished desperately for the mirror I broke the day before, wanting badly to check my hair, but not wanting to take the time for a trip to the bathroom. I satisfied myself with cleaning out my locker, which contained the usual assortment of empty Dinosour Egg cartons and Chic-o-stick wrappers. I hoped my tidiness would impress Jewel.

I wanted to impress her, bad.

The school's double glass doors swung inward and my breath caught in my throat.

Jewel?

Sex Type Thing by Stone Temple Pilots filtered to me, turned way too loud for practical listening.

Billy rolled over the top.

He walked around the corner, his locker being two down from mine. He wore jeans, ripped in the knee, and a black Marilyn Manson T-shirt that read *Smells like children*. He held his tape deck with the mono speaker up to his right ear.

I wondered why he wasn't deaf.

He saw me. "Yo, Jason man, you're in early," he screamed, much louder than necessary to compensate for the music.

Before I answered, the janitor lurched out of his supply closet and shouted, "Turn that shit off. STP is for pussies. Try White Zombie, man, they're the new shit."

Billy turned the music off. The button made a metallic snap. Laughing, he said, "I hear ya, Morris. Mom won't buy me any though, says they're too evil, they worship the devil or some bullshit. I had to steal this Manson T-shirt from my brother."

Morris, cool in his way, liked to preach about music and girls. We all liked talking trash with him.

"You little punks need a real job like I got here. You can buy all the fucking metal you want, man. Beer, too. The girls love it."

Billy laughed. "You don't have no girls, man, who you kidding?"

Morris shot him a look—and the bird.

"Do they worship the devil?" I asked.

Billy shook his head. "I doubt it. Parents lie so you don't listen to it and rebel."

"Damn straight," Morris added. "The man wants to keep us under his thumb. Big brother's always watching."

"Mom says she doesn't like the new bands," I said, "but if we censor them, we're going against what America stands for."

"Huh?" Billy grunted, obviously confused.

Perhaps those words had been a little big for him.

Morris understood though. He said, "God bless America, man." He raised both hands with his thumb, index, and pinky fingers in the air. "God bless rock n' roll, rock on dudes." Morris returned to work.

Billy watched Morris go back into the janitor's closet, and eyed me curiously. "You get in any trouble?"

I played stupid. "What do you mean?"

"What do I mean? Shit, what you did is all over the whole school."

Billy lifted his eyebrows and turned his palms upward. "Harvey? Yesterday? You beat his ass to protect Jewel?"

"Oh that," I said. "I didn't get in trouble. Mom thought I was protecting someone. No big deal."

"No big deal?" he asked. "They had to bandage Harvey's whole head, cart him off on a stretcher. He's still in the hospital, dude."

I didn't want Billy making a big deal out of this, not with Jewel due to show at any moment. She wouldn't like me bragging. "I'm not proud of it, Billy," I said, trying to discourage him. "Let it slide, okay?"

"But, you leveled the school bully, man. You're a hero."

Anger gripped me. "Yesterday he was your buddy. We all ran in the gang. You were gonna touch the three-titted woman right along with him. You watched him try to rape Jewel. Besides, you tricked me into going out and being confronted by the group, simply because Harvey told you to. Now you're praising me for beating Harvey's ass?"

"Calm down," he said, arms extended, palms out. "I mean, shit, we all did what Harvey said. You were the only one tough enough to stand up to him. I was following orders, you know?"

"No, Billy, I don't know. You were supposed to be my best friend. We all should have stood up to him, long ago. He's an asshole and he talked us all into stealing stuff from little kids. He might even be a killer. He thinks raping people is cool, and that we would go along with him. Fuck. Most of us did, if I hadn't come along." I let a tear slip from my eye. I remembered everyone huddled around the fort, just watching. It made me sick to my stomach. I wiped at it with a furious swipe of my hand. "Aw shit."

Billy, silent for a moment, not knowing what to say and looking sick. "I'm sorry. I should have done something. I knew it was wrong but I was scared. We all were."

I grinned at his apology. "Did Tracey whoop your ass?"

Billy's eyes went huge. "Dude, I swear she is nuts. She about cleaned my clock before I talked sense to her. I thought I was gonna end up in the hospital, roommates with Harvey."

I grinned bigger. "Hey, at least she stood up for what was right. She came to her senses. She's the one who came and got me from the lunchroom."

"She did," he agreed. "She talked sense into me too, Jason." He looked sincere.

"I believe you, Billy. I'm gonna miss the gang, you know? We're all friends because we were stealing and shit, but we were all close. I can't imagine being closer to anyone except—"

Billy put a hand on my shoulder. "Except Jewel, I know, man, it's okay."

"I don't know why but . . . when I'm with her . . . "

Billy grinned, his teeth gleaming. "You got it for her bad, bro," he said. "I think it's cool you got yourself a chick, even if she's weird."

I avoided eye contact. This was weird, new territory for all of us. "Thanks, Billy. It means a lot."

"No problem. So, what's up with Jewel, anyway?"

"Whad'ya mean?" I asked, but I knew.

"You know . . . the bruises and all?" he asked. "Her ma beating her or what?"

I cringed. I didn't like talking about Jewel like this, without her around. "I don't know, Billy."

"Why not? I mean, you talk to her all the time."

He could be real stupid sometimes. "Do you think I asked her where the hell all her bruises come from? Sometimes I wonder about you, man."

"Simmer down, man," he said. "I didn't mean nothing, thought maybe you knew, that's all."

"I don't—I wish I did. It's complicated."

"What's complicated?" he asked.

"Nothing—everything, I don't know. Everything's FUBAR, man, all kinds of fucked up."

"What's fucked up, Jason? You can tell me."

"Some of it I can't," I said. "I'm worried about her is all, about her dad passing on, all them bruises, a crazy mom—all that. Then Harvey tries to stick his big fat hog in her. How much grief can one person take?" I teared up.

Billy gaped. He managed, "That's messed up, man."

"I'm trying to help her but—"

"You've already been there for her, done more than anyone else has, anyway. Keep at it. What else are you gonna do?"

I wanted to sweep Jewel off her feet, kiss her softly, and take her away. Maybe take her away somewhere where no one could ever hurt her. "You're right, Billy."

Busloads of people entering the school broke the silence. It also broke the trance, and the sentiment floating between Billy and me, peer pressure a bitch.

"You'll figure the shit out. I'm gonna run, bum a chew off of Tracey."

"Catch you out in the yard."

Billy took off as the new arrivals came walking around the corner to the lockers.

I searched for Jewel. As usual, she wasn't anywhere I would have predicted, like a ghost. Maybe she was a mirage, something my mind conjured up. Maybe I still slept at home in my bed, having dreamed up the last two days completely. It all felt surreal enough.

A tap on my shoulder turned me around. "Dude, can I rip your White Zombie disc—"

"I don't like White Zombie," Jewel said. It wasn't Morris.

I jumped. "Where did you come from?"

"You sure are a nervous person," she said. "Are you always hiding something?"

"No, no, of course not. I— "

"I make you nervous. It's me, isn't it?"

I tried hard to breathe. Her hair, pulled back in a loose bunch in the back, cute as hell, made my stomach flutter. Her full-length bangs swept like feathers to the front of her ears, her gorgeous ears, so small and delicate. She wore a black turtleneck despite the warmer spring weather. The contrast of the black material against her red hair, made it hard for me to breath. "No, Jewel. It's not you—we covered that yesterday."

"Covered what?"

"You know?" I asked, dumbfounded. "That I care about you?"

"Yeah, I remember. Thanks." She turned to her locker and opened it, ignoring me.

My heart sank as Jewel brushed me off. "How are you today? I mean . . . you know?"

She turned to me. "I'm fine, no lasting damage." She turned back to her locker.

"I didn't mean. I meant—"

Jewel's eyes narrowed. "You mean you're worried because your mom's shrinking me?" she asked. "She told you I said it was okay to remain friends?"

"Yes but we don't have to talk about it."

"No we don't, Jason," she said. She turned to leave. "Now, if you'll excuse me."

"Wait—" It came out more desperate than I intended.

"What the fuck do you want me to say to you?"

"I—I want..."

"I want, I want. Is it always about what you want, Jason? If you care about me like you say you do, maybe you should stay away. I attract trouble, it follows me everywhere. Your mom knows. Or did she tell you already?"

"Absolutely not, Jewel," I said truthfully. "She would never talk to me about her clients. It's called client confidentiality."

"I know what it's called. You know how many shrinks I've been to see, Jason?"

I shook my head.

"More than I can count."

"I don't care, Jewel."

"Why?

"Because I care—"

"No. All I am to you, Jason, is a client. I'm everyone's little client."

"No, Jewel—"

"Go ahead, Jason. Fix poor little Jewel, she's so helpless, can't take care of herself, needs help from everyone."

"No, Jewel."

"Then what, Jason? What do you want from me?"

I grabbed her shoulders, desperate.

"You going to hold me down too? You want to pin me to the locker, have your way with me, and walk all over me?"

"No."

"What do you want from me?"

"Nothing. I don't want anything except—"

"Except? There's always an exception, isn't there, Jason?"

"No—I"

"You what?" she challenged.

I remained silent, my breath coming hard, chest heaving. A group of people had gathered around us. I didn't care.

Jewel waiting for my answer, eyes fierce.

"Love you," I whispered.

She shook, her frozen façade melting. "What did you say?"

People around us murmured, their gossip blooming like a flower in the spring.

A surge of energy jolted me. I nearly screamed to the world, "I said I love you, goddamn it." My chest heaved as I stared into her eyes, trying to understand.

Jewel's eyes rimmed with tears.

Intent on each other, neither of us saw the throng gathering.

Even Morris, pretending to clean gum out of the water fountain, watched in anticipation.

Jewel's lip trembled. "You've gone from like to love quite fast?" It was more of a question than an observation.

"It's the truth," I said. "I didn't want to let you walk away from me. I needed to tell you."

Staying silent, Jewel took my hand, leading me down the hall, somewhere more private.

My heart beat faster.

The bell rang and the other kids reluctantly went to their homerooms.

Only Morris looked on, eyes wide, until I made eye contact with him. He scurried away, too, with a self-conscious shuffle—heavy stuff even for him, I guess.

Jewel ducked into the gym doorway and pulled me in after her. She said, sternly, "Are you trying to trick me, Jason?"

I shook my head back and forth, unable to tear my eyes from hers or speak.

"You'd better not be. I've had enough people lie to me to last a lifetime." Her eyes flashed as though she remembered the betrayals.

"Never, Jewel, I'll never lie to you. I love you."

"Unconditionally?" she asked, more a demand.

"What?"

"Do you love me unconditionally? No matter what, for always."

"Definitely, unconditionally, always."

"No matter what I tell you?" she asked. "No matter what the truth turns out to be?"

"I promise. But I don't know what could be so horrible."

She lowered her head and stared at me from the tops of her eyes, ominous and serious. "Lots of things. Bad things."

She swallowed hard. "I was about to tell you about one of them at lunch yesterday, before . . ."

"Before I had to take down Harvey." I didn't want her to have to say the words.

"My sweet, sweet hero," she whispered. I loved her soft voice. "I'm sorry I got mad before. I needed to know you would always be here for me, and not because you see me as a victim."

"You're one of the strongest people I've ever known," I said honestly. "Anyone else would be nothing but a quivering pile of mush, all things considered."

She smiled sweetly. "That is the sweetest thing anyone has ever said to me. Thank you." She reached for me.

My heart felt as if it would burst.

She kissed me, right on the lips. My first real kiss—our first kiss, wonderful.

I'm convinced the angels sang as little bits of light sparkled all around us.

Jewel took her lips away. "You want to talk at lunch today, this time no interruptions?" She smiled.

"Yes."

"Good, I'll meet you at your room this time."

My heart felt like it might turn inside out it was flopping around so hard. Things were back on track. I wished she'd quit flip flopping on me, causing me no end of worry. But she'd been through a lot so I forgave her.

"We'd better get to class," she said. "Oh, and Jason? You still..." She waited for me to finish her sentence.

I smiled. "Make your brain tingle."

"Yes, you do."

"Jason? Jason."

I snapped out of my daydream and the rest of the class laughed.

Mrs. Melchen stood with her hands on her hips. "Jason, you've been daydreaming all class period. I know it's nice out, but—"

"Sorry, Mrs. Melchen. I can't wait for lunch." I wanted to see Jewel.

Jodie Harms, from the back corner, spouted, "I'll bet he was thinking about Jewel. They're in love." She made kissing faces with her lips.

Mrs. Melchen smiled. "Is that true, Jason? Is Jewel special to you?" She hadn't meant her comment to be malicious, but the whole class erupted with laughter all the same. Most of them had already had at least one serious relationship, but not me. They all knew it.

I blushed. I glanced at the clock, three more minutes. I prayed no one would tease Jewel when she met me for lunch. "I guess she is . . ."

Jodie crowed, "He beat up Harvey Kuchenbecker yesterday because he was gonna hurt her—or something."

I despised Jodie more by the moment. Her smirk infuriated me. "Shut up, Jodie."

Mrs. Melchen yelled, "Hold on. No need for anyone to get upset, the incident is over and taken care of."

Jodie smirked. "Yeah, Jason, hold on."

I shot out of my seat.

"Mrs. Melchen, help," Jodie squealed.

Mrs. Melchen put up her hand. "Jason, sit down please."

I complied immediately, wanting no more trouble.

She continued, "As for you, Jodie, I suggest you mind your own business, young lady. Bad things happen to people who can't keep their little mouths shut and be nice."

Jodie opened her mouth wide, but nothing came out.

The bell rang. *Thank God for small favors.*

Mrs. Melchen said, over the din of shuffling papers and books, "Class, don't forget your essays are due at the end of next week. Don't procrastinate."

Students filed out of the room, and I fell into the back of the line. It was almost time to see Jewel.

Mrs. Melchen caught me before I exited. "Jason, I wanted to apologize about Jodie. She's a busy body."

"No problem. Thanks for helping."

Mrs. Melchen said, "I want to warn you."

Here we go. I flushed.

"You can expect a degree of teasing, having a girlfriend. Most of your classmates have already had opposite-sex friends."

I winced. "I know, I'll watch my temper."

She smiled. "I know you will. It takes a big person to let things roll off their back. Especially in your case, when Jewel has been through so much."

Not surprising, she knew about Jewel. "She is a sweetheart. Who better to befriend her than you? Take good care of her."

I damn well was going to try.

Jewel popped her head in. "I hope I'm not interrupting?"

Mrs. Melchen smiled. "Not at all. I was telling Jason what a sweetheart you are."

Jewel smiled and laughed. A beautiful little tinkling laugh, like ice pushed up on the shore of Lake Bemidji in the spring. "Ready to go outside?" she said like a singsong bird.

With a smile, I took Jewel's hand and walked her to the playground, ignoring the stares.

We walked, quietly at first, across the street to avoid our peers, then around the perimeter of the playground. Little kids played about wildly on the tar and eyed me warily. We stuck to the gravel indicated by the line—the line between the safety of the asphalt and the "forbidden" forest which surrounded the school. The memories were too fresh to take her back to the fort.

We walked, instantly comfortable with each other and without the need to chat unnecessarily.

The birds, fresh arrivals along with warmer weather, chirped and hopped about merrily, searching for worms beneath last year's foliage. The worms Harvey burned up came unbidden.

I glanced at our hands. Her white and red freckled fingers, long and thin, intertwined with my much larger ones. It felt good, right somehow. Like they belonged together.

Jewel stared intently off into the forest, like perhaps someone hid out there in the brush and pines, someone only she could see.

It pained me to admit it, but she looked pathetically temporary, like she were somewhere precarious between ordinary and the unknown, threatening at any moment to teeter into oblivion.

I would do my best to keep the scales balanced. But one never knew—never. Jewel was fragile, but, at least for the moment she was at peace.

Suddenly, everything changed.

Jewel whirled to face me so quickly her red hair flung about her head like a helicopter blade.

Startled, I took a step back.

Her pupils enlarged to the point of consuming the blue irises entirely. Her usual penetrating gaze turned even darker and sharper.

Maybe she decided I was trustworthy or maybe her personal demons became too much to contain; I don't know. Jewel opened up to me.

The words came pouring from Jewel's mouth like a monotone hum. "I see him sometimes."

Bewildered and taken completely by surprise, I asked, "See who?"

"I see Daddy." Jewel's chest heaved as if under the weight of the words, her voice thick, as if she spoke through a mouthful of blood.

I needed to be casual—not surprised or skeptical—so I simply nodded in understanding.

Inside I felt destroyed, beat to shit. This wasn't anything innocent like telling me her brain tingled.

As if she questioned my sincerity, perhaps with good reason, she said, "I do see him, Jason. I wouldn't lie to you."

I chose my words carefully. "I—I know you wouldn't, Jewel, not intentionally," I said, "but—but your dad's . . . your dad's dead, Jewel." The realization of what she said sent chills up my spine. "Do you mean you see him on your Facebook page?"

Jewel turned her head slightly and peered from one eye, an eye partially covered by a lock of ginger hair, as if she were sizing me up. If she were surprised about me knowing of her Facebook page she didn't show it. Instead, she corrected me. "I didn't mean that, Jason." She said it menacingly, angrily. Her black pupils danced with a brilliance I'd never seen, as if newfound life bubbled from them like a black fountain.

The rest of the world stopped and my heart pounded. It'd been a simple statement. In another situation, it may have rung rather innocuous, but not coming from the mouth of Jewel, not from a temporary life, a life I loved far beyond my own.

I ventured into a territory that nobody, let alone an immature eighteen-year-old, should be venturing. I asked, "Wh—what did you mean?" I stood still as a cornfield before a storm, mouth agape, not wanting the answer.

Her piercing eyes heckled me despite her invitation. In a whisper she hissed, "Are you sure you want to know?"

I didn't but I did. I loved her. "Yes, Jewel," I said. "I do, real bad."

Jewel looked over her shoulder into the woods. The shadows within the trees grew deeper and cryptic. The sun lost its intensity as if what Jewel was about to tell me might be so sinister even nature would feel compelled to bow to it's will.

Still facing the woods, Jewel mumbled with words that died in her mouth, barely audible. "Yes, daddy, he's a nice boy," she whispered. "He's my friend."

What the hell was going on? "Are you talking to me?"

She wasn't.

Goose bumps formed on my neck and my throat went dry. My nausea reminded me I could never take my words back.

Slowly, so slowly it pained me to watch, Jewel turned back to face me, disapproval written on every essence of her face.

Her frown contained too many wrinkles for someone so young.

She said in a dark whisper, "Please don't interrupt when Daddy is speaking."

Realization reared its ugly head. Jewel was insane, stark raving mad.

But I loved her.

Like an out of body experience, I said, "Jewel, your dad isn't there. Nobody is there."

Ready for Jewel to behead me for my insolence, I cringed. Instead, I got a surprise, as usual. She smiled delicately, a smile her eyes didn't quite reciprocate.

Jewel whispered barely loud enough for me to hear. Anyone looking our way would have thought we were standing around, looking at each other. "Of course he's there, silly, right there in the woods. Can't you see him?"

I stared hard, believe me I did. I wanted to lie and say I did see him, but I said, louder than I should have, "No; no, I can't see him. I'm sorry."

"You still don't believe me do you?" She looked about to cry.

I drew her closer. "I do love you, Jewel. . I want to understand and believe you, so help me. Help me believe."

"You're exactly like your mom. You don't believe me. You think I'm crazy."

I did, though it wasn't important anymore. "Okay, I'm sorry I interrupted your dad. I'm sorry, okay?"

Jewel's eyes brimmed with tears, chest heaving. She looked insane. Her eyes searched mine for sincerity. She must have found it because she said, "It's okay. I'll smooth things over for you. Dad's not always good at forgiveness."

I stayed silent. What the hell was I supposed to say?

Jewel turned to the woods. Every so often, she nodded as if responding to someone invisible.

I wasn't sure if I should join her or walk away. Luckily, the bell saved me the decision.

Jewel remained, staring into the dark woods.

I reached out to her to remind her the bell had rung. Jewel whirled around and blurted, "Daddy says you can come over. He'll let you see him."

Trickles of sweat started at her temple, snaked down her neck, and disappeared into the collar of her shirt. Apparently, speaking with her dead father took a lot out of her.

I hesitated. "You know I'd love to come over . . ."

Chest still heaving, pupils still dilated, Jewel said, "Do it. Please come over—please. I need someone else to see—"

"See what, Jewel?"

"I need you to see Dad. So you know I'm not crazy."

"Jewel, I don't think you're—"

"You think I'm crazy. I would, too. Come see for yourself, please."

"Why do I need to come to your place to see him?" Deep down, I knew why—but I cared about this girl.

"Daddy's funny. I thought you might have been able to see him in the trees, but he didn't allow it. Most times, only I can see him."

I glanced at the woods. A cold shiver started in my lower back and worked its way to my shoulders—odd. If what she said was the truth, not a delusion from a grieving girl, well, it wasn't odd, but downright scary as hell. "I'll talk to my parents tonight and see if they'll let me. No promises."

"You promise, Jason?" She said this with such pleasure I couldn't let her down. I was her only friend—and now more than that.

"I said no promises but I promise to ask." My words had more angst than I'd intended.

If she noticed, Jewel didn't let on. She smiled and, to my surprise, hugged me—right there in front of our classmates, teachers and God. She let out a small squeal of glee, and, without another word, sprinted for the door to the school.

Chapter 12

I always had time to kill after school. Mom picked me up on most occasions, but not until after work. Jewel always went right home. Billy and the rest of the gang drove or took the bus. Today left me and Morris hanging out in the janitor's lounge, if it could be called that.

In reality, the lounge, little more than a corner of the sub-basement with an old, musty carpet remnant thrown down for comfort, resembled something more like a junkyard. Spare electrical parts and old ductwork littered the floor. A calendar full of nude women hung on the wall.

Morris enjoyed talking to me—enjoyed teaching kids the facts of life, as he understood them.

Although most of the guys, especially Billy, viewed Morris as a god, I took the-world-according-to-Morris with a grain of salt. In my opinion, anyone twenty-five, and for no good reason still lived at home, was a douche bag at best.

Morris currently prattled on, trying to teach me about women. "Ya see, dog, if a girl gets bored with you, the shows over, man, one-hundred percent completely over. You got to keep them interested, dude."

"Whad'ya mean, Morris, like I should entertain her or what?"

"Fuck no. You a fag or what? You gotta get in their shirt, their pants, keep them on their toes, man."

Still pretty new to all this sex talk, I didn't know all the slang yet. "You mean, like touch their privates?"

Morris shook his head. "Dude, you can't be saying shit like 'privates' no more. You're too old, makes you sound like a dick-weed. Call them what they are, pussies and cocks—cocks go in pussies. You'll learn soon."

"That's where babies come from," I said. "I don't want any babies."

"First off, just cover up, then you don't need to worry about babies."

"What?"

"You know, condoms."

I shook my head, unsure of what to say.

Morris got impatient. "Fuck dude, it's so your jizz can't get to her ovaries. Don't tell me you're not old enough to know what a condom is."

"Jizz? Oh, you mean sperm." I said it purposefully lame. If my dreams were any indication, I might need to wear two.

"Dude, I told you. Stop saying shit like that. It's jizz not fancy sperm."

"My dad calls it sperm."

"From now on, you come to old Morris. I'll shoot it to ya straight. I'm a straight shooter. You'll be in college next year, with college chicks. They'll be all over ya."

I wasn't so sure. But I had nothing better to do for another twenty minutes. I said, "I'm pretty sure Jewel's not the type. She doesn't like me touching her without her asking me to."

Morris shook his shaved head, his wiry frame turning with the motion. "You're all wrong. Women might say that but they don't mean it. Soon as you get across their state line, they melt like butter, putty in the hands."

"Mom calls it rape," I said sternly. "Harvey tried to do it."

"No, dude. I don't mean like make them do anything. You got to move slow and smooth, take yer time, wait till they beg you to touch them because they will, if you play your cards right."

"What do you mean?" He had my full attention.

"It's like this, man. Start with holding their hand, get them all cozy, maybe sit down with them somewhere on a bench at the park. You put your arm around them, talking to them, listening to them, all the while rubbing their shoulder and peering into their eyes—women love romantic shit. Before you know it, you got a handful of tit and she's begging for more."

I concentrated on not getting too worked up. No way did I want Morris to see he affected me. "My dad says I should be a gentleman. You know, like open doors and shit."

"Fuck yeah. How do you think he got to banging on your old lady? He opened lots of doors, bought her dinner. He ate a lot more than dinner."

"Fuck that, Morris."

"Dude, men romance women so they'll give it up...just the way it is. I always say, if a guy ain't going down, I know how to break up a happy home, know what I mean?"

I had no idea what he meant, but I let it go. He already thought I didn't know shit. "But if I have sex right away with someone, there's nothing left to do."

Morris smiled. "Sure there is, dog. You nail them again, 'cause it's even better the second time, ya last longer."

I changed the subject.

Already sick to my stomach, mostly from trying to not get worked up, but also because the truth was hard to hear—at least Morris' version—I dug for a reason to leave. Glancing at the clock, I had it—time for Mom to come. Thank God for small miracles. "Look Morris, thanks for the talk, but I gotta go. Mom will be waiting upstairs."

"Sure thing, dude. You ever got any questions, any at all; you come see old Morris. I'll get you all straightened out on whatever it is you wanna know."

"Sure, Morris, thanks." I ran up the stairs as fast as possible.

With no sign of Mom in the parking lot yet, I went outside, not wanting Morris to see me still hanging around and give me more of his bullshit on girls.

I crossed the street to the Middle School, then walked up to the big wall. My favorite, the one I would miss the most when we were all gone—our violent version of dodge ball, Gauntlet, where kids with tennis balls lined up the whole length of the wall. One hundred feet of pure terror. The bravest would run across. Being one of those—the brave ones, like those guys from *"The 100"*—put me in pretty elite company. It made me feel good inside to know I'm like a hero. Sure, I took my share of balls, got some bruises. But never was I too scared to cross.

The game toughened me up, taught me life isn't always perfect, and there's always another day—usually. We didn't stop to think about the day in which the next day doesn't come, the great equalizer, the new dark days . . . Death.

At least I didn't—not yet.

But I would.

I wondered how resilient Jewel was, how much of a pounding she could take. How much could one person take before they gave up? I shook my head. I needed to help her, maybe the only one who could.

As my thoughts turned dour, Mom pulled up to the curb.

I took one last look at the wall, which didn't look grand anymore but decayed, sad, as if it knew the end was near. No more tennis balls, no more kids—not us kids anyway. We were young men.

No more Jewel.

Chapter 13

Right in the middle of clanking silverware and dishes, idle discussion about everyone's day, and the sucking noises Dad makes when he's trying to clean between his teeth, fear drifted through me. My little brother, unaware of my problems, smacked on his mashed potatoes like a little heathen. Worse yet, he chomped between bouts of screaming, "Hulk smash." The Hulk, his latest obsession, had turned my brother into a maniac. As if to prove it, he launched a fork of peas and hit me in the face.

"Nate, man, watch where you're throwing stuff," I yelled. "Mom, tell him."

"Nate, please keep your peas to yourself," she said patiently.

"Hulk throw peas, Hulk smash," Nate screamed.

Mom smiled and ran a hand through her wavy brown hair. "Mr. Hulk, would you please tell Nate he needs to come back, because if he doesn't, he'll be going to bed right after dinner."

Giggling, Nate said, "Here I am, mommy, I'm back. The Hulk had to go."

"Good, now stop throwing your peas."

"Sure mommy, I'll stop, the Hulk is gone."

"You're pretty quiet tonight, anything on your mind?" Both my parents were being respectful enough to not directly ask me about Jewel. But they were both dying to know how things went today.

"No, not really, you know." My rambling invited Dad to pry.

"You haven't said anything since you got home. Why don't you tell me?"

"I don't know where to start. Jewel"—I shrugged—"is a little weird since her dad died." I glanced at Dad.

He smiled. "I know it's not easy to think about but try putting yourself in her shoes. You might be acting a bit weird too, huh?"

I didn't want to think about losing Dad. "No, yeah, I know—"

"You aren't sure what will make a difference?" my mom asked.

She'd broken her own cardinal rule of not putting words in people's mouths. I didn't feel like correcting her. I didn't have the energy and I didn't know how to articulate my words. I said, "It's fine—everything's fine. She invited me to her house."

Mom's eyes brightened, and a smile teased the edges of her mouth. "How nice. Do you want to go?"

Good question. I said, "I guess—"

"You guess? A cute girl asks you over and all you can say is, I guess?" Dad said.

I shrugged. "I want to and all but—"

"—but what, Jason?" Mom said with concern.

I contemplated telling them everything but I couldn't. I said, "Her mom is weird."

Mom smiled big. "She's hurting inside too. She'd enjoy the company as much as Jewel. She'll be there, right?"

"I'm sure," I mumbled, not knowing or caring if the stinky bitch was there or not.

"You know the rule," Dad said. "If you're at a girl's house, their parents have to be home. But go have fun," he said happily. "I know you like her and she enjoys your company.

"It'll be good for her. She needs a friend. Besides, it won't do you any harm to socialize with a girl. Learn to be a gentleman."

Dad smiled and winked.

I recalled my conversation with Morris and almost vomited right there at the table.

"Are you okay? You look green," my mom observed.

"I'm fine, Mom. A little nervous." Far from being a complete lie, just not the whole truth, my statement served to mask my current strongest emotion—fear. "Can I be excused?"

Dad said, "Sure, sure son. So, when does she want you to come over?"

"Tomorrow, I think."

"Perfect," Mom said. "Take the bus home with Jewel and I'll pick you up, say around eight. Sound good?"

"Great, mom, can I be excused?"

"Sure, Jason, sure. I'll come see you before bed."

"Mom, I don't require you to check in. I'm eighteen."

"You will never be too old to give your mother a hug, mister," she said with mock sternness.

I smiled, sheepish. "Fine, you can give me a hug."

"Okay, you may be excused."

Part of me hoped my parents would have said no. Couldn't they see I was scared? No, I guess they aren't mind readers. I contemplated speaking with them about Jewel's claims, but every time I attempted it, my legs refused to walk downstairs. I didn't know how to tell my parents my girlfriend talks to her dead dad via a website in which she stares at his corpse.

The knock came at my door, but it wasn't Mom. "Come in," I said.

"Hey, Jason," Dad said too cheerfully, like I was still ten, "you getting excited yet?"

I blushed.

"Sorry, I meant nervous, anxious excited," he corrected.

"I know what you meant," I snapped, way too quickly.

"No need to snap at me. We can talk about anything, you and me."

"I know but—"

"You're embarrassed? It's natural to be embarrassed at your age. I was, too."

My embarrassment remained part of it but there were more issues Dad didn't know anything about or how to deal with—nobody would.

"What is it, son?"

I couldn't bring up Jewel's dad, so I brought up something else to garner Dad's interest. Something Morris had said. "Me and the guys talked about girls and . . . you know."

He smiled. "May I assume Jewel is more special than a friend?"

I laughed. He made it sound like Jewel and my relationship was like one of the kids from the alternative education department. I said, "Is 'special' the best word you could come up with?"

"What I meant was, you think of Jewel as a girlfriend, not as a female friend."

"I guess that's right."

"This is your first crush, your first love, so to speak."

The word love shocked me. I used it with Jewel, somewhat reluctantly, but to have Dad say it brought it to a whole new level. "I guess I must love her. I care about her an awful lot."

"Do you think about her all the time, dream about her sometimes?"

I was amazed he understood.

"You've got it bad. It's normal, Jason, completely normal. I didn't have my first girlfriend until I was your age either. And I didn't sleep for days."

"You didn't?"

"Nope. She was on my mind day and night. That's the way it is sometimes, when you care about someone."

"Was it that way with mom?" I asked, sincere.

He rubbed his chin, contemplating. "Let's put it this way: I met your mom in college. I'd had several girlfriends so I knew what I wanted in a girl. As you get older you'll date more than one girl until you find the love of your life. Everyone else is practice."

"I don't want anyone else, Dad," I said. "I want Jewel."

"I know but at your age, love isn't the same as when you get older. Certain things change."

"Like sex?" I exclaimed. "That's what you mean, right?" Exactly like Morris said.

Dad eyeballed me closely, choosing his words. "Yes, that's one of the things. But that's not all. The type of love changes, too. You're experiencing puppy love, cutting your teeth on the idea of girls being more than friends."

What I experienced didn't feel like puppy love—more like a full blown case. But I didn't correct him. Sometimes I still wonder what constitutes love.

He went on, "We all mature as we get older, priorities change, and the importance we put on relationships increases. Boys and girls settle down, want to have a family, start the cycle—all while building a life together."

I guessed what he said rang true for most people but it didn't make my life and death feelings less powerful.

I said, "I know you're telling me the truth, dad. But I can't imagine anything happening that would make me not want to be with Jewel. I care about her and I can't see her saying she doesn't want to be my girlfriend anymore."

Dad smiled sympathetically. "I know these new feelings are strong. But as time goes along, sometimes feelings change. That's the way love is."

"How do they change?"

"It's hard to explain," he said. He ran a hand through his dark hair. "It's like this: When a relationship is brand new, you can't sleep, eat, and everything else pales in comparison. But later, the newness of it wears off. The overwhelming love and attraction can diminish. If you find the person enjoyable even after the newness is gone, you have found your soul mate."

"What's a soul mate, dad?" I asked. I wondered if it was anything like a kindred spirit that made your brain tingle.

"Like me and mom," he answered. "The person you were meant to be with forever. The one you want to start a family with, build a life."

"What about divorce? Did those people think they'd found their soul mate?"

Dad placed his hand on my shoulder and sighed. "They may have thought they did. Or, maybe they did, but things happened."

I needed to know exactly what I was getting into. "Like what?"

"Sometimes people get married too soon, before they know the other person. We had the sex talk, Jason. You don't have to be married to have a baby. Sometimes, people get married because they get pregnant. And the relationship doesn't work out, sometimes anyway."

Morris had said the girls got bored. I asked, "What about boredom, dad? Do people get bored sometimes and not love the other person anymore?"

Dad rubbed his chin and furrowed his brow. He let out a breath and said, "Unfortunately, some people need variety, and those people never settle down—or when they do, they end up hurting someone when it turns out they can't do it."

"But, how do I know which people need variety?"

He shook his head. "That's murky water, buddy. Sometimes you don't know, at first anyway. The only way to know for sure is by getting to know someone."

"But they might hurt you," I said.

Dad smiled. "They may. It's likely you'll get hurt. Or, you might do the hurting. I hate to say it but it's the truth."

The truth—everyone told the "truth" lately. "I don't want to hurt anybody. I don't want to be hurt, either."

"The only way around it is to never have a girlfriend," he said with a shrug. "Is that what you want?"

"No," I said. "I have a girlfriend but I never want to hurt her."

Dad frowned, shook his head, and smiled. "In all reality, you only control your own behavior," he said. "If you find your feelings for Jewel have changed, communicate respectfully with her. Take the time to explain why the relationship didn't work for you, so she knows. She may learn something in the process, which she can use in her next relationship. It should work."

"Does it always?"

Dad shook his head. "No, sadly enough, it doesn't. Sometimes people move on without a good reason or no reason at all. There are hurtful people in this world, Jason. I hope you never have to meet one. But you might."

"Why do people get bored?" The boredom thing was eating at me. I wish Morris' talk hadn't bothered me so much, but it had.

Dad let out his breath.

He didn't want to answer me—probably thought it stuff I didn't need to worry about yet. Too damn bad. I expected an answer.

He shrugged and rubbed the palms of his hands together thoughtfully. "Like I said, some people seem to need the variety, enjoy being with someone new all the time. Remember what I said about the strong feelings at the beginning of relationships? Well, some people get addicted to those strong feelings," he said. "The only way to keep getting that rush is starting over with someone new."

I hoped to God Jewel wasn't a love addict.

"What about sex?" I asked.

"What about it?"

"Could someone, you know, hurt me, if they got bored because I didn't have sex with them?"

Dad chose his words. "Tough one, son. It could happen. If someone hurts you because of that, they weren't worth being with in the first place. Communication is key."

I remembered what Morris had said about talking and listening, but I presumed Dad meant it in a different sense. "Dad?"

"Yes?"

I blurted out, "What if Jewel wants to have sex?"

Dad's eyes flew open. "Why?" he asked suspiciously. "Has she talked about it?"

"No, I don't want her to get bored with me."

Dad returned his hand to my shoulder. "You're a little too young to worry about sex. There'll be plenty of time to worry about sex when you're older, like in college."

I wanted to remind him that was next fall, especially since Morris had made it sound like it could happen at any moment. I decided not to remind him. "Okay, dad, thanks."

"You bet, Jason, anytime," he said. "I enjoyed our chat."

A bit uncomfortable, I said, "Me, too."

He hugged me and left the room.

I still had questions but they'd have to wait. Maybe there was such a thing as questions without answers.

Justin Holley

I woke up. A storm raged, flashes of lightning transforming my room from pitch black to daylight—and back to pitch black once more. The black seemed darker, like the other night, the night of the dream.

Jewel.

The lightening flashed once more and my closet door stood wide open even though I always kept it shut.

Was I dreaming?

I glanced to the corner, the darkest spot in my room, an inky, tar-like blackness. It pulsated with darkness, as if tendrils of black matter were being thrust out like tentacles, coming and going, searching.

Searching for what—me?

I shuddered. My room felt cold, much colder than it should have, several degrees colder than when I fell asleep.

I stared at the corner for a long time, like I might miss something. Maybe I wanted something to happen—perhaps I willed it to.

A rumble of thunder boomed in the distance.

I caught a shimmer of movement and my heart about sputtered out with the shock. I looked more closely, despite my fear. The memory of my last dream had me oscillating between fear and a foreign emotion. The white of her bandages radiated from the dark corner like they made their own light. She whispered, "Jason, Jason, Jason."

"I'm here," I whispered. "Jewel?"

She stepped out of the deeper shadows. Her bandages were so white they nearly blinded me. Jewel's red hair hung over her eyes, bottomless black tiny pits. Self-conscious, I concentrated hard on those eyes; with the exception of her bandages, Jewel wore nothing else.

"Yes, it's me," she whispered. "I've come for you."

My concentration shot straight to hell in direct correlation to my growing sexual excitement. "Wh—what do you mean?"

"I've come for you," she said, "to be with you. Hold me, Jason. Hold me tight—keep me safe from the storm."

"But—but, the storm can't hurt you. I—"

She didn't seem to hear my stammering. Or she ignored it. White vapor slid from her mouth like fog, obscuring her naked body, roiling about her like a snake. Jewel walked closer to me.

The fog obscured Jewel completely, like a vacuum sucked her back into the dark corner of my room.

Alone, I was thrown off balance by the whole situation.

"I must be dreaming."

My closet door creaked, softly at first.

"J—Jewel?"

No answer.

"N—Nate?"

The door crept open. A figure outlined in the doorframe.

"Dad?" Shivers raced up and down my spine. I was ice cold.

The figure stepped out of the closet.

I tried to scream, but nothing came out.

The figure, a man, had no eyes. It shouted, "Jewel, what'd I tell ya about being naked around boys? Do I need to teach you a lesson?"

As he walked up to my bed, coldness radiated from him and enveloped me.

I pulled the blankets over my head.

Jewel said, "Jason, I'm so cold—hold me."

I didn't know what to do. I hesitated.

"Jason, stop being boring—hold me," she said.

Shaking, I lifted my covers to see out into the room. To my horror, I was naked too. When had I taken off my clothes?

Jewel's dad, half way to the bed, said, "You getting naked with my Jewel, boy?"

"I don't remember taking them off, I swear." I searched the room for Jewel and my clothes.

Her dad ambled toward me like a sightless zombie, blood pouring from his eye sockets. He had a pair of steel handcuffs in his hands. "I'll teach you a lesson you won't soon forget, boy."

Jewel joined me under my covers, her absolute coldness almost unbearable.

Almost.

"J—Jewel, what are you doing in my bed? You're dad's going to kill us." Her dad's red eye sockets bore into my eyes like lasers.

"Stop fussing," she said. "Don't you love me? Don't you want to touch me?"

"Yes but your dad—"

"I'm gonna tie you both up, like I tie up Jewel." Jewel's dad leaped at us.

Jewel screamed and climbed completely under the covers. I never felt anything so cold in all my life. Our bodies touched beneath the covers. My excitement grew. I wanted it, but not like this. Not with a ghost—not with her dad—right there. They had to be ghosts—what else?

"What's the matter, Jason?" she asked. "Don't I feel good?"

"Yes, but, I'm not sure"

"Sure of what, Jason?" she asked. She touched me, touched me like she knew what to do.

The buildup threatened to make me lose control, like the last time. My breath came faster and louder.

"Oh Jason, I can tell you like it," she whispered in my ear.

"I do . . . I do." Pressure built, faster, hotter. Without much warning, the release I'd ached for, and everything was over.

Jewel and her dad were gone.

All remained dark and silent in my room—and beneath my covers, too. I still didn't dare look. I needed to sleep. But an unintelligible sound, garbled like someone speaking through a mouthful of blood stopped me.

I lay still, hoping whatever it was would go away.

It didn't.

Suddenly the voice became clear. "I told you I would get you. You broke the oath—the blood oath."

I recognized the voice, and I shook with fear and cold, my naked body frigid beneath my covers—my safe haven.

"Jason, you son-of-a-bitch, you pussy-whipped fucker— I'm gonna kill ya, slit yer guts, like Mumford's and my sister's."

I wondered what lay in the clutter around my bed that I could repurpose into a weapon, but nothing came to mind. I pulled the covers off my head to look.

There stood Harvey. At least it looked like Harvey from the shoulders down. Above his shoulders, a nightmare loomed. Where Harvey's head should've been, a skull—the skull from the gang's bonding by blood—sat grinning like a hellish nightmare. The red candle still protruded from the hole in the top of its head and the eyes flashed red.

"What you staring at, Jason?" he asked. "You fucked up my old head, so I got a new one. What's the matter? Don't you like it?"

I crawled to the far side of my bed, horrified.

"You gonna answer me, pussy boy?" Harvey walked toward me. He had the aluminum baseball bat in his hands. He didn't seem to notice I was naked.

"Harvey, no, please. I'm sorry"

Harvey shrugged. "Look, I know this is a tough spot, buddy, but you gotta make things right with me and the gang . . . satisfy the oath. Take your medicine like a man, Jason."

"N—no."

Harvey lunged at the bed.

I closed my eyes.

I awoke, breathless. Sunshine streamed into my room like rays of pure warmth, the cold replaced by radiant heat.

The sudden change confused my senses. "I—I must've been dreaming," I whispered. I glanced under my covers. Naked, my boxers on the floor next to my bed; I shivered as the cool air hit my body. I quickly picked my boxers up and put them on—but the sticky fluid on my stomach stopped me. I took a deep breath and exhaled. "Another stupid wet dream," I whispered.

But I didn't believe it. I still shook with fear.

Chapter 14

As usual, I got to school early. I wondered if Jewel would be in—and what it would mean if she wasn't. At best, I had a fifty-fifty chance. After the dream I had, I hoped to look her straight in the eye without blushing.

We Die Young by Alice In Chains, coming to me quiet and muffled at first until the outside door opened, and it hit me full force. Billy must've gone at it with his old man, because he arrived at school early. If he got cuffed, he came in early. The quarrels with his old man were becoming more frequent.

Billy turned off his music and walked up to me. He looked tired. "Hey, Jason."

I searched his face for signs of a scuffle, to see if his old man had belted him.

"What the fuck you staring at, Jason?" he said. "Shit, I know I'm hot, but—"

"Get over yourself, man," I said. "I was looking to see if your old man cuffed ya is all."

"He cuffed me. What of it?"

"You should turn him in," I said. "It can't go on like this."

"Are you Jason the shrink or something? You're starting to sound like your old lady."

"What, you been seeing Mom on the sly, know how she shrinks people?" I asked with a grin.

Billy smirked. "Hell no, dude, I know if you've seen one shrink you've seen them all."

"How many shrinks you been to?"

"One fucker—he was a real asshole, tried shrinking our whole family and shit. My old man told him what he wanted to hear, got him the fuck out of our house. My old man hated those home visits. Anyway, my ma lipped off and told my old man the sessions wouldn't work if he wasn't honest with the shrink. Shit hit the fan. My old man cuffed her good, told her if he ever saw the shrink in the house he'd kill him—and her. No more shrink."

"Fuck dude," I said, "you never told me."

"There's lots of stuff I don't tell you, Jason," Billy said. "No need to."

"But—but we're best friends, boys, homeys, you know?"

"Who wants to hear about messed up shit? I mean, fuck Jason, you're my escape from it all. I don't want to fuck up by bitching to you about it all the time."

Maybe I was like Pollyanna, viewing the world through rose-colored glasses. My life, in comparison to Billy's, was a hundred percent better. My parents were fair and kind, his brutal. I got plenty to eat. It never occurred to me it may be different for my friends, other members of the gang, and Jewel. I said, "I'm sorry, Billy. We all got problems, but..."

"Look, dude, everyone knows you got a future," he said. "Your family lives here by choice. It's not that way for the rest of us, dog."

I had never viewed it that way. "I feel like I belong. I'm no different than you, man, just part of the gang."

"You don't need the gang, Jason. Everyone knows. We're all waiting for the day you walk away. That's what pisses Harvey off more than anything. He can't control you because you got stuff the rest of us don't. It's called money, Jason. The rest of us don't have any. What we get, we get from taking it."

"It can be different, Billy."

"Sure it can, dog," he said. "For you, but not for all of us. I know it's hard for you to hear."

"It's tough," I said slowly. "You guys are my friends, friends forever."

Billy shrugged. "Times are changing, Jason, I can feel it. Anyway, don't feel bad, bro. We still have a month all together, and you got your Jewel. It'll all be good for you."

"What about everyone else?"

"Don't sweat it. Let's not talk about all this heavy shit. Let's go see Morris."

"Fine." But I was far from fine.

We hadn't been sitting down in Morris's office for five minutes and he already prattled on about women. "Dudes, you should've seen the chic I was banging on last night. Shit man, she had a body that wouldn't quit."

I thought Morris was lying. "You weren't doing shit. Why do you make shit up?"

"Hell no, I ain't lying man, shit. What kind of guy do you take me for? Of course I was banging her. I wouldn't lie about it."

Billy glared. "Why do you say stupid shit? Morris won't talk to us no more if you keep lipping off."

I shrugged.

Morris continued, "I don't need no highschooler calling me a liar."

"Don't worry about Jason," Billy said. "He's wound up on account of he's going to a girl's house after school." Billy mockingly thrust his hips up and down.

176

Morris grinned. "Right, little man? You gonna try to score?"

"Damn it, thanks a lot, Billy." I was pissed.

Billy held out his palms in mock surrender. "Hey, cool down, dude. Morris is all right. He'll have advice for ya."

"Like the advice I got yesterday," I said with a moan.

"Damn straight, dude," Morris said. "I was giving ya the clear shit, the real deal. Sex is where it's at, man."

"I don't know, Morris," I said.

"Fucking aye, little dude," Morris said. "You want to pop her old cherry or not?"

I shrugged. "I don't think..."

"Stop thinking and act. Be a man of action. What do all the posters in your guys' classrooms say? Dare to be a *man*? Dare to *be*?"

Morris worded things so cool. Still, I stayed silent.

Morris fiddled with something wrapped in tinfoil. "So, who's the gal?"

I shouldn't have told him but I did. "Jewel."

"You mean the depressing little redhead you were talking to?"

"She's not depressing. I like her."

"Dude, she's all beat to shit—pretty sorry excuse for a piece of ass."

"Fuck you, Morris." I lunged at him, but Billy got in the way.

"Whoa, chill," he said. "He didn't mean nothing by it, did you, Morris?"

Morris shook his head. "Fuck no, I didn't. Shit, dude, take it anywhere you can get it. Who am I to judge?" He put his palms up.

Still pissed, I shot daggers with my eyes. If Billy hadn't been in my way, I would've popped Morris right in the nose.

Morris changed his tone. Looking back, I'm sure he didn't want any negative attention from the school. He said, "Look, man, sorry I dissed on her. Here, as a peace offering, take this with you when you go to her place. It'll get her in the mood, if you know what I mean." Morris grinned and extended his hand with the tinfoil in it.

"What's in there?" I asked.

"It's a little something to soften her up—A little aphrodisiac, bro. A little insurance never hurt anyone, right?"

It was drugs. "Fuck no. I ain't giving her no dope—I can do it by myself."

He snatched the package away. "Hey, suit yourself. More for me this way."

With wide eyes, Billy said, "I'll take it, if Jason doesn't want it."

"Billy, what're you doing?" I asked. "Drugs will kill you."

Morris grinned. "We gotta die of something. Might as well go down getting naked and high."

"I want it, Morris, please, give it to me," Billy said. "I wanna try it."

Billy couldn't take meth or pot. He wasn't smart enough to avoid addiction. Plus, he might be stupid enough to get caught. "Fine, Morris, I'll take it," I said. "Give it to me, but keep it away from Billy."

Hey, what the fuck?" Billy squealed.

"You don't need to get caught," I said. "Your mom already found your chew can. Now you have to borrow from Tracey. Your dad will beat you to shit."

Morris said, "Okay, okay, I won't give none to Billy. Shit, you're worse than an old woman, Jason." He handed me the tinfoil.

I stuck it in my pocket.

Morris said, "I won't even charge you this time. But next time..."

"There won't be a next time. If I see you with drugs, I'll tell Principal Hammond."

Morris stood up, looking like he might kill me. He moved forward, pinning me to the wall.

I tried to wiggle free, but Morris was too strong. I smelled his sour breath and saw the madness in his eyes. "Mor— Morris, what the fuck?" I said. "Get off me, man."

Morris kneed me in the groin. I fell to the floor, sobbing, unsure if Billy was mad at Morris—or surprised.

Morris knelt down to where I writhed in pain. He spit in my face and hissed, "You even *hint* about any of this to Hammond, I'll kill ya. Better yet, I'll kill your parents, kill them deader than shit. And your precious Jewel, too."

"Leave her out of this." I tried to sound tough but I failed.

Morris knew he'd found the key to my silence. "I'll gut her, little man—gut her like a fucking little pig."

Terrified, I believed he would. Jewel didn't need someone else trying to hurt her. Morris's features softened. "Good, we understand each other so we can maintain our friendly relationship. Now get outta here. I got work to do."

Wiping off my face with my sleeve, I stood up slowly, not even glancing at Morris. My balls ached like hell. Almost doubled over, I grabbed Billy by the arm and dragged him up the stairs. I needed to keep him away from Morris. Hell, I needed to stay away from Morris myself—he was bad news.

Chapter 15

Thoughts of Jewel danced through my head. She was late for school, and I wondered if she'd come at all. I fidgeted at my locker, worried. Flustered by the drugs in my pocket, I would've acted weird anyway. She would've known because she always knew when I was up to something.

Jewel was good.

Once she knew, she'd make me tell Hammond—or she would herself. Morris would kill her, maybe my parents, and for sure me. I was screwed.

I limped out into the playground, drugs in my pocket and reckless—a dangerous combination. Voices from *Gauntlet* floated to me like a drug from across the street. I walked over to kill some time, hang out with the little kids without extorting them.

The line of kids with tennis balls were jeering at a little kid who lay crying in the middle of the wall. The throng sounded like animals, predators, not caring about this little hurt kid, but wanting him to get up so they could pelt him.

It reminded me of the book, *The Lottery*, which we read in English. Worse yet, it reminded me of the bad things happening to Jewel—and the predators hunting her.

On this day, it all made me sick to my stomach— probably because of what I went through with Morris. I couldn't take the bullshit anymore. I walked up to the spot in which "Gauntlet" began.

The throng started chanting, "Go, go, go, go—"

I glared at them as I stepped out in front of the wall, daring one of the sons-of-bitches to throw a ball at me.

They didn't. They breathed hard, angst and crazed lusty hormones palpable. It floated off from them like a primordial mist.

I walked over to the little kid. "You okay?

He wiped his eyes. "I think so," he said. "Thanks, Jason."

I helped him up. "Why'd you run Gauntlet?" I asked.

"Cause you do it. You're so cool. Everyone thinks so."

I shook my head, realizing the impression I bestowed on other kids. Why did I take responsibility for everyone's actions? Everything I did ended up a mistake—the gang, the gauntlet, and the drugs in my pocket.

I took a deep breath. "I outta remember it, but what's your name?"

"Jamie."

"I'm going to share a secret with ya, Jamie. This isn't cool. In fact, it's stupid. Someone could get hurt, more than a sore muscle."

"But—but, you're a hero."

I helped him up. "No, I ain't no hero," I said. "I take stuff from little kids."

"You're not like the others, Jason. You ask nice."

"Don't matter; it's all the same shit no matter how I try to wrap it up. It's bullshit. I'm sorry."

I'm not sure if anything I said actually sank in. But I hoped so.

I took Jamie by the hand and led him off the wall.

The throng jeered its discontent.

Fuck them.

I hadn't known where to stash the drugs where a teacher or kid wouldn't find them. I didn't put them in the toilet because of the tinfoil. I sure as hell wasn't going to open the tinfoil—who knew what the hell I'd find in there. Scared to throw it away, worried a poor little kid would find it, I couldn't decide. Worse yet, an adult could find it and have the tinfoil fingerprinted. I was for sure screwed, blued, and tattooed. After running every scenario through my mind, I left it in my pocket, the only place I could hide it where no one would find it. The dope being in there creeped me out though, made me paranoid—so I might as well have taken the shit and got it over with, got high and said screw it.

But I didn't.

I didn't see Jewel until right after home-room period. At her locker when I walked up, I approached her quietly. I took a deep breath and put my hand on her shoulder.

She whirled around, quickly, startling me. "Get off me, get the fu—" She saw who it was. "Oh my gosh, Jason, I'm sorry. I thought..."

"It's okay, Jewel. I forgot you don't like being touched. Sorry."

She smiled. "It's okay, Jason. I don't mind you touching me. You make me feel safe. You're a nice guy. You can touch me," Jewel said shyly.

I blushed, the blood rushing to my face and elsewhere. Surprised I didn't pass out, I took a small step back. But the last thing I wanted was for Jewel to think me afraid. So for good measure, I reached out for her hand.

She gave it to me and suspiciously watched me out of the corner of her eye.

"I—I talked to my parents."

Jewel smiled, the suspicion gone from her face. "What did they say?"

"It's okay with them if I come over after school. Mom said she would come pick me up at eight, if it's okay with your mom."

Jewel frowned. "Anything's okay with Mom, Jason. She isn't much of a mom, not anymore. I spend more time taking care of her it seems."

"Oh, I'm sorry, Jewel," I said. "If you don't want..."

"No, I do want you to come over, bad. But don't expect Mom to make popcorn or anything."

"No, of course not, we'll do our own thing. We'll have a great time."

Jewel squeezed my hand. "I'm so excited, I can't wait. I never have anyone over. I'll show you my room."

I blushed, my latest dream coming back in full force.

"I'm not embarrassing you, am I?" She smiled.

"Not at all, Jewel. I'm, you know, excited."

Jewel giggled. It was beautiful and wonderful to see the joy in her eyes. Unbelievable. A girl handed so much crap— she deserved to be happy. She turned a bit more serious. Jewel said, "Maybe you can meet Dad."

I didn't know what to say. "Maybe, we'll see if he . . . comes around."

It must have been an appropriate thing to say because it made Jewel smile. "Well, he said he would. He wants to meet my boyfriend, the boy who makes me so happy." Her eyes lit up with happy radiance.

The thought of seeing a ghost sent a chill up my spine. But there would be no backing out now. "I—I'm glad I make you happy, Jewel. You make me happy, too."

She grinned, wide, showing all her teeth. She leaned toward me, meeting me half way.

I reciprocated and our lips touched—the electricity incredible. I almost burst right there on the spot.

She pulled away, leaving a void in my heart. Jewel said, "I have to take a make-up test today at lunch, so I won't see you until Lit. Will you pass me a note?"

I grinned. "What if Mrs. Melchen grabs it?"

"Do you care?" Jewel giggled.

I smiled. "Not at all."

"Good, I'll see you there." She blew me a kiss.

Like she walked on air, she ran away until she disappeared up the stairs.

Billy walked up to me and broke the spell. "Dude, you got it grade-A bad, man," he said. "You gonna do like Morris said, bang her?"

"Fuck you, Billy. Don't bring up Morris to me. Anyways, I care about her. I don't wanna ruin things. You ain't been banging anyone, either."

"Dude, you pissed Morris off is all," Billy said. "I mean, he's kinda turning into a douche bag but he's trying to help us. Sorry about what he did to you though—that was tough love." He paused. "I'm gonna though."

I was pissed. Morris had kicked the shit out of me and threatened about everyone I love. He might be worse than Harvey. My words came out harsh. "Gonna what?"

"Bang a chic," he proclaimed.

"Who?" I asked. I had no idea who it could be. Maybe he'd lined something up with one of the carnie chicks but I doubted it. What would they want with a scrawny guy with no money?

"Tracey," he said.

What a douche. "What the fuck, dude?" I asked. "Why you saying stupid shit? She's part of the gang, and besides, if you even tried she'd wipe her ass with you."

"Fuck no, Jason, she digs me," he said. He believed his own bullshit. "I'm gonna bang her, for real, dude."

"She got done kicking your ass day before yesterday, because you were being stupid. Now you're being stupid again."

"No, dude, it's no problem. Morris told me what to do."

"I told you to shut up about him," I said, much too loud. "Screw Morris, Billy. He's a loser, still lives at home sucking off mama's tit. He don't know jack."

"It seems like he's got it all laid out. He gets high too, super cool."

"There's nothing cool about getting high, so shut up."

Billy slipped into his own little world. "Get naked and high, toking and screwing, man, the good life. Like my brother, man."

"You'd be a loser like Morris, living at home, working as a half-assed janitor at a high school, and being friends with students. The guys a jackass, dude. He threatened my whole family."

"Stop saying stupid shit, Jason," Billy whispered. "Morris didn't mean it, I bet. Just because you're scared of your own shadow. I'm gonna get Tracey in bed, man, for sure."

I shook my head. I didn't know what in Billy's head made him say shit like that—hopefully it wasn't contagious.

Ironically, Tracey walked around the corner—sweet justice. "Did I hear my name?" she asked. She had a smile on her face, which wasn't unusual if she wasn't pissed about something.

"Hell yes, Billy was talking about you," I said, "weren't you, Billy?"

Billy looked about ready to die. "I was saying you beat my ass the other day, I have lots of respect for you, I swear."

"What are you so worked up about?" Tracey asked. "I didn't hurt you permanently, reminded you to mind your own business is all."

"He was saying more, Tracey," I said. "Go ahead and tell her what you told me, Billy. Don't be afraid of your own shadow."

Curiosity etched her face. "What, what was he saying?" Turning back to Billy, she said, "Do I need to kick your ass for real?"

I made the obscene gesture Billy made earlier, but I stopped abruptly when Billy mimed puffing a joint.

"You going weird or something?" she asked. "What the hell?"

I needed to change the subject. "I'm fooling, Tracey," I said, "He didn't say Jack. Let's hang out in the yard. We haven't got to do much lately."

She calmed down, and I let out a breath.

Tracey didn't need to know I carried a tinfoil of dope in my pocket.

"Anyone heard when Harvey is coming back to school?"

Billy said, "They said he couldn't come back until they fitted his teeth with a retainer, so they don't fall out and shit."

Tracey whistled. "Damn, guess he's not so tough after all."

"Guess not," Billy said. "There's at least one bad ass a little badder than him." Billy smiled. He was trying to kiss my ass.

"Badder ain't a word, Billy," I reminded him.

"Whatever, dude, you beat the fat ass but good."

"You messed him up—good for you bro," Tracey said. She shook my hand. "You get in any serious trouble?"

I shook my head. "Nope, no one called the cops and both Mom and dad said it was okay since I was sticking up for Jewel."

"I was scared for her. Harvey was gonna tap her if you hadn't come to save her. I would've tried to help, but he'd probably try to tap me, too. He'd better not though, I'll kick him square in the junk." The scowl on Tracey's face left no room for doubt.

I shot Billy a quick glance, and grinned at him.

Billy didn't grin back.

Tracey saw the exchange. "Billy, you sure there's nothing you wanna say to me?" she asked slowly.

"I was wondering if I could bum a chew off ya."

"That's it?" she asked. "I think someone's fucking with me." I giggled, which pissed Tracey off. "What the hell's going on?"

I lost my willpower. "Billy's got it bad for you."

Billy cringed. He wanted to do the joint bit, except it was too late.

"Slap me full of shit, Billy," Tracey said. "I didn't know you liked me. I think you're cute, too. Maybe we can be like Jason and Jewel."

Billy turned pale, things happening faster than he ever expected.

Tracey turned to me briefly and winked. She turned her attention back to Billy. "I bet you wanna go in balls deep, don't ya, Billy? Come on, let's go see Morris, he must have condoms down there. Damn, maybe we can do it right down there in his office. Wouldn't that be the shit?"

I grinned. Only Tracey would've known how to beat Billy at his own game. Billy looked ready to run for it.

He stammered, "I don't know, Tracey. I mean, we're friends and all..."

"You mean you don't want to bang me, Billy?" she asked. "I mean shit, you boring or what?"

I almost choked, barely stifling a laugh. She had him going—hook, line, and sinker.

"No, fuck no, I ain't boring. I, you know . . ."

"What, you're a big man? Gonna be a big time player like Morris the pig? Come on. Now's your big chance, let's get it on." She made like she banged a gong.

I laughed so hard my gum popped out of my mouth.

191

Tracey laughed, too, right at Billy.

Billy smiled. "Screw you guys."

All three of us laughed until we were blue in the face. It felt good, the first time in a while nothing felt upside down.

But it wouldn't last, of course. Tracey got serious. "I hear the cops are gonna search the swamp for Harvey's sister."

We looked up. "They think she's dead?" I asked.

"I heard," she said, "they gave it forty-eight hours. I guess they figure she didn't run off banging a carnie."

"You think Harvey killed her?" I asked, vocalizing what I was sure everyone was thinking.

Billy looked spooked, eyes big and white.

"I do," she said. "It's been a while since we've done anything exciting, probably since we took the blood oath. We been so busy taking and protecting, know what I mean?"

My turn to nod.

Billy kept on staring at Tracey like she had a skull for a head.

"So I was thinking," she continued. "Whad'ya guys think about finding her before the cops?"

"You mean out at Buck Hill?" Billy asked, a hitch in his voice. "You mean her corpse?"

"I hear Leonard was gonna look, too. I want to beat him to it, find her first, and get all the glory. What do you say?"

"When?"

"Tomorrow night, just us," she said. "It'll be like old times."

Billy looked like he might die of fright. I wasn't keen on finding a corpse either, but Tracey was right. We needed to do this. The chick deserved to be found by someone other than a bunch of asshole cops who'd shove her in a bag. And who better than the remnants of the gang, whose leader probably offed her.

Chapter 16

The rest of the day played out uneventful. I wasn't sure if I was more nervous about going to Jewel's house, the drugs, or going to find Harvey's sister. Anyway, I'd made Jewel a note in math, which made her giggle. Neither of us cared if the teacher read it in front of the class anyway—everyone already knew we were an item.

I hadn't ridden a bus in a long time, not since maybe the ninth grade. I had my driver's permit, but Mom picked me up most of the time. As a consequence, I remained a little fuzzy on the whole bus thing, where to go, where to sit. Jewel took complete charge, made it easy.

Jewel and I sat in the back seat. By the body language of other kids they also wanted the back, but had, somehow, lost the right to do so, the pecking order never clearer than in the back of the bus.

Jewel reveled in it with a steely glare, making things plain. This seat belonged to her and her friend, stay the hell away—or die.

"You always sit in the back?" I asked.

"I do now."

I had no idea what she meant. I didn't ask.

Jewel told me anyway. "See that boy over there?" She pointed at a boy with a Nike windbreaker and short cropped, black hair. "He used to sit back here. I persuaded him I should, instead."

"How?"

"I would have shared the seat, but—"

Prickles of fear crept up the back of my neck, a warning.

Jewel's somber expression melted her smile like wax. "But he didn't like it when I spoke with Daddy. It made him scared. He got so scared he wouldn't sit back here anymore. He said I was crazy. Maybe I am."

"Of course you're not crazy, Jewel. I don't understand why you can see him, you're dad, and nobody else can. But that doesn't make you crazy. Maybe everyone else is, you know?"

This made Jewel smile, briefly. "No, I can't blame people for getting scared off. I didn't believe in ghosts either, until recently—until daddy went away. And came back."

The hair stood up on my head. Despite my rising terror, the desire to lessen her burdens overpowered it. "We'll figure it out, Jewel. I'll help."

Jewel's bottom lip trembled. "Do you promise?"

"I promise. I won't be scared, Jewel." I hoped it was a promise I could keep.

She laid her head on my shoulder.

I'd protect her, no matter what. I would've walked through hell and spit on the devil himself if I needed to.

She whispered, "Thank you."

I turned to her and ran my fingers through her ginger hair. To me, Jewel glowed with a beautiful aura, someone I loved, not someone who needed my help.

She was my girlfriend.

The rest of the bus ride, Jewel chattered about school. She didn't mention home, not even once. Jewel never mentioned home, not to anyone but me anyway.

The bus stopped, the brakes screeching with their wretched honk as the air breaks released.

My heart pounded as the doors slid open.

Jewel and I stepped into the sunshine. A glimpse of her house from the road, otherwise obliterated by the dense grove of trees. We trudged the long dirt driveway and the loose gravel crunched beneath our shoes.

Believe me when I say I peered long and hard into those woods. I wondered what story the trees could tell, the things seen and unseen.

We approached her home, a one-story rambler with peeling turquoise paint. Shingles sat cockeyed on the roof, the railing on the front porch long since fallen, the front step missing multiple boards.

Maybe she was embarrassed, or maybe she caught me staring, but Jewel offered, "Since Daddy died, we haven't been able to keep up with the chores. Sorry."

Her eyes took on a black hue, absorbing the twinkle they normally flashed. Sometimes her eyes scared me.

"No, it doesn't bother me at all," I lied.

I had no idea why they moved from wherever it was they lived before, other than Jewel not fitting in. Whatever the reason could be, it wasn't pleasant. No one moved into a ramshackle place for no good reason—not in my world.

"Is your mom home?" I asked, feeling like I didn't belong.

Jewel stated with distaste, "She's probably drunk. She drinks a lot since Daddy's death."

"Doesn't she see him?" I asked, regretting it immediately.

Jewel whipped around and faced me, her ginger hair falling into her face. "No. Don't you mention it to her. Daddy would be very mad."

"Why?" Stupid question but the first to enter my mind.

Jewel stared as though I should know the answer.

I didn't. But who in their right mind would?

She answered gruffly, "Daddy doesn't like it when people talk about him without his permission. He might punish me."

Her statement sent the ice spiders crawling about my scalp. Was it possible? I tried to talk but my mouth felt welded shut.

We entered the house.

Jewel surprised me and stood up straight as we entered, her shoulder slouch less pronounced, her confidence seeming to grow to infinite proportions when in her personal domain.

I wondered why.

We walked through the front door, which creaked open on one rusty hinge. The first room we entered, the kitchen, was layered in various forms of organic filth.

Dishes were piled a good three feet high. At least they were placed next to the sink where dishes belong, in my world anyway. The greasy gold linoleum, cracked and tearing, made crunching noises beneath my tennis shoes. A block of moldy cheese sat on a stained countertop. A bloody hamburger meat wrapper sat stinking in the open door to an antiquated microwave; the flies made love to it as they crawled.

Jewel's mom sat at the shabby, chipped Formica table filled with past due bills and three empty bottles of Irish whiskey, the ashtray in front of her piled high with spent cigarette butts. She held one cigarette, still smoldering, in her mouth and another, unlit, in her hand, ready for immediate kindling when the tobacco was spent from the other. Her hair, once black, was laced with grey wisps like ghostly streamers, unkempt and wild.

She may have been attractive once, but the deep lines in her face spoke to a hard life. She wore a ratty, light blue terrycloth bath robe barely covering her. She bent forward as if hoarding her filthy cigarette butts. I forced myself to look away so as not to gawk at her cleavage, which stuck out prominently, the robe loose enough to reveal large breasts complete with nipples sticking out like pencil erasers.

I couldn't risk Jewel's mom catching me staring. Worse yet would be if Jewel caught me. I prayed to God my penis would mind itself—it was acting strange lately.

Jewel approached her as if her mother were a child. She said somewhat cheerfully, "Mommy, this is Jason. He's the friend I told you about."

The woman looked up from the table briefly. Before returning her gaze to the mess before her, she muttered, "I've seen you before, at the school."

I tried to smile, ignoring the woman's stench. "Yes, after school the other day."

Her eyes lit up briefly before she frowned. "After the little rapist tried to ball my little girl, you mean," she said. "The little bastard ought to be castrated."

"But Jason saved me, Mommy, saved me before Harvey could do anything."

"Ain't you boys all the same?" she sneered. "You might go about the game a little different but in the end, sex is all ya want."

"Mommy."

"It's time you learned the truth. Men are filthy pigs. Your friend's eyes here lit up when he gawked into my robe. He tried not to look but he's a pig too."

Shocked, I remained speechless.

"Mother, stop." Jewel exclaimed. "I love Jason. I don't mind if he touches me. He didn't look at you. I was watching him."

"Ha. Are you jealous of your old mother? Maybe you should be. After all, I was hot to trot in my day."

"Mom, stop it. You're embarrassing me."

She frowned and picked up a half-empty whiskey bottle. She took a pull right from the neck, and she wiped her mouth on the back of her terrycloth sleeve. "Nothing like good booze. Helps keep them damn voices quite." She laughed.

I didn't know if the "voices" quip was a joke or if she laughed for no real reason.

"Mom, you need to stop drinking," Jewel said. "It's making you say horrible things."

"No, not the booze, Jewel," she corrected. "It's life. Life's a bitch, then you become one, then you die. Simple."

"Stop it, Mom. Daddy won't like..."

"Daddy won't like what, Jewel?" her mom challenged. "Me drinking and laying around like a lazy bum? Fuck him. Fuck him to hell, Jewel. He left us with nothing, not a pot to piss in. So, don't you tell me—"

"Mom!" Jewel shouted. "Stop, he'll punish us—me."

"You hear that crap about her dad haunting her from beyond? She tell you her old man is giving her those bruises on her arms? It's a load of bullshit. Shit, she does it to herself. Hell, your own mom knows."

In shock, my mind reeled. Jewel's dad wasn't causing the bruises? I managed, "Mom doesn't speak to me about confidential things."

"Don't go acting all nice, little piggy boy." She made snorting noises through her nose.

"Please stop, I'm not a pig," I stammered.

She whipped open her robe, for a moment, and her rather large tits shook up and down. "Go ahead, take a good look. No good looking out of the corner of your eye."

"Mom."

I turned away.

Jewel grabbed me by the arm and started walking briskly down the hall.

Her mom bellowed from the kitchen, "Fine, go screw her. She obviously wants you to. Go get it done with. You won't want her afterward, anyway, and I won't need to see you around anymore."

Jewel kept going, determined to get away.

I followed Jewel down a dark hallway, too dark to see the dust and cobwebs. Beyond a doubt, they were there.

Between the filth and Jewel's mom, I felt sick and contagious.

At the end of the hallway, a light through a crack in a door shone like a laser beam. Jewel opened it and we spilled into the sunshine filtering through the cracked windows. There were no screens anymore, but the cracked glass at least kept the bugs and weather out. Jewel's room, otherwise tidy—perhaps the only thing tidy in the whole house—spoke to her responsible nature. Her bed sat neat and made up, and her old toys were stacked neatly on shelves on the wall.

As if noticing my observation, Jewel stated, "Daddy says I should keep my room clean. Cleanliness is next to Godliness."

A statement, if it came from the mouth of my grandmother, would have sounded comforting, came across quite the opposite when quoted from someone dead—and who might still be coming around.

Jewel sighed. "I'm sorry about Mom. She's fragile is all, hasn't been the same since daddy left us. Don't pay attention to her, she doesn't know you."

"Jewel, I wasn't looking."

Jewel touched my shoulder. "I know you weren't, Jason. She's lonely and a drunk, says stuff she doesn't mean."

"It sounds like she means it."

Jewel shook her head and looked ready to cry. "She wasn't like this before daddy died. She was a good mom, like yours. It's all my fault, Jason."

I grabbed her hand. "No, Jewel, it's not your fault. You didn't kill your dad, it was an accident."

"But I yelled at him, made him mad. He would have paid better attention if he wasn't mad. He's not good when he's angry." She held up her arms and sobbed.

I let her arms rest on my chest, her hands landing gently on my shoulders. "Is he doing this to you, Jewel?"

"Y—yes," she sobbed.

I held her closer.

Jewel buried her head in my shoulder, extending her arms and pulling us closer.

Her chest heaved as she sobbed. Her tears dampened my cheek.

She curled her body into mine. I held her, letting the powerful sun warm us.

Jewel picked her head off my shoulder. Her blue eyes danced with tears, and a beautiful internal light, any hint of the blackness of her pupils gone, tiny dots of pitch. "Thank you,

Jason—for holding me, for being here," she said. "You have no idea what this means to me."

I wanted to kiss her, badly. But I didn't want Jewel to think what her mom, Morris, and Billy thought—I was only interested in sex.

Somehow, she knew. "It's okay, Jason, I know your heart." She turned her nose sideways and kissed me, soft and gentle.

I kissed back. It was wonderful. The warmth started in my heart, moved into my stomach, and downward, a wave of pleasure and happiness, unlike anything I had ever experienced.

Maybe I still haven't.

I pulled my mouth away, not far, but far enough to whisper. "Jewel, we don't have to do anything. I love you no matter what."

Jewel ran her fingers through my hair. "I know, Jason. But we could. I mean people who love each other do, sometimes, right? We're eighteen..."

"I guess so." My breath came harder, the warmth increasing.

Jewel turned her body, slightly, so my knee slipped between her legs and hers between mine. She pressed against me.

She sucked in air as my knee touched her.

She pushed harder.

"What if your mom—"

"I don't care, Jason. I'm sick of her. She can't care for me anyway but you can, Jason, you can." She kissed me.

I gave in and pulled her tight to me, all our parts touching.

Without warning, Jewel pulled away. "Daddy."

I whirled around, panicked, expecting to see her dad's empty eye sockets. But nobody stood there.

"Daddy, no. He's a nice boy and he loves me." Silence. "I don't believe you, Daddy. You're not the only one who can love me." She pulled away and faced her stereo sitting on a small table.

"Jewel, who are you talking to?"

She turned to me. "Please, Jason. Please don't interrupt him. He'll get mad, and hurt me. Maybe he'll hurt you." She turned back to the corner. "Please, daddy, don't hurt him. He doesn't understand."

My skin crawled and I desperately wanted to go home. But I needed to help Jewel. Something terribly wrong had happened in this house. "Is he saying I have to leave, Jewel?" I asked as calmly as possible.

"No. Yes, but I don't care. I need you here. I need someone else to see." Jewel screamed with terror. "Please, Jason—look."

"Look where, Jewel, at who?"

"My Dad, please, I'm not crazy. Daddy, please show him." Jewel wailed desperately, imploring a dead man to show himself.

I trembled with fear. My insides felt like ice.

Then it happened.

Across the small room, Jewel's stereo turned on. Korn's *Coming Undone* blasted.

I yelled over the din of the loud music, "How did you do that?"

The music turned up higher as if it didn't want Jewel to hear my words.

"I'm not doing anything. It's Daddy, can't you see him? He's right by the stereo."

"I don't see anything."

The stereo went silent so quickly I nearly fell forward into the noiseless void.

Jewel ran to her window. "He ran through the back yard. By the garden shed. Come on."

Jewel grabbed my arm and pulled for the door. My fear dissolved, and I resolved myself to see this madness to its conclusion. Something inside my head snapped. I chased after her desperately, as if my life depended on us catching this apparition.

Perhaps it did.

We bounded down the dilapidated back steps and across the back yard.

"Daddy, please wait, show him," Jewel screamed.

We came to a screeching halt at the edge of the bushes shrouding Jewel's overgrown yard. Obviously a mower hadn't touched it all summer. Our lungs heaved as they begged for oxygen. At least we were still breathing.

"Which way did he go?" I asked.

Jewel scanned the underbrush. "He's standing right in the bushes. Can you see him?"

We ran for the spot.

"I can't see anything," I stammered. For a second, I thought I did see something move with a subtle stir of the fabric of reality—perhaps my imagination or a trick of the evening light.

Then it vanished—if it were ever there at all.

Jewel stopped with her back to me and put out her hand into the brush. She pulled it out tentatively.

She sobbed and whispered, "He says he can't stop bleeding. Sometimes he leaves it on the bushes."

Sometimes he leaves it in your bruises.

Jewel turned and showed me the hand she stuck in the foliage.

A cold splinter of fear ran up my spine as I eyeballed the crimson smear on her fingers and forearm.

I didn't want to but I needed to know. I reached into the bushes. There I felt it, warm and wet on my cold fingers. I pulled away and stared at the crimson liquid pooled in my palm.

I can still smell the irony residue and salty bisque of its physical presence.

Jewel's shock nearly gagged me as she looked at me in the way people do when they share a secret—a dark secret.

Chapter 17

My mom's car hit the bumps in Jewel's driveway. I couldn't feel them. I was numb.

Mom never did come inside to get me or to speak with Jewel's mom.

Thank God for small miracles. Who knows what Jewel's mom would've said to her?

But I had no idea where Jewel's mom had even gotten to, no longer in the kitchen when Jewel and I returned to the house—after finding the blood on the bushes.

I wanted desperately to tell Mom there was a lot more shrinking for her to do, especially with Jewel's mom. Afraid of what Jewel's mom might say in therapy, I kept my mouth shut. If she said anything like the bullshit she told me, well, dig my grave.

Leaving Jewel was difficult. She understood but still, I wanted to be there for her. When Mom pulled up, I left Jewel sobbing in her room. She hadn't wanted to kiss anymore, fine by me. Chasing after a ghost didn't exactly make for a romantic afternoon. I sufficed with a hug and promised her I would see her in the morning, at school.

The morning was a long way off.

To her credit, because I know she died to, Mom didn't ask any questions. But when I opened the door to the house, Dad, full of them, jumped me immediately.

"Hey, man. How'd everything go? Did you have a good time?"

I took a deep breath. "Everything was great, dad. We listened to music and I spoke with Jewel's mom a little."

"Oh, right on," he said, "is she an interesting lady?"

Oh, sure, she's full of interesting things, I guess." I hoped I'd concealed my lie adequately.

"You guess?" he asked. "Hey, I know she's a little different, but she must be nice. Jewel is, right?"

"I guess she is. I mean, she's a bit strange, you know?"

Mom jumped in. "No need to rehash this discussion. Both she and Jewel are going through a tough time. They'll be fine—eventually."

I had my doubts. "Can I be excused?"

"You okay, Jason? You look like you lost your best friend—everything okay with Jewel?"

"Jewel's great. I'm tired, that's all."

Mom smiled. "You do look tired. I hope you're not getting sick. Maybe you should get to bed early tonight."

"I think I should, mom," I said. "Maybe I'm getting the flu."

"Get up to bed."

"I'll check in with you a little later, Jason, make sure you're okay," Dad said.

I headed for the stairs, wishing he wouldn't bother.

Mom called out, "Before you crawl into bed, throw all your laundry down the chute. I'm washing tonight."

I trudged up the stairs to my room, hoping none of my dreams had left stains.

I lay in bed, waited for my parents to go to sleep. I had plans tonight, but it wouldn't due for them to catch me sneaking out. I wished I was sneaking out to see Jewel, but I'd promised Tracey and Billy I'd meet them to enter the swamp. Goose bumps spread across my flesh. I wasn't sure what was scarier, Jewel's dad or Harvey and the swamp.

I swallowed the lump in my throat, tried to think of other things. For some reason, I remembered back to Sunday school. When I was younger, I worried about the end of the world. The pastor at our church said Jesus would come in on the clouds when he came back on judgment day. After that, I never felt safe unless the weather was crystal clear. Clouds meant the end, my death. Kids don't understand things like redemption and salvation. They know alive and dead—period. There are other ways, much less pleasant. The worst part is, unless you're here at the very end of all things, the world ends different for everyone.

I must have fallen asleep, because I woke to familiar small bangs resonating off my bedroom window.

And little did I know my world was gonna end that very night.

Chapter 18

I listened for any reaction from my parents, worried they'd heard the rocks.

Nothing.

I parted the curtains and watched Tracey, who was dressed in jeans and a black hoodie, blonde hair concealed beneath the hood. She paced back and forth, hands in pockets, nervous.

I slid my window open slowly. Billy was standing next to his mountain bike, looking up at me. He waived at me with an impatient gesture. They were both keyed up and ready to roll. Strangely, I didn't feel as nervous about going to look for a corpse as I should have but seeing a ghost and getting its blood on my fingers might've desensitized me a bit. No, not a little—a lot.

As always, I went out feet first, found the edge of the trellis, climbed downward, my feet finding the holes not plugged by ivy. Soon, I was at the bottom.

Tracey and Billy were already on their bikes. "Hey, guys," I said lamely.

"Hey," Billy said, "You ready, man?" I guesses he'd been imagining the moment he found the body. He looked real nervous, his eyes wide.

I'd had other things to worry about. Besides, we didn't even know there was a body. Harvey's sister could be off banging some carnie. Happened all the time. "Let's get this done," I said. "I gotta get back before my parents wake up. I'm still in a little hot water over Harvey." I grabbed my bike which leaned against the house.

"Let's go," Tracey said. "The cops are already out there, and I don't want them to find her first."

Most people would wonder why the cops would search the swamp at night. Sure, us kids did, because it was exciting, against the rules, what we needed to do, whatever, pick your poison. But wouldn't the cops want to search during the day? Not in our town. The night of the oath, things were different at the swamp at night, like creatures existed in the dark that couldn't be found in the day. Whenever the cops found a body in "the house" or the swamp, the sun was down.

The implications made my skin crawl. The coyotes started screaming already. I thought about the bloody bushes, and goose bumps plagued my arms and neck. The swamp probably ran all the way to Jewel's back yard, and I wasn't sure how I felt about that. On one hand, the fact would make me feel closer to Jewel. I could almost visit her. Walking through the swamp and crawling in through her bedroom window excited me. But on the other hand, corpses, ghosts, and killers awaited me. My stomach ached.

I remained quiet as I rode, lost in thought.

"What's wrong?" Tracey asked with genuine concern in her voice. "Everything okay with Jewel?"

I pedaled faster, knowing she wouldn't see in the dark anyway. "She's fine."

"You bang her?" Billy asked.

"For fuck sakes, no," I said. For good measure, I added, "But I know who you want."

That shut him up.

"Who?" Tracey asked. She had a peculiar and unidentifiable lilt to her voice. Maybe curiosity, maybe jealousy, maybe something else altogether.

"Nobody," I said, "I was fooling with Billy again."

She turned toward Billy but didn't say anything. Something might be brewing between them but now wasn't the time to point it out.

We stayed quiet for a couple blocks, no sounds except our wheels on the tar, the wind in the trees, a few early crickets. They were probably thinking about the corpse. I was thinking about Jewel—and blood. A cascade of colored lights reflected off the trees. Sirens broke the silence for a moment but all went silent again. We were close to the swamp.

"Cops are congregating by Hell House, but we should be able to sneak past them," Tracey said.

Billy said, "You guys think Harvey killed her?"

Harvey's threats, odd behavior and violence. My body went cold. If he could try to rape Jewel, had actually killed his sister, what else might he do to the girl who dared stand up to him? Was Harvey still at the hospital, at home in bed, or out here in the swamp? My skin felt like a sheet of ice, not because I was concerned for our own safety, the cops were out here after all, but that of Jewel's.

"Well?" Billy repeated. I didn't want to be the one to supply his answer out loud.

Tracey saved me the effort. "I think the chick is dead—deader'n shit—and I think Harvey did it."

Billy didn't answer, but he watched the looming swamp like Harvey might be out there. I wondered what the hell I was doing out here. I already had enough problems. If the chick was dead, finding her wasn't going to make her any less so.

As if in answer to my concerns, Tracey said, "We gotta find her. She deserves better than for her body to lie around out there—out there where animals can eat it and stuff." Tracey squished up her face, like she was trying hard not to cry. "We gotta find her," she repeated, quieter this time, like she had other reasons for doing this. Maybe she wanted to see Harvey go down.

Voices cascaded to us from the swamp as we approached Hell House. So we wouldn't be seen, we got off our bikes and pushed them behind the old Baptist church and left them leaning against the off-white walls. The church yard butted up to a little jag of high-ground which stood between the deeper swamp and the yard of the house. We should've been able to get there without alerting the cops to our presence.

"Where should we start?" Billy asked. Good question. Buck Hill Swamp covered several acres of black spruce and tag-alders. Lush ferns grew anywhere the trees did not, obscuring even large items. Finding a body in the dark would be like finding a pin in a swimming pool full of rice. We needed to be smart about this if we stood a chance at all.

Both Tracey and Billy looked to me. "Where should we start?" Billy asked. "I—I mean, we can't search the whole swamp."

"Maybe he stashed her in Hell House," Tracey suggested.

When we were young, we explored everything together, Billy and I: the Mississippi river, our ever expanding neighborhood, and even houses we considered to be haunted. Houses like Hell House. In addition to Bigfoot and UFO's, Billy loved the idea of ghosts. He'd love Jewel's house.

After confirming the cops were searching elsewhere, we soon stood outside 'the house', with the peeling white paint and mostly-boarded windows.

Billy said, "The rumor is, a guy blew his wife and kids' heads clean off and hung himself."

I shook my head silently. We'd all heard the stories, but Billy still sounded like a goddamn tour guide. He could be dramatic, no question.

"When?" I asked. I needed to be sure he wasn't making the shit up.

"It all happened on Halloween years ago," he started. "I guess a metric-fuck-ton of people tricked and treated here that night, the man giving out candy like nothing was wrong or anything. A little past midnight, someone heard the gunshots, the screaming . . . and the awful silence."

Billy eyes went big.

The awful silence? Billy's story sounded rehearsed, like he'd practiced for this very moment. "So, of course, everyone says it's haunted, right?" I asked, sarcastic.

"Hell yes," Billy said. "Even Mom said she's heard tell of homeless people found dead in there, scared to death. One of Harvey's brothers, Leonard I think it was, told me during a full-moon, when it's high overhead, you can see a shadow of the man hanging from the noose. He said the shadow sways back and forth. When there's no breeze." Not even with a hint of a smile—dead serious.

The mention of Harvey made my stomach hurt worse.

"Bullshit," Tracey hissed under her breath, but she believed Billy, at least in part.

Only one way to find out. My flashlight ate little of the darkness away as I shined it into the open basement window. All three of us listened but heard only cops shouting from somewhere out in the swamp.

I held Billy's sweaty hands as he slid, belly first, through the broken window and down into the basement. I helped Tracey next. Her hoodie slid up and exposed her stomach and ribs, and something inside me stirred. I'd have to watch myself. I slid through, my belly scraping on the splintered wood frame while Billy pushed up on my feet, slowing my descent. My feet hit the floor, and pieces of old concrete crunched beneath them.

Spray-painted signs and symbols covered the concrete walls. A triangle with bisecting lines reminded me of the food group pyramid. *Ding-dong* was spray painted above it, as if to signify a doorway. A large eye painted above the words watched us.

"What the hell do you figure that is?" I asked.

Billy whispered, "It must be a satanic symbol or something." Billy ran his fingers over it, tracing the lines.

I got the impression Billy liked the idea if it being a satanic symbol. In fact, he'd been the one to embrace the blood oath, had become increasingly more interested in the occult as we got older. So had Harvey.

"To me it seems more like a doorway," Tracey said. She wanted to downplay the satanic angle, and I hoped it wasn't too late.

"Whad'ya mean?" Billy asked. "A doorway to where? Hell?"

It'd backfired on her, and by the light of the flashlight, Tracey shuddered and look away. "Never mind, Billy," she whispered.

"Ugh," Billy said, "gross."

Tracey and I turned around. "What's gross?"

Billy simply pointed at the floor so I walked over. Laid out on the floor beneath the drawn doorway on the wall, three pairs of white men's underwear lay with a short black candle atop each pair.

"Holy shit," Billy breathed. "Someone's worshipping tighty whiteys."

Tracey stared down at them, silent, looking like she might cry.

Something about the arrangement reminded me of the blood oath, made me nervous. "Let's get this over with," I said. "Let's go upstairs and look for the chick."

"Why you think they're down here?" Billy asked from behind me.

I wanted to get upstairs before we found out the reason they were down here.

Broken glass crunched beneath her feet as Tracey walked toward the staircase. Billy's flashlight beam streamed past her but did little good. The dark staircase looked haunted, a crimson stain at the base of it stood out in a dark splotch.

Tracey said, "It's a blood stain. They must've sacrificed an animal. Undies and sacrifice, they must be worshipping the devil, sure as shit."

I wondered who *they* might be. Harvey? My skin crawled, goose flesh erupting on my arms. We'd all seen blood but I didn't know if that's what this was or not.

"We should've had the blood oath down here," Billy whispered.

I ignored him. Tracey frowned like she tasted something bad but stayed silent. We stood at the bottom of the stairs, on the red splotch, and peered up into the darkness.

BRUISED

"It's black as ass up there," Billy said. "You think it leads to hell?"

I shrugged, trying to be cool. "Probably," I said, sarcastically.

"You think so?"

I rolled my eyes.

"You go first since you don't think it leads to hell and all."

"You've seen the house above ground plenty of times. Are you in hell when you see it? No," Tracey said.

Billy scowled. "You only get to hell from the inside, from the basement like."

Tracey groaned.

I went first, started up real slow, nervous and scared. The stairway creaked, cobwebs pulled at my hair, and my heart thumped. The blood vessel on my temple throbbed with every heartbeat.

Darkness reached out and slowed us down—as if alive, long tendrils of thick sticky blackness.

"Damn, are we ever gonna get to the top?" Billy asked. "I mean, what if the stairs keep going forever?"

"We'll get there, calm down," Tracey assured him, playing the mother card, always taking care of Billy. But I didn't feel as certain inside as she did, not in the least.

"You sure seem calm for someone who's trudging up the stairs to hell," he said.

I contemplated the irony of his statement.

"Wait, there it is, Jason," he said. "I see the landing. Let's be careful, in case the devil's there."

"Don't be stupid," Tracey said. "The devil ain't up there, for crying out loud." I hoped to God it was true, but the blood oath. Anything might be possible.

"Don't be so sure," Billy warned. "Lots of people died here. Could be ghosts."

"Sure there could, Billy," Tracey said, "and that's why we're here—to find a corpse."

Billy didn't say anything. Weird. He always has something to say.

The hairs on my neck stood up. "What?"

"I thought I saw something up there."

"What?" My skin crawled with burgeoning fear.

"Dunno—maybe a ghost," he said. "Or a shadow—kinda dark."

"Quit trying to scare me." I was getting pissed.

"No lie. I saw something."

Tracey breathed heavily behind Billy, not quite drowned out by my own heaving breaths.

Enough of this. I took the remaining steps two at a time, and despite the sticky darkness and our fear, my right foot hit the closed door. I turned the knob slowly, letting the door creak inward. The gutted kitchen loomed before us, bathed in shadows.

I let out a breath. "I don't see the devil or a ghost."

"We ain't out of here yet," Billy said. "What if we end up with our blood stained all over?"

He was referring to the ceremony. "It's a little late to worry about that, jackass," I whispered. "We're already in here. Let's look around and get out as quick as we can. The body probably ain't here, anyway."

Billy's paleness made him look like a ghost himself.

I tiptoed past the rusted appliances and over the cracked linoleum, Billy right behind me, Tracey behind him. It appeared like the rust had run from the appliances onto the floor—at least I hoped it was rust. Billy was eyeballing it too.

"Is that blood?" Billy asked.

"No," I said. "It's rust from the metal."

"You sure?" Tracey asked in a high-pitch voice.

I wasn't but I didn't say so. "Yeah, now let's go. We gotta keep moving."

After a few more strides, I peered into the empty living room. I crept in slowly, the floorboards creaking beneath our feet. The living room smelled musty, the air dead. Shadows everywhere, especially in the corners, blocked my vision. Dirty white sheets covered the few pieces of furniture. The staircase to the second floor, where the man supposedly hung himself, loomed savagely ahead of us.

"There's the second floor landing," I said, trying to sound nonchalant.

"Man, guys think," he said, "the poor fucker swung back and forth, right up there. What could drive a man to off his family and himself?"

Billy had a way of putting things.

"Who knows—could've snapped, I suppose," Tracey said.

That's when it all happened—hell descended on us, perhaps the beginning of something bigger. But was this the beginning or a continuation?

Billy pointed to the top of the stairs. "Oh shit, there it is. A shadow, like a corpse swinging."

"Where?" I asked, confused. "I don't see." Why couldn't I ever see the ghosts?

Something clattered above us on the landing—footsteps, coming toward us.

Billy and Tracey turned and ran. Billy yelled, "Run, Jason, it's the devil."

I froze. A figure dressed in rags, maybe a homeless person appeared—then vanished like a ghost. I turned and ran.

BRUISED

I followed Billy and Tracey, my feet pounding the dusty hardwood of the floor, down the hall and around a dead-end corner to what must've been the mudroom. The kicked-up dust made us cough. Panic surged through me—we couldn't find the exit. "Where is it?" Tracey yelled frantically.

I shook my head, brain spinning, and my body slowly turning in circles. The glassless window-frame gave me an idea.

Close enough. Desperate, I dove out head first with no regard to what I might land on, crashing awkward on the grass outside. With grass leaving its green residue on my arms, I rolled and came up running, arms and legs pumping, lungs working overtime. We ran blindly until our feet sloshed through water. I stopped to listen, heard nothing, not even the cops anymore.

Tracey and Billy breathed hard next to me, hands on their hips.

"Where are we?" Billy asked.

"The swamp," I said.

Billy's feet shuffled in the muck. "Maybe it was Harvey's sister's spirit."

Tracey's breath came out as a cross between a hiccup and an annoyed gasp.

I shrugged. "Maybe," I said. But it hadn't looked like Harvey's sister.

"It could've been," Tracey said. "If her body's in there, the cops will find her."

"I don't even hear the cops," I said.

"They have to be on the street, getting ready to go in, or else we'd hear them out here," she said. "The swamp isn't so big we couldn't hear them."

"Sometimes it seems as big as the whole world," Billy whispered.

People got lost all the time—some were never found.

"Stop talking like that," Tracey said. "It'll scare the shit out of us. Let's go find the body."

"Finding it out here is like finding a needle in a haystack," Billy said.

I sighed. I knew where she might be, and I didn't wanna go there, but if it got us out of the swamp quicker...

"What is it?" Tracey asked. Suspicious, like she knew I was on to something.

"Where else besides Hell House would Harvey," and this next part I had a hard time getting out of my mouth, "kill someone?"

Tracey nodded. "The blood oath tree," she whispered.

When she said it, a gentle breeze came up and set the oak leaves to rattling together like dried out beetle husks. Goose bumps spread across my skin. Had the breeze been a coincidence? From somewhere out in the swamp, a screech, maybe an owl, maybe something else, erupted and ruined the otherwise-silent wilderness.

"What was that?" Billy asked. He didn't sound scared out of his mind, exactly, but the nervous lilt conveyed fear. When he got anxious, Billy always asked unnecessary questions.

Tracey quietly took a round tin out of her hoodie pocket, opened it carefully, and deposited a Skoal Bandit into her lip. "Doesn't matter what it is. We gotta get moving, before the cops get done searching Hell House and start into the swamp."

"It matters to me," Billy said, but Tracey started further into the swamp before he could finish. Billy and I followed. I secretly hoped she knew where she was going. We couldn't risk getting lost in the swamp . . . end up like all the dead homeless people.

The ground gave beneath my feet, the moisture not far beneath the earth's surface. In some spots, the springs breached and we'd have to be careful, because the frost had disappeared, so you never knew what was what. We were a long way from the channels we rode bike on, but there were ponds and puddles everywhere. Later in the summer, when the alga bloomed, it'd smell to high heaven.

The chatter of the police officers swarming over Hell House faded into the distance, and disappeared completely, like someone dropped a curtain. Unnatural silence, like the inside of a vacuum. My ears popped with the pressure. I expected to see a black veil above us but instead, a full-moon stared back—an unblinking eye. The pines rustled, a pantomime of speech.

"How come the trees are moving when there's no breeze?" Billy asked.

I shrugged, but nobody could see. It was a good question. Something was off in the swamp. My hair felt like it was standing on end, goose bumps plagued my arms, and the back of my throat tasted like the copper penny Billy had said would mask the smell of a beer I drank once. It hadn't.

By the light of the moon, Tracey slowly turned in a circle while staring up into the trees. I'm sure she was trying to figure out the riddle but something told me we wouldn't find the answers up there. I thought of blood on bushes, ghosts of dead dads, insane gang leaders, coyotes and fairy lights. The swamp whirled around me like a psycho merry-go-round. In my ear, someone said, "Jason." A wave of electricity hit my skin like a blast of cold air.

"What?" I asked.

"Whad'ya mean, what?" Tracey asked. "Nobody said anything."

Even though neither Tracey nor Billy had said my name, my mind wouldn't allow me to truly believe it. "Come off it," I said. "What did you want?" Somewhere deep inside, I had recognized the voice. It's sounded a lot like Jewel's. Was I going crazy?

"Did you hear something, Jason?" Billy asked. "If you did, that's cool."

He backed back away toward Tracey and slipped his fingers through hers. She didn't pull away.

"Nothing," I said. "My mistake." But it wasn't nothing. Somebody, or something, maybe Jewel maybe not, had shouted in my ear. Nobody else had heard it.

"Are you sure this is a good idea?" Billy asked. "Maybe we should come back during the day."

Billy could be a douche, a follower, but he was brave to a fault. Hearing him sound scared frightened the shit outta me.

"Hell no," Tracey said. "We ain't bailing on her now. If Harvey killed Krysta, we gotta find her body, set her soul at peace. If we don't, her spirit will walk the swamp forever."

Tracey put a comforting arm around Billy. They'd make a beautiful couple, looks wise and in other, more intangible, ways. I wondered about what Tracey had said. Could spirits get trapped? Was Jewel's dad trapped? "Let's get this done," I said. "If my parents wake up . . ."

"Which way?" Billy asked.

Tracey said, "This way." But I didn't think she sounded so sure. In any regard, she started off, still hand-in-hand with

Billy, and I followed, continuously looking over my shoulder. I wished the cops would appear but they were nowhere in sight.

Within minutes, my shoes, and the bottoms of my jeans, were soaked. Water squashed beneath my feet. To make it all worse, I was constantly waiting to hear my name. How would I ever sleep?

On cue, Billy said, "I don't remember the path to the blood-oath tree being so wet. You sure this is the way, Tracey?"

I followed Tracey's gaze. The tree resembled a monster, tipped in blood and backlit by the ever-rising moon.

"Holy shit," Billy whispered. "There it is." He breathed hard.

The three of us walked slowly toward it. Here was where we'd all pledged our allegiance to Harvey, made promises we'd since broken. What happened when you went against a blood oath? Academically, Harvey couldn't be here, was still in the hospital, but who ever said the mind was rational? Maybe it'd been Harvey who whispered in my ear. Maybe he'd become an evil deity, punishing us for our treacherous ways. He was no longer a teenage boy, but a monster—a creature of the darkness who wanted nothing more than to take us to hell with him.

"What's hanging from the tree?" Tracey asked in a near-whisper. She kept walking closer.

As my eyes adjusted, I noticed a square-shaped object hanging from a rope. The rope swung despite the absence of wind, like someone was pushing it back and forth. The rope squeaked as it swung.

"It's a bag," Tracey said. She sounded nervous. She spit into the leaves, probably to act tough, bolster her courage.

"What ya think is in it?" Billy asked. "You guys think Krysta's head is in there?"

I had to admit, the bag was the right size and shape, like a bowling ball could be carried to the alley in it. As we approached, our wet shoes scuffing the moss and grass of the small clearing, the moss had been disturbed, even thrown around like a buck had scraped the ground with its hooves. The scrapes weren't random, but had been disturbed in a pattern, geometric shapes and symbols scraped into the ground. By the light of the moon, *widdershins* was scrawled directly beneath the slowly swinging sack. My hair stood up. It had to be magic.

"What the hell does that mean?" Billy asked.

I shrugged in a darkness so cold I could see my breath. What the hell had Harvey been doing out here?

"Witchcraft," Tracey whispered. "It's a word used in witchcraft. I read it in a book Mom has next to her Ouija board."

"Who did it?" Billy asked.

"Who you think?" Tracey asked. "Who planned the oath?"

Nobody answered—didn't have to.

"We should look in the bag," Tracey said without excitement.

"I'm not chicken shit or nothing," Billy said, "but I don't wanna see Krysta's head. The whole bag thing reminds me of the swinging corpse of Hell House."

"Stop bringing up that scary shit, Billy." But she didn't let go of his hand, and didn't move any closer to the bag.

Like I was hypnotized, I walked toward the swinging bag. The ropes groaned louder, like the weight of the bag might snap them. Suddenly, I had to know what was in there. I stood before it like I was in a trance, but I snapped out it quickly and reached toward the hasp.

I spread the material of the bag open slowly, not wanting to look. For a moment, blackness. Then the shocking stench hit me and nearly knocked me to my knees—and I saw.

I'm sure I wobbled, because Tracey yelled, "Quick, grab him."

I staggered away from the bag, the sight of what I'd seen emblazoned into the space behind my eyes: the red hair, the blue eyes. I didn't realize I'd puked until it splattered off my shoes.

"What's in there?" Billy asked.

A keening wail began in the back of my throat and exited my mouth like a banshee into the night. "Jewel," I howled. The tears started down my cheeks.

"What the hell?" Tracey said. She sounded far away, like in another dimension. I was pretty sure I was dying. Tracey, like she were in slow motion, illuminated by the very-bright moon, walked slowly toward the bag with her flashlight. She reluctantly grabbed it with one hand and looked in. She flinched, turned around with a frown, her eyes locked on mine, shaking her head slowly. "It's not, Jason, it's not Jewel."

"But—but—" I managed, but I wanted her to be right too bad and nothing else would come out.

"Is it Krysta's head?" Billy asked.

Tracey shook her head. "What kind of dog does Harvey have? What is Mumford?"

"Irish Setter," I said. I understood the red hair, the bluish eyes. I felt stupid but relieved all at the same time. I nearly fell, but Billy caught a hold of me.

Tracey's eyes never left mine.

We left, to hell with Krysta. She was probably getting laid, anyway. Harvey was a psycho.

When I snuck back in, the lights were still on downstairs, my parents still up, but I managed to sneak in quietly. I slipped beneath my covers and fell asleep. I'd been asleep when my world ended—Armageddon.

Nearly being yanked from my bed by my hair, I struggled. I had no idea what'd happened, or who was trying to kill me.

The screaming started. "Did you and Jewel do this? Is this the kind of girl she is?" It sounded like Mom, but my eyes wouldn't open.

For a moment, I thought she knew about Jewel and I making out. I thought she knew I'd snuck out.

Dad yelled, "Get up, Jason. Now! What is this shit? I thought you knew better."

I pried my eyes open. In the palm of Mom's hand—the tinfoil, unwrapped. In the center of the foil were the rock-like pieces of crystal-meth.

The cause of my parent's anger.

"Mom, I can explain. It's not mine."

Dad screamed, "You'd better damn well explain, Jason. This had better be good, real good. We raised you better than this."

I can't believe I didn't see this before," Mom yelled, nearly hysterical. "Does this belong to Jewel, Jason? Is this why she's acting so strange?"

"No, mom, no," I pleaded. "It's not Jewel's. She doesn't even know I have it. I swear. Please, mom, don't tell anyone it's hers. It isn't."

Dad balled his fists, his eyes wide. "Whose is it, Jason? You'd better tell me the truth, right now. Come clean."

I paused, not sure what to do. I remembered what Morris said about killing my parents—and Jewel. I couldn't imagine Morris killing anyone, and I didn't want to rat out Billy. But someone had to go down. "It's—it's the school janitor's drugs. He tried to get me to take them, but I refused. I hid them in my pocket so no little kids would find them, and take them."

"These are Morris's drugs?" Mom asked, angry as sin.

"Y—yes, he gave them to me yesterday morning, wanted me to take them. He said he'd kill you guys—and Jewel if I told. So I took them. I was gonna throw them away, but I forgot."

"Don't you lie to us, Jason," Dad screamed.

"I'm not lying, dad, honest. I swear. Look, the tin is full, I never took any. Please, Jewel doesn't even know. I swear."

They softened, chests still heaving in anger.

"I'll be taking this up with Principal Hammond in the morning," Mom said.

"Be careful. Morris said—"

"Screw Morris. If he so much as looks at your mother or me crossways, I'll rip his lungs out," Dad said.

I grinned despite myself.

Mom put a hand on his shoulder. "Easy, honey, violence won't solve anything."

"It'll give the punk what he deserves." Dad spit as he talked. "How long has he been dealing out of the school? Why didn't you tell us?"

I shrugged. "That's the first I'd seen of any drugs, dad, I swear. I would have told you."

"When?" he asked, "when would you have told us, Jason? Would you have told us at all if we hadn't found it?"

I shook my head, slowly. "I—I'm sorry, no. The answer is no. I would have thrown them away and been done with it."

Mom asked, "Do you understand the destruction that someone like Morris can cause? Drug dealers are the reason I see half the families in my office."

"I was scared, mom," I said. "He said he would kill you guys—and Jewel, too."

Dad glowered but he spoke quietly. "Don't insult me, Jason. At your age, you believed him? We've been through this before."

"It was bullshit, Dad. I didn't want to get—"

"Get someone in trouble? Do you give a shit about Morris?" Dad shouted.

I'd said too much. "No, nobody—

"Bullshit," Dad thundered. "Was it Jewel? Don't lie to me, son."

I whimpered. "Okay, okay. It was Billy." I sobbed louder.

"Billy Stratham?" Mom asked.

I didn't answer.

"Oh my sweet Lord, not Billy," Mom said.

Dad hugged her. "It'll be okay. At least it's not Jason."

I sobbed, wanting Jewel with me like never before. I hoped she was okay—wasn't receiving any new bruises.

Chapter 19

Principal Hammond sat staring at me from across his desk like a vulture, his fat fingers threaded together. He tapped his desk.

With my parents, I'd already seen the police take Morris away in handcuffs, defeated. He wasn't going to kill anyone, let alone gut them or anything else.

The next part, the hardest, Billy walked with the cops, his parents walking beside him. The look of disbelief, of betrayal, on his face being the worst. I'd been with him on an adventure last night, and I'd ratted him out.

Principal Hammond said since Billy never carried the drugs in his possession he wouldn't get in too much trouble—not with the law anyway. In his old man's glare however, I foresaw the beating, which would be worse than what the legal system could ever impugn.

Thankfully, Billy wouldn't have to go to juvenile hall. I let out a breath of relief. He and I would never be close, the trust gone. Billy would never understand why I did what I did.

Maybe I wouldn't have, if not to protect Jewel.

Jewel wasn't at school—just as well.

Yet, I worried. About both my friends.

After what happened at her house, I didn't want to think about the wounds Jewel would have now, whether inflicted by her father or herself. I wanted to be with her, to hold her, protect her from herself, her dad, Harvey. But here I sat, stuck, ratting out Billy Stratham, instead.

"What have you learned today, Jason?" Principal Hammond asked.

To always throw the drugs away before I get home. "Any time I see drugs, I need to tell my parents or a teacher." I sounded like a little kid.

It nearly made me vomit.

"Good, Jason, good—you did the right thing today, telling the truth like you did. Morris is gone for good. And Billy will be better for it."

Fuck you. Nothing was going to be better. Not for Billy. Not anytime soon, anyway. Nobody had known his parents like I did. Billy would've been better off with me looking out for him. But that wasn't going to happen—not now.

I reminded myself I still had Jewel, which brightened my outlook.

What else could I say?

Hammond smiled. "Since we're all in agreement, I see no need to put you through any more, Jason. I'll leave your punishment up to your parents."

"Oh, there will be consequences, count on it." Dad was nodding like he was already conjuring up how my time would be spent.

I cringed, imagining myself spending the whole summer mowing and landscaping. I hoped they wouldn't take away Jewel or our time together.

"Run along to class," Mom said. "We'll talk about this tonight at home."

I nodded, anxious to see if Jewel was at school yet.

She wasn't. Nor had she arrived by the time lunch came around. By the end of the day, I knew I wouldn't see her.

Chapter 20

Worried and helpless, I felt reckless. I sat in my tree. I didn't think things could get any worse. I ratted out my best friend—and he would be beaten because of it.

Jewel is MIA. I was sure the school had called her mom at home. How would she be punished? What would her dad have to say about this? How would her dead dad punish her this time—because of me? And her mother worthless, couldn't protect her if she wanted to. I needed to do something. Nope, things couldn't be worse.

Who was I kidding? Of course they could get worse—much worse.

I slipped down the rope ladder instead of using the wood steps, almost supper time. As usual I wasn't much hungry, but this time I'd be forced to eat. Grounded teens couldn't sneak off to their bedrooms.

"Jason?" Mom called. "Wash your hands and come to the table."

Nope, no skipping supper.

I washed my hands and sat down. Nate, already eating, chewed silently for once. Even *he* was subdued, like he knew I was in hot water. For the first time ever, he left me alone. Eerie.

We ate silently—or not so silently. For the first time, I heard the gnarly sounds my family made while eating. Teeth collided with forks full of food. It annoyed me. How the hell could people eat so loud? Every sound rattled me, amplified by my annoyance. Milk guzzled down my brother's throat, his sippy cup making little whistling sounds. Dad sucked at his teeth to get the stuck food out. Mom's sounds were more eloquent, softer, and her bites smaller. She chewed with a gentle calm that culminated into an unbearable cacophony.

I broke the noisy silence. "So, how long am I grounded for?" I wanted to know when I'd see Jewel.

Mom and dad exchanged glances.

They must have talked about it—but something else danced in their eyes as well.

Dad cleared his throat. "We haven't decided yet, Jason."

"What do you mean, you haven't decided?" I said. Now I was worried.

Mom put her fork down. "Honey, a difficult situation arose today. We'll have a decision by tomorrow so you can plan accordingly."

My spirits sank. Worried about Jewel's absence from school, I wanted to help her. But, being grounded, what could I do about anything?

"Can you give me a ballpark?" I asked.

Dad smiled. The old ballpark figure—a phrase used in our family quite often.

"Not this time, buddy," he answered. "A ballpark isn't going to cut it. This is a serious issue...very serious. We're talking drugs here."

I sighed. No use arguing, the crime is still too fresh—maybe tomorrow.

"What about Jewel?" I asked. "Will she get in any trouble?"

Mom shook her head. "I'm sure the school called, to follow up on Morris's threats. It shouldn't be a problem for Jewel, not if she's innocent."

I searched Mom's eyes. She appeared to be sincere. I wondered if she'd met with Jewel today but I refused to ask.

"Of course she's innocent, mom," I said. "She didn't know anything about it. I told you already."

"Yes, of course you did, Jason," she said. "I'm sure Jewel's fine."

I wanted so damn bad for her to spill her guts. But no way would she— not with confidentiality rearing its ugly head.

"I hope so," I said. I glanced at Mom to see if she would tip her hand in any way.

She didn't.

About to excuse myself to my room, I halted when the phone rang. No one ever called at this time of the day.

Mom answered. "Yes, this is she. What? Are you sure?" Mom couldn't hide her shock.

I went cold. My insides turned to mush like they might ooze out of me.

"Oh no, this is horrible," she said. "Do they know who did it?"

"Does this have to do with Jewel?" I asked.

Mom waved at me to be quiet.

I shouted, "Mom, please tell me."

She shot me an angry look and walked into the kitchen, mumbling. I sat, head on hands, beside myself.

"Calm down. I'm sure everything's fine." But dad didn't look like he believed it himself. He peeked into the kitchen as I did, curiosity plastered on his face.

"Does this have to do with Jewel?" I asked. "Why she wasn't at school today?"

He shook his head. "No, of course not," he mumbled. "I don't know."

Dad fidgeted, his facial movements uncomfortable. I let the issue ride for the moment.

Mom hung up.

"What is it?" Dad and I said it at the exact same time.

"Please take your brother and go to your rooms for a moment. I need to speak with your father."

"What? Why?" I asked.

"Because I asked you to," she answered.

It was unusual for Mom not to give me a good reason, which scared me even more.

"Mom, is—is it Jewel?" I asked.

"Go to your room," she said firmly. "I'll be up to talk to you in a minute."

I grabbed my brother who fought only briefly and trudged him up the stairs to his room and closed the door. Then I remembered the old furnace grate—the one I'd used to eavesdrop on Mom and the babysitter. We had since gotten a new furnace, but the old grating, still in place, still would work perfect. I curled up next to it and listened.

"What is it, honey?" Dad asked.

Mom let out her breath. "Morris is dead."

Relief spread through me in warm waves. Who cared about Morris the douche bag?

Silence hung in the air. My dad asked, "Overdose?"

"No," Mom whispered so I barely heard her. "He was murdered."

"What? By who?"

"They don't know, Michael. But—but they found him close to Jewel's property, on the edge of the swamp. He had a gun with him. It was lying next to him in the underbrush."

My blood turned to ice. I could barely breathe. Morris was murdered at Jewel's?

"How the hell did he get out of jail so quick?" Dad asked. He sounded furious about it.

"The sheriff let him out when his parents came to get him," Mom answered. "They didn't consider him a risk to flee and he's well known to have mental problems, so they let him out under their supervision."

"A risk to flee?" Dad asked, incredulous. "How about a risk to commit murder? He'd already made threats."

Mom remained silent. I assumed she didn't have an answer.

"He could have come here as easily," Dad exclaimed.

I thought back to Morris and his threats to kill Jewel. I guess he'd meant them.

"They don't know who murdered the asshole?" Dad asked.

"No. They spoke to Jewel's mom. She was confused and upset about the whole thing. The police think Morris was following through on his threats to Jason—and someone killed him before he got a chance."

I thought about Jewel's dad—and his anger. The blood on the bushes, the bruises on Jewel's arms. Harvey? I shook with fear for Jewel. What would her dad do to her?

"My God," Dad said. "Right here in our little town."

"That's not the worst of it, Michael," Mom said softly, her tone worried. She paused. "The killer took Morris's eyes."

"What the fuck?" he exclaimed.

"Michael. Shush. Nate or Jason might hear you. They don't need to know about this, at least not Nate for God sake."

A heavy weight lay on my chest. I tried to move, even at risk of being caught, but my muscles froze up. The picture of Jewel's dad on Facebook—the picture with quarters for eyes. I was pretty sure I knew who'd killed Morris. Who else would be protecting Jewel? With too much to think about, I let my head sink to the floor. It felt warm and soft.

"Needless to say, this town is getting bad, Michael," Mom said. "We've got gangs, drugs, murder like the big cities."

"Maybe worse," Dad added. "We need to tell Jason about this. He's going to find out tomorrow anyway, when he speaks with Jewel."

"Yes, I know. I wanted to speak with you first. How should we handle this, Michael?"

"You're the shrink," he answered with humor in his voice.

I started down the steps. What difference did it make anyway? Already grounded, they couldn't do much more to me.

Mom sighed. "There's no need to tell him about the eyes. Let's stick to the basics."

"Jason already knows about the eyes," I said as I walked around the corner.

Mom glanced up at the old furnace grate and frowned. "I should have known," she said.

"Jason, you shouldn't spy on us, son," Dad said. "Sometimes adults need to speak in private about things."

"What difference does it make, dad? Morris is dead."

Dad let out his breath, but otherwise stayed silent for once. I suppose he understood my shock.

"How much did you hear?" Mom asked.

I stayed silent.

"Everything?"

I considered telling them Jewel's dad was a psychopath from beyond the grave, but how do you tell your parents a ghost is killing people?

"You know he was killed over by Jewel's place," she said.

"Or the body was dumped there," I added.

"Jason," Dad warned. "You're not the police, so stop speculating."

I shrugged. "Is Jewel okay?"

"The police spoke to her mother. They're both fine from what I understand."

Those words made me feel better. The police were at Jewel's and she was okay—for now. "Do you think she'll be at school tomorrow, mom?" I asked.

Mom shrugged and sauntered over and hugged me.

Dad stood with his arms folded like a sentry whose thoughts revolved solely on our safety.

I only worried about Jewel's.

I awoke in the night and wondered if I were awake or dreaming. I stood up.

My closet door shut, a good sign, I breathed easier. The dark corner of my room appeared normal with the usual shadows.

My computer had switched to sleep mode, so I wiggled the mouse.

The screen lit up and I brought up my Facebook page. I searched and found Jewel's page. I clicked on the icon for the one she'd made for her dad.

I held my breath as I waited for it to boot up, which took longer than normal.

When the image appeared, the sight made me gag and choke, almost throw up.

The picture of Jewel's dad remained the same, but underneath the picture, the caption read, "Dad—my hero." Jewel, in her own way, praised her dad for what he'd done.

The image made me sick. But I still loved Jewel—with all my heart. It wasn't illegal to love your dad for murdering someone. I wondered how I'd feel if Dad murdered someone while saving my life. My heart lightened. Of course I'd love him. I supposed it didn't matter if ones dad were dead or alive. If he saved you, he saved you.

I shut my computer down and tried to sleep. Thoughts of Jewel swirled around me. I touched myself, but remembered what Jewel's mom had said and so lifted my hand from my shorts.

I fell asleep, hoping Jewel would show up at school the next morning.

Chapter 21

Neither Jewel nor Billy showed up for school. I didn't know what to do—so I wandered. Tracey ran up to me.

She got right in my face so I smelled the tobacco on her breath, could see the brown chunks between her teeth. Her steely eyes showed she was pissed off. "I heard about Billy and Morris," she barked.

I took a step backward. How did she know about Morris? "Morris had it coming," I said. "He's a douche bag."

"Yeah, he had it coming," she said, her hands waving. "But what about Billy, Jason? Did you have to bring him down, too? He's your best friend. We were all together last night. One minute we're on an adventure, the next your ratting him out."

"So," I said slowly, "you didn't hear yet what happened to Morris?"

"What do you mean, Jason?" she asked. "He's in jail, right?"

I shook my head. "Not anymore he's not."

"You mean he got out?" Her eyes darted around like Morris might be lurking around the schoolyard.

"They let him out when his parents came to get him."

"So, he was selling drugs, but now he's running free?"

"I didn't say that."

"What the hell are you talking about?" she exclaimed. "Spit the shit out."

"Morris is fucking dead, Tracey. Murdered, his eyes ripped out."

Tracey remained silent, strange in of itself. "That pig Morris got offed?"

I nodded.

"The killer took his eyes?" she asked. "What crazy fucker—Harvey?"

I shrugged. I didn't mention Jewel's dad or else *I* would have sounded nuts.

Tracey scuffed the tar with her hiking boot. "Where'd they find the pig?"

I hesitated. "At Jewel's, in the woods."

"They found the pig at the house of your piece of ass?" she asked. "No shit, Jason? Wild. Did they catch Harvey?"

I shook my head. "The police don't know for sure who did it. Jewel and her mom were as shocked as everyone else."

I wanted to bring up Jewel's dad but I couldn't. Harvey could have done the deed—for sure he could've.

"He got what he deserved, I guess." She furled her brow. "What about Billy? He's probably at home because he got beat so bad he can't walk.

Guilt picked at me. "They made me tell my parents," I said.

"Couldn't you have said Morris gave you the drugs, and you didn't know what to do with them?"

"I didn't think fast enough," I said, ashamed and humiliated.

Tracey spat a Skoal Bandit onto the ground. "How did they find the drugs, anyway?"

"Mom found them in my pants pocket when she washed clothes," I whispered. She added, "I forgot about them."

"So Billy had to go down because you made a stupid mistake?" she asked. Her self-righteousness pissed me off.

I snapped. "It was an accident, okay Tracey? Fuck, you think I would've ratted out Billy on purpose? I misspoke and my parents caught it and made me tell them who I was protecting." Quieter, I said, "They thought I was protecting Jewel. I couldn't let her go down for no reason."

Tracey spat a wad of fibrous juice onto the asphalt. "You ratted out Billy to save your piece of ass?" she asked, incredulous, eyes wide.

"She has enough problems already," I said. "She didn't need this, too."

"What about Billy?" she asked. "Did he need this? His parents will kill him. You've known him all your life. You met Jewel this year, so what the fuck?"

"What the hell do you know? How many big decisions have you had to make?"

Tracey shook her head. Her blonde hair shimmied back and forth,

"You've never had to make a decision bigger than where you were gonna sneak your next chew, so don't bitch to me about decisions."

"But—but—"

"But nothing, Tracey, don't push me," I yelled. "I've had a real bad few days. I had to see Jewel's fucked up mom, Jewel's bruises, and talk to her fucking dad who I couldn't actually see. My parents found drugs in my pocket and I was forced to give up the goods on Billy. I found a dead dog that was killed by the leader of the gang I run with. Morris got himself murdered, which is fine. But Jewel's missing from school. No, don't push me—not today."

Tracey took a step back. "What do you mean, you couldn't see her dad?"

I glared at her.

Even Tracey knew when to quit, sometimes anyway. She softened. "I guess you only told the truth. Fine, I can understand why you did it. It doesn't mean I like it any, but I get it."

"I don't like it any either." It was the truth. My stomach hurt unbearably from stress. Half of it was from worrying about Billy, the other half from worrying about Jewel. Powerless to do anything about either one. "Fuck." My fury grew.

Thinking I was coming unhinged, Tracey took another step back. "What the hell, Jason?" she asked.

"Nothing, everything, I don't even know anymore, Tracey," I answered. "Everything's fucked up."

"Calm down, everything will be okay," she said. "Relax, dude."

I doubted my ability to relax—I doubted it very much. "I'm sorry," I said. "I know you care about him. I'll do whatever I can to make sure you guys can still be together."

Tracey's mouth moved like a fish out of water for a moment. She set her jaw and swatted a tear away from her eye.

Huge spotted us and headed over. If it were even possible, my day was about to get worse—much, much worse.

We called Eugene "Buddy Huge" or Huge. At five-foot-ten and a hundred seventy pounds, he was the biggest kid in school and towered above the rest of us.

He was the strongest, too. He didn't even take shit from Harvey.

One day, the year before all this, a boy named Larry picked on me one day, shoved me around and shit. Larry, at the time, was considered the toughest kid in the school, a year older than us. Buddy Huge walked up and clocked him good. Huge popped the kid right in the temple, and Larry went down like a sack of potatoes. He didn't even breathe hard, Huge, rubbed his knuckles a little. He wasn't the brightest, but sometimes Buddy Huge came in handy.

This would prove to be one of those times.

"Tracey, Jason, what you guys up to?" Huge shouted. "You both look pissed as shit."

"Jason's just worked up is all," Tracey answered. "You know, about Billy and Morris."

"I don't care shit for Morris, but why Billy, man?" he asked. "He ain't no drug addict."

I shook my head. "Do I gotta explain everything, for fuck sakes?"

Tracey stepped in. "Huge, man, Jason here has had a real bad day. You hear about Morris, yet?"

"You mean he's in jail?" Huge asked.

"The fucker's dead—dead as shit."

"No shit. Dead, huh?" Huge asked. He looked up like Morris might be floating around up there.

Tracey said patiently, "Found him over by Jewel's place. I guess he was gonna off her but someone offed him instead. They took his eyes." Tracey looked Huge in the eye. "It might've been Harvey. We found Mumford . . . dead."

Huge nodded like none of it surprised him much, maybe too much for him to think about. Or maybe he'd already reached the same conclusions we had. He asked, "Why would Morris want to kill Jewel? What'd she do to him?"

"He said he'd kill Jewel if I told about the drugs," I said. "I guess he was following through."

"He got offed, huh?" Huge squinted in thought and gazed up. He glanced at me.

"What about Billy?" Huge asked. "Anyone seen him?"

I shook my head.

"I still don't know why you had to tell, Jason." He stepped toward me, angry.

"Look, Huge, I've had a real bad few days, remember?" I asked. I put my hands up in front of me.

He bellowed, "What about Billy's bad day?" Huge's temple started throbbing under his skin, about two seconds away from nuclear meltdown.

Huge's tantrum reminded me of my brother saying, "Hulk smash." Only it would be much more believable coming from Buddy Huge.

I tried to calm him. "Huge, dude, listen," I said. "I didn't mean to rat on Billy, okay? It was a fricking accident."

Tracey backed me up. She wouldn't have had to. But she did anyway. "Eugene, look me in the eye. Jason didn't mean to give up Billy. His parents were gonna finger Jewel, and of course Jason wasn't gonna let that happen. Of course, they demanded to know who he was covering for. Jason had to tell them or else the cops would be hauling Jewel away."

"Jewel?" Huge asked like he'd never heard the name before.

"Jason's main squeeze." Tracey smirked. "His piece of ass."

I flipped her the bird.

Huge nodded his big head, something running through his muddled mind. It took a long time for something to get through his thick head.

Huge looked at me thoughtfully. "That's right," he said slowly. "Hey, Jason, someone told me something about her last night, when I was out messing around."

I tried to act casual but I wasn't going to like what Huge had to say. "What Huge?" I asked. "What'd you hear? Was it about the murder?" I'm sure it came out impatient. Tingly feelings zipped up and down my spine. My grandma would've said someone stepped on my grave.

He didn't seem to notice. He was too busy concentrating hard on his wording. "No, it wasn't like that," he said. "I was walking, minding my own business, when I ended up over by Harvey's house. I don't like the dink, and he got what he deserved by my thinking. But I thought I'd stop in anyway. You know, we all been part of the gang for a long time, so why not, right?"

I shrugged. "Sure."

"Anyway, his parents' car wasn't in the driveway. If they're home, it's always there because Leonard has all his weight lifting shit in the garage, you know?"

"What are you saying?" I asked impatiently.

"I'm getting there," he explained. "Someone was talking in the garage, assumed it was Leonard with his buddies, right? I walked up to the walk-in door to see if Leonard knew if Harvey was still in the hospital. I listened and it sure as hell wasn't Leonard, it was Harvey. Not cursing while he was lifting weights—sometimes he does that—but it was something else. He wasn't cursing at the weight. He sounded like he was bitching someone out."

"Who, Huge?" I asked. "Who was he bitching at?"

Huge frowned. "I snuck inside the garage, nice and quiet, and I peeked around the wood divider they got up so no one can see them lift weights. There he was, naked as the day he was fucking born, everything but his face that was still bandaged up."

Tracey frowned. "He was naked?" she asked. "What the hell for? He got a woman in there or what?"

"Hell no, he didn't." Buddy Huge flailed his hands. "If he did, hell, no big deal, right? Everyone's entitled to a little chunk of A. But shit, he was pounding his donk right into a hole in his wall. I mean, he was going to town."

My eyes went wide. "No shit, he was sticking it in a hole?"

"I wouldn't kid about that. But there's more."

I shook my head. The tips of my fingers were getting cold.

"I didn't want to watch or nothing, but I wanted to hear what he was saying. It was gummed with all the hardware he's got on his busted teeth, but I understood. Harvey's teeth are real fucked up."

Tracey smacked Huge in the arm. "For fuck sakes, Huge, spit the shit out already," she said. "What was he saying?"

"He was reaming that hole in the wall, all the while screaming obscenities about Jewel."

My mouth dropped. "What? What the hell did he say?"

Huge looked around as if afraid someone might hear. "I don't wanna sound gay, but here's what he said." Huge paused. "He was saying, 'how you ya like my big cock in ya, huh? This'll teach you to mouth off to me, bitch. I'll keep your punk-ass-mouth busy.' Then he kept right on a pumping his Willy into the hole in his wall."

Tracey scowled like she wanted to know more. "So he was getting off, pretending he was hurting Jewel?"

Anger paralyzed my lips. Harvey was capable and crazy enough for damn near anything.

Huge said, "I didn't stick around for him to finish, but he finished while I was there."

"We know you ain't gay, dude. Spit it out." I was about to burst a blood vessel.

"As he finishes, I hear him say, 'You wait for tomorrow night, Jewel. You're gonna get yours. The blood oath's gonna be satisfied.'"

"You sure that's what he said?" Tracey's eyes widened.

"You're saying you think he might hurt her tonight?" I asked. "You sure he wasn't having a fantasy or something?" I was grasping at straws. Two people attempting to murder Jewel in two consecutive nights—too much.

Huge shrugged. "Dude, your guess is as good as mine," he said, palms up. "I didn't stop to ask for clarification, if you know what I mean. I got the fuck out before he saw me. But the last thing I saw was the weirdest. While this was going on, Harvey was twitching like he was getting rid of something in his head. Like he was hearing voices and shit. This time was real bad, like his head was full of bees."

Tracey said, "He's been doing it a lot more lately," she agreed. "Maybe the fucker *is* crazy. He's been taking this oath thing way too serious. He's been doing a lot of fucked up shit. Killed his dog. He might go after Jewel."

I wasn't going to leave Jewel's salvation up to her dad. I said, "Jewel didn't make it to school today. You guys gotta help me tonight. We're The Three Musketeers of the gang. You need to sneak over to Jewel's with me, make sure she's alright."

Tracey lifted one eyebrow. "Dude, she's your girlfriend," she pointed out. "What are me and Huge gonna do?"

"Back me up," I said softly, searching their eyes, looking for support.

Huge shrugged. "Oh, you mean in case Harvey's there," he said with a rumble of anger. "You need me to clock him. And you need Tracey to calm Jewel down and shit, right?"

They were right. Huge and I could beat Harvey's ass, and Tracey could comfort Jewel. But what about Jewel's dad?

"Close enough," I said. "Look, you guys in or out? You gonna help me or not?"

"What if Harvey jumps us?" Tracey asked.

Huge pumped his fist into his palm. "Don't sweat it."

I shrugged. I wasn't about to tell her Jewel's dad killed Morris, but he must've. Harvey had no reason to kill Morris. Of course, he had no reason to kill Mumford, either.

She didn't look convinced. "Aren't you grounded, Jason?" she asked. "How you gonna get out of the house with your parents watching you like a hawk?"

"I'll figure something out," I said. "I've got to."

"You could get in a shit load of trouble," Tracey reminded me. Maybe she was looking for a way out.

"I know," I said. "But I love her."

Tracey whistled. "You got it bad, real bad." She shot me a concerned look.

So do you, I wanted to say, but now wasn't the time. I didn't want to explain Tracey and Billy to Huge. Tracey shook her head. "I'm in. What the hell else are friends for?"

Huge said, "Shit, ain't nothing much exciting been happening around here. Not in a long time," he said. "One last hurrah before we graduate. Let's do this."

A tear leaked out. "Thanks, guys."

Huge backed up and stuck his arms in the air. "Don't get all gay on me."

Tracey stepped up and wiped my eye quickly. "Where do you want to meet?"

"Jewel lives out of town, so we'll want our bikes," I said. "Let's meet under the old water tower. It's a short ride from there."

"What time?" Huge asked.

"I'll be grounded so my parents need to be asleep. How about ten-thirty, work for everyone?"

Tracey gave a thumbs up.

Buddy Huge grinned big. "Let's raise hell." He raised his hands above his head as in triumph. He pounded his fist into his palm.

Chapter 22

Jewel never showed up for school. By the time I got home, I was worked up. But as much as she meant to me, Jewel remained the furthest thing from my parents' mind. They may have understood what I needed to do, if I gave them the chance to listen, but I doubted it.

And I didn't.

Because they kept their parent-blinders on—blinded by the need to administer correction—I had no faith in their judgment. My friends and I would take care of the situation, our way, like we always did. Parents could be stupid, not seeing the forest for the trees, not seeing when their oldest son showed signs of worry, bothered by something bigger than he was. They weren't able to tell I felt scared—nearly scared to death. I hoped to God I'd recognize it in my own children. The children I made with Jewel.

I felt completely alone.

"Hulk smash."

Peas splattered against my chest. I looked up slow, in no mood. I said, "Keep the peas to yourself. Why the hell do we have peas every goddamn night?"

Dad snapped up from his paper. "Curse again and I'll wash your mouth out like you were twelve!" he said. Quieter, "Be patient with your brother. He's only six."

I let out my breath. "I'm only eighteen."

Mom sighed, ignoring my comment. "Jason, what's wrong?"

"What do you think?"

"Do you still feel bad for telling on Billy?" she asked. "Are you worried about Jewel?"

I rolled my eyes. "Yes, of course."

Dad said, sternly, "Watch your tone young man. Don't forget we caught you with drugs, drugs in your possession." He slammed his fist on the table so hard our plates rattled.

"Jason the pusher, Jason the drug addict," I said, ignoring his tantrum. "I'm the criminal element like Morris was."

Dad stood up, probably to throttle me. Maybe I deserved it. "Don't talk about the dead."

Mom stopped him. "Honey, please, sit down," she said softly. "This is hard on all of us. We already know why Jason had the drugs. Nobody thinks you're a user or a pusher, Jason.

Morris probably got what drug dealers have coming to them. Nobody blames you."

"Dad does," I shouted.

He let out his breath, trying damn hard not to get up and punish me. Through clenched teeth, Dad said, "If you would listen to me, you'd know I said you used poor judgment. I didn't say it was your fault."

"I don't listen?" I asked. "Me? What about you? Even if I explained stuff until I'm blue in the face, it wouldn't matter to you."

"You can't walk around with drugs in your pocket," he exclaimed.

"I made a mistake, so sue me. It's not like I'm gonna do it again or anything."

"I would hope not," he hissed, his eyes red with anger.

"Michael, enough," Mom said. "Jason's trying to apologize, aren't you, Jason?"

I mumbled in agreement.

"What did ya say, son?" He knew.

"Nothing dad," I said. "Okay—I'm sorry."

"Sorry you got caught?" he asked, quieter.

"No, damn it," I said, angry all over again. Damn he could be an asshole. "Sorry, I put the damn drugs in my damn pocket in the first damn place."

Mom jumped in. "Jason, stop swearing," she said, therapist voice vanished. "I don't want to sound prudish, but you need to show respect."

She smiled. "I know how you speak in front of your friends. Know your audience, like we've always told you."

I knew she told the truth. She heard how my friends and I talked to each other. I remembered my eleventh birthday party at the Holiday Inn. Billy, Huge, and Tracey were cussing up a storm.

Scared Mom would overhear, I made them swear underwater. Hilarious actually, watching all those damn bubbles come up, like they were all farting in the pool or something, I laughed like a lunatic.

They giggled incessantly when Mom walked up.

"So, making your friends swear under water, huh?" she'd asked.

"What?" I'd asked. "How did you know?"

"Oldest trick in the book, my boy."

"Are—are you mad?"

She smiled. "No, as long as you know your audience, Jason, I don't mind at all. I know you and your friends swear to each other. It's part of your culture. But what happens if you swear in front of an adult?"

"I get in trouble?"

"Bingo." She walked away.

My memory over, I said, "Sorry mom, dad. I've had a rough day. My friends are a little pis...er...mad I snitched on Billy. They'll get over it."

Mom eyed me closely.

I knew better than to lie. "Jewel didn't show up for school today. I'm worried she'll hurt herself. I'm worried about the murderer."

"I'm sure she's safe and sound, probably sick. I have an appointment with her in the morning. I'll find out."

She wasn't sick, I knew. Not physically anyway. Morning was a long way off—an eternity. But I kept my mouth shut.

"You could call her, son, if you're worried," Dad said, much calmer. "You're not grounded from the phone."

"Yeah, 'cept she and her mom don't have a phone. At least I didn't see one."

"Shoot, they do have a cell phone but it's unlisted. I can't divulge it to you."

I shot her a look. Sometimes, having a mom for a therapist sucked. But other times it rocked I guess, so I always took the good with the bad. I'd be seeing Jewel soon anyway, one way or the other.

I hoped like hell we beat Harvey there.

Dad must have detected my anxiety. "Maybe she'll be at school tomorrow."

"I hope so." I paused. "How long am I grounded for anyway?"

Dad glanced at Mom.

"We've been discussing that," she said. "We decided to leave it up to you."

"What?" I asked.

"We want to see if you know how to be fair, allow you to utilize good judgment."

I groaned to myself. I obviously couldn't pick something too light. Nor did I want to go too rough on myself. Shit, what did it matter anyway? After what I had planned, I'd be grounded for the rest of my natural life. I said, "I think two weeks would be good, long enough for me to learn my lesson but not so long as to be unreasonable."

Dad smiled. "Right on, sport, I think you get it."

Mom agreed.

Two weeks it was—for now anyway.

Chapter 23

The unbearable wait kept me imagining the horrid things that could be happening to Jewel. The possibilities swirled through my head, like her dad hurting her, giving her more bruises. Morris had wanted to kill her, but got offed by someone else. Now, Harvey wanted a piece of her. What had this poor girl done to deserve any of it? On top of it all, Mom believed Jewel, hurt herself. If she was, who could blame her? I wanted to end her pain for her—be her hero.

I sat at my desk and wrote the message for the insurance we needed— in case things went downhill.

Dear Mom and Dad,

I'm sorry I broke the rules and snuck out, I am. It's I need to save Jewel. If you're reading this, it means I didn't make it back, and I need saving, too. Please call the police, no the army, if you get this note and I'm not back yet. It means we'll probably need them out at Jewel's house, where I'll be. Sorry, but you wouldn't have listened. You would have thought it a big joke. Please come to the rescue. I love you.

    Jason

I placed the note on top of my pillow.

My parents went to bed. I cringed when they their bed springs creaked, headboard banging softly but steadily. I hated listening to that shit. But that night it proved exactly the diversion I needed.

I crawled out of bed with my shoes already on and ready to go. Sliding my window open, I edged my way out to the trellis. I found the familiar foothold and started working my way down. The window I left partially open to crawl in upon my victorious return.

My left foot hit the ground first. I breathed a sigh of relief, having made it without too much commotion. My parents were still so hard in the throes of it, and cannons could've gone off without them knowing.

I'd taken the same escape route the night before. Even that hadn't been the first time I ever snuck out—we did it all the time in the summers. Billy would ride over, pitch a rock at my window, much like Tracey had, and out we'd go.

I remember the last time, only last summer. Ages ago. Billy heard that his neighbor grew weed under black lights in his basement. I didn't wanna go, thinking it better when all

Billy wanted to explore was Buck Hill Swamp for Bigfoot, and haunted houses. It should have given me a clue of things to come.

Like this night, I waited until my parents were in bed before hitting the trellis. Billy waited for me at the bottom. We biked over to his neighbor's house, Craig—a real douche bag.

We hid the bikes deep within bushes capable of concealing them well, yet provided a quick escape route. Billy brought cheap infrared goggles that made us look like we were from space or something. I felt stupid because there remained plenty of light to see, but Billy enjoyed using them—so we did. Billy's brother told him the best way to sneak in, somewhere near the basement steps, so that's where we went.

"What if he's at home, Billy?" I asked. "He might kill us, man."

Billy shook his head. "My brother said he would be gone, Jason. Don't sweat it. It'll be okay."

"We're sneaking in to spy on a drug dealer," I said. "Drug dealers kill people for less than this."

"Go home," he said. "I need to do this. I want to ruin his stash before he can sell it to little kids."

I sighed. "Fine, let's get this done quick."

We slid the sliding glass door open after making sure no one lingered around the place. From there we made a quick turn and snuck down the carpeted basement steps. The steps made noise, but no one was home to care anyway. Once we hit the basement, the black light glowed like a cavern to hell, easy to find. There were pot plants everywhere, hanging from the ceiling, sitting on the floor—the find both scary and exhilarating. That's when Billy dumped them all out, potting soil and all, right onto the grey cement floor.

"Holy shit, Billy," I said. "What're you doing?"

"I'm ruining the stash, man," he said with a grin. "Good luck trying to sell these plants." Billy laughed. He had the time of his life, his laugh contagious.

I laughed too. "Oh, this is fun. Craig the douche bag is gonna be pissed. I bet we've ruined hundreds of dollars."

"Maybe thousands," Billy added.

We both laughed, throwing plants and soil everywhere. We stomped on them and tore them up. It was awesome—something great and good that we did together.

Times changed.

Billy believed that we'd be doing the world a favor if we killed the plants—probably right.

But now, all Billy wanted to do was smoke them. Times were changing.

It made me sad to think of it. Billy had been my best friend and I ratted on him.

Those days were over. Maybe they would've been over whether Billy still wanted to be friends or not. We were getting older. Soon we wouldn't need to sneak out. Everything changed, given enough time. But it felt sad all the same— change always happened.

Either way, my carefree life was ending, and I hated to think of the future.

Jewel.

Suddenly, caring about something was important. I thought loving girls might be a welcome change, part of the new life. If Jewel were part of the change, everything would be worth it.

I needed to kill Harvey Kuchenbecker.

I glanced at my parent's car, considered it, then forgot it just as quick. I was in deep as it was. I ran to my bike, where I stashed it under the lilac bushes. Off I went, careful not to peddle until half a block away, in case the chain rattled.

A nice late-spring evening greeted me as I rode. The warm night air stroked my face. The lilacs smelled wonderful. Oak leaves cast shadows that danced like black fire.

It might be my last bike ride for a while.

Riding hard, I was a little out of breath when I got to the old water tower. I stopped to catch my breath. I didn't see Huge and Tracey anywhere. Did they have a change of heart? Did something else happen?

A bright red cherry off the end of a cigarette in the distance caught my eye. I made out Huge's outline in the bushes, the cherry pulsating as he inhaled. I breathed a small prayer. Huge must've bummed a coffin-nail off his big brother again.

I breathed a sigh of relief—should've known my friends wouldn't let me down. Tracey stepped out of the bushes. "Hey, Jason, we're here," she said, "had to hide in the bushes to smoke when a cop drove by."

"Thanks, guys," I said. "This means a lot to me."

Tracey glanced behind her, biting her lip. "Someone else is here, too," she said, "besides me and Huge."

"Who?" I asked.

Billy walked out of the bushes, hands in his pockets. He slipped an arm around Tracey's shoulder. "What up, dog?"

"What the fuck?" I asked. "I thought you'd hate me forever." My heart beat fast with surprise and joy.

"I was pissed," he said honestly. "But Tracey called and explained everything. Everything's cool between us."

"Tracey told you why I had to rat you out?"

Billy shrugged. "It was either me or Jewel. I've known for a while. Why fight it? If Jewel means this much to you, well, let's go save her. It's time to put Harvey down, anyway." He patted Tracey's shoulder to show me he understood.

"But aren't your parents pissed, Billy?" I asked.

"Sure they are," he agreed. "Probably beat me even worse. But your parents are pissed, too, and you're here, aren't you?"

"Yeah," I said slowly, "but mine won't beat me."

Billy lifted up his shirt and showed me the bruises on his back. "They can't beat me any worse without killing me, so who gives a fuck? So let's stop wasting time and roll, kick Harvey's ever loving ass."

"Did you hear about Morris?" I asked.

Billy quieted for a moment. "I guess he got what he deserved. I mean no one deserves to die, but..."

"I know what you mean, Billy." I put my hand on his shoulder.

I looked at everyone, one at a time. "You guys' sure about this? You're not afraid of Harvey, or the guy who offed Morris if it wasn't Harvey?" I didn't wanna tell them about Jewel's dad.

Huge walked out of the bushes and flicked his cigarette butt into the street. Orange sparks cascaded around the tar. "Hell no," he answered. "Let's get the party started. I'm smoked up and ready to bash skulls, bro."

Billy and Huge would have a problem making the transition to life after High School. Glad to have them along, though, especially Billy, my mind went through the possibilities. I needed some muscle. "We'll bike to walking distance and sneak in the rest of the way."

"We winging it after that, or do you have a Plan C?" Tracey asked.

"We need to find Harvey, maybe search Jewel's yard and the swamp like we did last night." I thought of Mumford, the blood on the leaves at Jewel's, and Morris with no eyes. I shuddered.

"Can't wait to lay a fist into Harvey." Huge said. "How'd it feel to club the dude?"

Huge could be blunt.

"I ain't proud of it," I said. "I was saving Jewel's life."

"You ought to be proud," Huge said. "You took that jerk down good. You put the smack down on him, bro."

Tracey shrugged. "Yep, he got what he deserved all right. But, we gonna stand around here and discuss it, or we gonna go save your piece of ass, Jason? Harvey could be there now."

Billy spit out his chew. "Enough chit chat, let's do this thing."

"Okay, let's cruise," I said. "Jewel's place is only about a mile away. Let's get any talking outta the way because once we get there, we need to go in quiet. Any questions?"

Nobody had any—or they didn't ask.

We rode like our lives depended on it. I prayed to God Jewel's didn't. Our tires hummed on the pavement, and Tracey's bike made clanking noises like it was in disrepair.

The mile went by quicker than I would've expected. Tracey, Billy, and I were sweating, but Huge's sweaty body was pouring like he stepped out of the bathtub with all his clothes on. He smelled bad but I didn't care—as long as he wasn't too tired to fight Harvey.

I hunted down Jewel's mail box, remembering it was bright blue. I got off my bike, and the others followed suit.

Huge's breaths came so hard, I was afraid he might die on us right there.

Tracey whispered, "Is this the place?"

"Yeah, this is it," I answered.

Huge, between big breaths, said, "Hold on one sec guys, let me catch my breath, shit, you guys ride too damn fast."

"Fucking A, fat ass," Billy said, "we always waiting on you, bro." Billy, impatient too, and on a mission.

Huge puffed, "I can't help it, man, hold on a sec."

We waited.

When Huge nodded his eagerness, I led the way into the woods—the very, very dark woods. We stopped at the edge for a moment. Everyone paused to look for the spot where the police had found Morris's body but I kept moving.

Complete silence within the confines of the oak trees and black spruce, the atmosphere like a vacuum. The full moon flickered through the dancing leaves and created myriads of glistening movement all around us, near impossible to tell what constituted shadow—and what might be danger.

"Where's the house?" Tracey sounded scared.

I didn't blame her.

"It should be straight this way," I said, "and slightly to the left, a little over fifty yards."

Huge kept walking past us, his feet sloshing through past years' leaves, like if he stopped he knew he'd never move again. But he made too much damn noise.

"Pick up your feet, for fuck sakes," Billy whispered. "You're being too noisy."

"Okay . . . sorry," he said. "I wanna get to the fighting, you know? Before I'm too tired out. Harvey's not exactly a pussy."

"Follow me."

We walked slowly until we saw the glow from Jewel's yard light. It remained faint, but there all the same, like an apparition. I shuddered. I wondered what other, more real, apparitions might be floating around out here—ones that left blood on the bushes. The ones that killed the local dope pusher. Jewel's dad, not Harvey, had killed Morris.

"There's the light from Jewel's yard," I said. "Let's start moving real quiet like."

"I don't see no sign of Harvey, man," Huge said. "Maybe he's not even here." He was breathing hard.

Billy looked grim. "The dink's here; I can smell him."

"If we get up to the house, we'll peak in," I said. "If everything's okay, we'll leave, okay?"

Huge shrugged. "Fine by me."

We covered the last distance through the woods, reached the edge of the yard. Everything remained quiet—too quiet. The oak leaves and pines all remained still.

I glanced over to the utility shed where Jewel and I discovered the blood—nothing out of the ordinary.

The long, unkempt grass, covered our Nikes with dew. The wetness felt cold and harsh on our feet, summer still a ways off. We kept the few oak trees in the yard between the windows and us, in case someone peered out from inside the house.

"Look, there's one window with a light on in it," Tracey whispered while pointing. "The shade's drawn, though."

I followed the direction of her finger. Sure enough, a faint glow flickered, like from candles or a small fire.

"Her mom's room," I whispered. "Jewel's window is on the other side of the back porch."

"That's where Harvey will be," Huge said. "He'd peak in first, the chicken shit pervert."

Billy said, "Damn coward. Let's get them."

"What if Harvey was casing the joint last night and killed Morris. What if Harvey's the murderer, like the cops think?"

"It sounds like him," Billy agreed. "He has been nuts lately."

Nobody said anything. There wasn't any need to. This was what Huge was here for, after all.

I hoped I was wrong about a lot of things. "Let's check it out," I said.

Tracey led the way across the yard, our feet rustling last year's leafs. We stayed low, using the sparse oak trees for cover. Between the weak yard light and the moon, it wouldn't have been hard to see us from the inside of the house.

At the base of Jewel's window, everything remained quiet.

Her curtains were still open like they were when I'd come over. I stood on my tip toes and closed my eyes. I hesitated, afraid of what I might find. Jewel sleeping, Jewel dead, a ghost, Harvey—anything. I took a deep breath and scanned the room.

"What do ya see?" Billy whispered.

I shook my head. "Nothing, no one's in Jewel's room," I said, relief in my voice. "She must be somewhere else in the house. Let's go look in the other windows."

"Wait," Tracey whispered.

"What?" I asked, impatient.

She held her hand up to me. "What's this shit?"

I couldn't tell what she held. I grabbed her wrist and held it in a spot with more light.

"You don't need to be so damned grabby," she hissed.

I ignored Tracey. My jaw dropped, Tracey's hand wet with fresh, red blood.

"What the fuck is that?" Huge whispered.

"Blood," I said. My knees buckled.

Billy gasped, too. "Whose blood is it?"

I had a pretty fair idea, but wasn't ready to say.

Tracey inspected her hand, then wiped it in the grass.

"Did you get it off?" I whispered.

She shook her head, panicking. She turned to me. "No. There's even more on me now." She whipped around and shook the blood off her hand.

Huge walked over and pointed at the grass. "Look, it's all over, like a trail."

The blood glowed in the full moon light.

"It is a trail," I said, "a trail of blood."

I feared what we might find at the end of the trail—Jewel? Her dad? Tracey nervously stared off into the woods. Huge looked impatient, Billy frightened, spoiling for a fight, hell bent on taking his frustrations out on Harvey.

"I guess we should follow it, you know?" I said.

"I guess . . . or maybe call the cops."

"Screw the cops," Billy hissed. "All they do is screw everything up . . . arrest me, my brother, and my old man; the list goes on—screw them. We can handle this ourselves."

"Billy, settle down," I said. "We'll handle this ourselves, but you gotta calm down. Lead the way."

"You bet your sweet ass I will." He stomped off into the trees.

Tracey, Huge, and I followed behind Billy as he followed the blood. He stopped, blocking my view with his wiry frame.

"Oh, shit," he muttered. His voice was high pitched and shaky.

"What is it, Billy?" I asked, afraid—so very afraid. "What did you find?" I tried to get around him.

At first Billy didn't answer. "It's Harvey," he whispered. "Someone offed him."

I walked around him. The remnants of Harvey's remains lay on the ground. His empty eye sockets reminded me of Morris—and Jewel's dad, and the quarters. Most of Harvey's throat appeared to be missing, too. Blood puddled around him.

Tracey said, "Oh sh—sh—shit—what the hell happened to Harvey?"

"He's dead," Huge said simply.

Tracey glared. "No shit, Sherlock," she said. "But who the hell would steal someone's eyes?"

Huge had no answer.

Neither did I. Or maybe I did. Either way, I shook my head. No sense in saying too much yet.

"What, Jason?" Tracey asked. "What is it?" Tracey's eyes pleaded for an answer.

"Jewel went crazy when the stereo turned on by itself. She said her dad was standing there but her dad's dead. Jewel ran out of the house, chasing after him. When we got to the edge of the woods, she said he was gone. But fresh blood glinted on the bushes. Jewel said he bleeds sometimes and leaves it behind."

Huge and Billy's mouths gaped.

Tracey erupted. "You're telling us *now*, Jason?" she shrieked. "You don't think we would've wanted to know that before we came here with you? What the fuck, Jason?"

"I'm sorry," I said. "I didn't think it mattered."

"Didn't matter?" she asked. "Didn't fucking matter, Jason? There's a ghost running around leaving blood, maybe killing people, and you didn't care?"

I sighed. "I should have," I agreed. "But I was caught up saving Jewel. I didn't even think about it until we were already in the woods."

Billy snorted. "Jewel don't need any saving from Harvey now. He'll never hurt anyone again. The blood oath is over." Billy spit on him.

The woods closed in on us, the shadows getting deeper.

"What if the killer is still here?" Tracey asked.

Scared, we made sure nothing snuck up on us.

"Maybe we should get the hell out of here, call the police or something," Tracey suggested. "I mean, Harvey's dead, man. Dead!" Tracey yelled loudly.

"Be quiet, someone will hear us." Billy looked around vigilantly.

Huge shrugged. "We can leave."

I had no argument. What difference did it make? I only needed to make sure Jewel was okay. "Go ahead," I said. "I can handle this on my own. Jewel's probably okay, unless—"

"Unless she's dead, too," Billy growled.

"Jewel's tough," I said. "She probably doesn't even know what's going on."

But we all knew someone didn't get their throat ripped out at your house without you knowing it.

Tracey whispered, "Maybe we can still help her. Come on, we'll help you, Jason. Won't we Huge? Won't we Billy? Huge is a big fucker, he'll keep us safe."

Huge looked around, nervous. "I've got our backs," he whispered. "But let's get this done quick. I don't wanna end up like Harvey and Morris, man."

"Let's go," I said. "We'll make sure she's okay and get out of here, call the cops, and let them deal with Harvey's corpse."

I led the way, cautiously. Morbidly enough, I used the blood trail, which glistened in the moonlight, to guide us back. Soon we were staring at Jewel's house from the edge of the swamp.

"Okay, how should we do this?" I asked.

"Let's go knock," Tracey said. "Say we're friends of Jewel's and ask to see her. Jewel's mom should recognize you, Jason." She shrugged as if it were that simple.

"That could work in our favor. Or it could be bad."

We walked up to the door and I stuck my fist out to knock.

But I never did knock, because the back door had a pentagram drawn with fresh blood. The red liquid leaked downward from the sloppily drawn lines, like the door was bleeding. I didn't want to, wanted to run like hell truth be told, but with a surge of adrenaline, and the will to save Jewel, I tried the knob. The door was locked, wouldn't even budge, not even a quiver from the solid wood slab.

"What is that?" Billy asked.

"Pentagram," Tracey answered, "you know, witchcraft stuff, like in the swamp."

"Did Harvey draw this before he bought the farm?" Billy asked.

No one answered. Huge yawned but otherwise stayed silent. Now that Huge knew Harvey was dead, he thought the threat had passed.

It hadn't.

Everyone stayed silent a bit longer, no noise except our heavy breathing. "This is getting real weird, Jason," Tracy said.

Fear shook her voice, scaring the shit outta *me*. I said, "I still need to make sure Jewel's okay"

"Can't we call the cops?" Tracey asked.

"All they do is make life worse," Billy said, "I say we bust in."

Huge took a step toward a heavily curtained window on the same wall as the door. "I think I can get us in through here."

"Don't, Huge," I said. "It'll make too much noise, alert the murderer to our presence."

"I say we still knock, if we're going in at all," Tracey said.

I shook my head at the dripping pentagram. The others were doing the same. No way were we gonna knock on a door with a pentagram painted in fresh blood.

"Hell House," Billy said softly.

"Whad'ya mean?" Tracey asked.

Billy pointed at the small rectangle of a basement window. It was cracked already, wouldn't take much to cave it in. Behind it was nothing but a pitch black void. The thought of squeezing into it sent shivers down my back. "We go in through the basement like at Hell House," he whispered.

"We'll go to jail for breaking and entering," Tracey said, but she didn't sound like she was convinced of it.

"You guys go," I said. "Go get help, and I'll find Jewel myself."

"No way, dog," Billy said. "I got your back all the way."

I wondered how far all the way was. I stayed silent for a moment. "Let's do it."

"Me, too," Huge said.

I wondered if he'd fit. He was a big son-of-a-bitch.

"Fine," Tracey mumbled, sounding none too excited. Neither was I but I had to make sure Jewel was okay.

Huge picked up an old mop handle next to the house, the wood grey and splintered. Carefully, more carefully than I would've gave Huge credit, he pressed the end of the stick against the corner of the glass until it poked through the already spider webbed pane. Glass tinkled down quietly, and I was pretty sure nobody upstairs could've heard it. Huge, using both hands, drug the handle around the outside of the window frame, slow but sure, until all the glass had fallen down into the basement below.

I took a tentative step toward the black, glassless maw for a few seconds before a musty odor—sweet and sticky, like rot and decay—made my nose scrunch up.

"I don't think anyone heard," Tracey whispered. She was looking over at the window with the light behind the curtains. "Nobody's moving, anyway"

With a nod and release of breath, I knelt down by the window and listened, and heard nothing but silence. It was now or never, because if I waited much longer I wouldn't do it, so I rolled onto my stomach and shoved my legs through into the darkness. When nothing grabbed a hold, I lowered them until my toes hit the wall, and I lowered myself down.

Huge grabbed my hands and lowered me the rest of the way so I didn't crash to the floor.

I stood in Jewel's basement, in the pitch black. It was cold—very, very cold, and quiet, save for the rattle of an errant pipe which pinged in its loose moorings. Down here the smell of rot was cloying, and it stuck to my sinuses like a liquid.

Someone lowered down behind me, their belly scraping on the old wood of the window frame, toes pushing at the cement wall, as my eyes scanned the darkness for danger. My heart beat in my chest like a piston. What we were doing was illegal, and dangerous. Not only could we be arrested, but also, if the killer had picked the basement to hide, we could be dead within seconds. We'd never see them coming. I thought about Harvey's empty eye-sockets and the blood on the bushes. I shuddered like an old lady in need of a shawl.

Billy was standing next to me, and another body filled the space of the window, probably Tracey.

"We need light," Billy said. By the sound of his shaky voice, he was fighting the stench too.

As my eyes adjusted to the dark, I made out an ancient washer and dryer, rust-covered. A laundry room.

Tracey dropped to the floor. "It reeks down here. Something must've died."

Light footsteps sounded from the floor above. A feathery voice, barely audible. Flat and monotone, like someone was mumbling to themselves.

"Let's go," I whispered in the direction of the busted-out window.

"I'm trying," Huge groaned. "But I think I'm too big to fit."

Huge's big head appeared in the rectangle opening. No way was he coming down through that small of an opening. "Wait by the back door. We'll let you in." I was scared out of my mind to be down here without Huge's protection.

Tracey hissed, "We're screwed, blued and tattooed. If we get attacked without Huge—"

"We'll be okay," Billy said, putting a comforting arm around Tracey. He sounded confident, like he could take care of shit, but I had my doubts. He'd say anything to calm Tracey down, whether it was true or not. But we'd come this far, and Jewel needed us.

My eyes adjusted to the dark to reveal a doorway on the other side of the room. Past it, a string dangled. A light switch. I made for it, one foot slowly after the other, careful not to trip or kick anything. As I did, someone up above slid what sounded like a piece of furniture across the floor. What the hell was going on up there? Huge was gone. *Dammit.*

I reached the string and pulled, as my nose registered the stench was even worse in this room. The space was surprisingly tidy, racks along the walls with various items, rugs running over the swept but cracked cement floor, neatly piled cardboard boxes not yet unpacked, and, in a corner, one helluva heavy looking old chest freezer. It was white, but streaked with red splotches of rust. The rust made me think of Hell House, empty eye sockets . . . blood. Immediately, I detected the smell. I walked toward it. The odor blanketed the freezer in a shroud, the light seeming to get eaten and bathe the appliance in darkness.

Tracey whispered loudly. "You crazy? Let's get upstairs."

I ignored her, compelled to look underneath that heavy lid. My hand fit snugly beneath the handle, warmer than I would've guessed a freezer handle ought to. I hesitated, took a deep breath, and slowly opened the lid.

I wanted to be careful, remembering full well what my mind had tricked me into seeing at the blood-oath tree. Another overreaction wouldn't help our situation, but the lid was up and I stared into a bloody red abyss. The bottom of the freezer contained a sea of coagulated crimson muck where shrink-wrapped packages floated, or sat half submerged, on the crimson tide. Maggots wiggled around like they do, and the rational part of my brain wondered how the flies had gotten in there to lay their eggs. The stench dropped me to my knees. I might've barfed, but I'd already seen a dead body tonight, so what was a freezer full of thawed hamburger?

Tracey asked, "What is it? What's in there?" She held a hand over her nose.

My head shook back and forth—an automatic reaction to Jewel not being in there. Tremendous relief. "The motor must've conked."

Tracey and Billy let out a breath. Billy grabbed her hand, and she edged closer to him. Billy needed that, someone who could act as a refuge outside his dysfunctional parentage.

Across the room, the only other exit sat adorned with strings of silver and gold beads, like a wall decorated for

Christmas. The staircase had to be on the other side, so I brushed past Tracey and Billy, who were embracing so tightly they looked like one person, and stopped before the silver and gold rectangle. The beads swayed a bit in the opening, the breeze from my movements disturbing them ever so slightly. I pushed through, the beads momentarily ensnaring me before I popped out the other side. Holy shit.

Not everything registered all at once, but came to me gradually like a landslide. The staircase was nowhere in sight, a pentagram with white candles sat on the floor in front of a ratty old couch like a coffee table, and a clothesline of men's underwear traversed the small room like banners at a used car sale.

The beads swooshed as Tracey and Billy spilled through the doorway. They began like I had, their brains processing what they were seeing. I had a small head start, already wondering if the altar belonged to Jewel or her mother. The card table next to the couch held framed pictures of Jewel's dad, and intermixed between them were more of the half-burned candles, these ones black. In front of those sat a Ouija board, the planchette sitting next to it like an obedient dog. But what now sat on top of the board was what spooked me, sent my balls shriveling back up inside me, the gooseflesh to rise on my arms, the urine in my bladder start to push its way outward. A monotone moan escaped my mouth—completely out of my control.

"Someone's gone full-blown nuts," Tracey whispered.

I moaned out loud. They hadn't seen what I'd seen—not yet. On top of the board, on what looked like an earring holder, held in place by their retinal chords, three sets of eyeballs glared accusingly. One set was old and shriveled like a two-year-old grape. The second set wasn't shriveled but had the dull sheen of death. The third set was the worst. They still seemed alive, like they could blink, moisture still glistening off them. They'd only been plucked maybe an hour before— maybe less. They belonged to Harvey—or used to, anyway.

Jewel.

Jewel was in big trouble, one way or another. Not waiting for Billy or Tracey, I hurdled out the doors and paused a moment before climbing the steps. My friends ambled behind me but I refused to wait. I reached the top and peered through the cracked basement door.

Bloody footprints seen through the cracks made my stomach flip. "Oh shit, guys, I see blood," I said, cold shock starting to sink into my belly.

"Fuck this, let's go get the cops," Tracey hissed. "They get paid for this shit."

"You guys go, but I'm going in," I said. "The killer's in there, and I've gotta save Jewel."

Tracey shook her head. "Damn it, dude, you do got it bad," she said, her voice trembling. Snot ran down her nose. "There's a maniac running around here. You're gonna get us all killed."

"Not if you, Billy, and Huge leave," I said. "I can handle this alone now that Harvey isn't here."

"It's worse," Tracey said. "There's a psycho ghost or homicidal maniac running around slicing people."

"I know, but..."

Billy stepped forward, put a hand on his love's shoulder. He was brave—stupid maybe—but brave. "I'm going with ya," he said. "Nothing like this ever happens around here, once in a lifetime chance for real action. Let's go."

Tracey rubbed her eyes. "Fine," she said. "I'm gonna regret this."

Her words rang in my ears.

Billy said, "Don't worry, Tracey. I won't let anything hurt you." He brushed past me and pushed the door open.

Bloody footprints rounded the corner—probably went down the hall.

"You know the layout of this place?" Billy asked.

"Yeah, why?"

"What's in the direction those footprints lead?"

"Jewel's mom's room, I think."

"If she's dead too, I'm outta here," Tracey said, "way gone." Tracey sounded scared. She was shaking, and tears filled her eyes.

Or worse yet, Jewel could be dead. I glanced at the back door and jumped outta my skin. Huge stood behind the curtain, backlit by the moonlight. I ran to unlock the door and let Huge in. I'd never been so glad to see the big guy.

"About time," he said. "What took you guys so damn long?"

"Found some psycho shit in the basement," Billy said.

"I'll explain it all later but we gotta find Jewel first, and quick."

Jewel was in grave danger, maybe already dead.

We rounded the corner and started down the hallway. Dark permeated everything, every light in the house switched off. The house remained silent, tomb like, not a sound. Nothing moved. We passed the kitchen. I smelled rotten food—the unclean stench of dirty dishes and open packages of raw meat. Nothing though, compared to the smell of the basement, and Harvey's fresh blood, which still haunted me.

Then I smelled Huge. He hadn't smelled good before, but I detected a combination of sweat, hormones and fear on him. It was glorious.

Billy, the only cool and calm one, like he was born for this shit, looked ready to split skulls. He grabbed Tracey's hand and kissed it.

Tracey didn't stop him but constantly watched our backs, convinced that's where the danger lurked.

Billy and I concentrated on the bloody footprints soaking into the threadbare carpet. We moved slowly, trying to be silent. We didn't need a stray floor board giving us away.

Partway down the hall, a glow emanated from beneath a doorway.

I pointed, and Billy and Huge crept toward it.

Tracey stuck her hand out and said, "Wait, we need a damn plan."

Billy shrugged. "We barge in, take them by surprise. Good enough plan for me."

"Surprise. That's our only advantage," I agreed. "We don't have any weapons."

"What if the murderer is in there—and—and has a knife?" she asked. "What'll we do? What if it's the damn ghost?"

Huge locked his eyes on Tracey's. "Then I take over," he said, "ghost or no ghost. That's what I'm here for right, to be the muscle? Shit, this might be my only chance for a good rumble, legal like anyway."

"How do you fight a ghost, Huge?" I asked.

Huge shrugged. "I'll figure it out," he said calmly. "Let's get this shit done before I lose my nerve."

"You're strong and tough, but—" Tracey looked worried.

Huge shook his head. "Don't worry about it," he assured her. "I got it under control."

Huge had overestimated himself. I should've called him off right there, too much going on—murderers, ghosts, blood. But I didn't.

Tracey peered down the dark hallway. Her eyes darted around like she knew where she stood. "What if the blood oath did all this, and killed Harvey?" she asked. "Maybe it's a curse because we broke it."

"Curse my ass," Billy sneered. "Curses are for little kids and superstitious people—old women and shit. So are ghosts. This killer is flesh and blood and it's time he met his maker."

I didn't believe in curses. But I didn't believe in ghosts either, before now. Maybe I should have. "Enough of this," I said. "I need to know, now. You in, or out? Once we open the door, there's no going back."

Billy put an arm across Tracey's shoulder. "I'm ready to kill, rock and roll," he said.

"Fuck the curse and the ghost, I'm in," Huge hissed.

"Damn it, Huge. You too, Billy." Tracey said. "Does someone else have to die before you two wake up?" I knew right then, she loved Billy.

I let out a big breath. "Look, Tracey, go ahead and get back out to the road," I said. "Hell, go call the cops. But I gotta find Jewel. It's something I gotta do. It looks like I'll have Billy and Huge to back me up. So it's fine—go."

Tracey shook her head, tears forming in her eyes. "Fine, I'm in," she sobbed. "I'll do this for you, Jason. And for you guys." She glanced around before looking Billy in his eyes. "But I don't like it, not at all. I've got a real bad hunch about this mess." She got right in my face. "I'm mother-fucking scared, Jason." She shook me by my shirt with a slight jostle, tears streaming down her face.

Tracey possessed great instincts. Even Harvey would listen to Tracey—not that he would listen to anybody anymore. I remembered back to one particular time, about a year before. We were gonna shake down a new kid for magic cards. Tracey jumped in and said not to do it, that the kid acted weird, too defiant, like he had an ace in the hole. We sure as hell were glad we didn't. The next day his dad, the county sheriff, dropped him off for school.

I should have listened to her this time, too.

But I didn't.

"Okay," I said. "If you're sure, Tracey."

She would do it despite her terror because she loved Billy.

We followed Billy and Huge, who walked quietly toward the door with the flickering light, all of our footfalls muffled by the thick carpeting. The light ebbed and flowed as if controlled by an unknown force. Shadows danced eerily.

I never remembered being so scared, and had the terrible premonition we were in a situation way out of our league. *No shit, Sherlock.* I felt small, fragile. If we didn't hurry I'd call the whole thing off.

Huge and Billy stopped at the door. The light from beneath the door reflected off their toes.

"We go on the count of three," Billy said.

Tracey and I held our breath; perhaps, something like a soldier feels before combat, something about the point of no return, the futility of it, like the crest of the rollercoaster, the rollercoaster of life and death.

"One. Two—"

Sirens sounded, and wild bursts of red and orange light cascaded off the walls. Police cruisers screeched to a halt on the gravel.

Sometimes, I wonder what would have happened had the cops arrived even a mere thirty seconds earlier.

But as it were, everything happened at once.

I said, "The cops" as Billy said, "three."

The door in front of us crushed in as Billy's foot went through it. He wasn't waiting for the cops, not missing his chance at excitement.

The front door crashed open. "Police. Get down, hands on your heads."

They fumbled their way through the kitchen but they were soon forgotten.

Huge and Billy gasped.

I fought to get around them, our bodies tangled for a moment. In front of me, a nightmare dredged from the darkest recesses of my mind. The culmination of all my fears. Jewel tied on the bed, her arms bound tight, bruising, and her ginger hair splayed out behind her, like someone'd posed a china doll. Surrounded by candles, her nearly naked body lay covered with blood, and the solemn grace of her features broke my heart.

I prayed the blood wasn't hers.

The scene of Jewel laying there on her bed has haunted me my whole life. She could've been beautiful if not for the ugliness of her situation, the absolute horror of it. I knew what caused her bruises. She looked so fragile, laying there helpless. Burned into my memory forever, the nightmare still visits me.

But the real nightmare hovered over her.

A figure in a black flowing robe and hood, wielding a dagger, ready to plunge, wavered in the shadows like a ghost, a murderer, the devil and the betrayer of all betrayers. I wasn't prepared for this scenario. How could she?

I screamed. "No."

Noticing us for the first time, the figure turned her head. "For the death of my husband, she shall pay her penance. Let God judge her for her actions, for what she's done to me. Her own blood will cleanse her soul." Everything slowed down:

The dagger plunged downward.

I dove for Jewel.

Huge grabbed Jewel's mom by the back of her hair and pulled her back.

Stronger than she looked, the woman struggled to escape Huge's stronghold.

Huge grabbed her tighter, trying to get better leverage.

The stinking old bitch struggled hard. There wasn't much to her save skin and bones, yet she had so much strength. Inhuman.

She crumpled under Huge's weight.

The woman's rib cage cracked. She cried out a wet guttural sob.

It was too late.

The dagger stuck out of Jewel's chest like a morbid, blood covered crucifix. Blood dribbled from the wound, quicker than I imagined possible, and saturated her bedding.

It was only the beginning.

I tried to put my hand over the wound but the knife stood in the way. I didn't dare pull it out.

Letting out a bellow of rage, Huge, rammed Jewel's mom's head into the narrow metal bedpost. Her eye, pierced by the metal, burst. Blood squirted everywhere.

A black shadow removed itself from the beaten body. I blinked.

It hovered in the air, then vanished.

I blinked, shook my head. *What the hell was that?*

"Get down, now." The police barged in the room and shouted.

A shot rang out, and Huge dropped the bitch's head and grabbed his guts. He stumbled.

Jewel's mom slumped to the floor, dead, her hair fanned out around her broken head like a busted straw bail.

"Jason, help. They shot me." Huge moaned. His eyes pleaded with me. Blood pumped out from between his fingers.

Tracey screamed. "Go down, Huge, go down."

He did, curling into the fetal position from the pain.

We had all forgotten about Billy. With a roar he charged the police. "Fuck you, bastards. You shot Huge." It wasn't for Huge, but for his brother, his dad, and for his own personal reasons.

"Billy, no," Tracey screamed as she reached for him. She missed.

One of the police fired. Billy's head exploded, propelling him and his gray matter backward.

I barely felt the piece of lead ricochet and hit me in the wrist, but later it would hurt like hell.

Billy fell to the floor with a thud. His eyes searched for me one last time, pleading. It broke my heart but Billy was dead and everything else was going straight to hell with him.

Tracey screamed and cried, then rushed to Billy and laid on him, weeping.

I turned away from Billy to Huge.

"Stay with Jewel, Jason," he moaned. "I'll be okay. It's not as bad as it looks."

I hoped to help her but too much blood lay everywhere, some of it my own. The irony bisque of it curdled my stomach.

I ran my fingers through Jewel's ginger hair. It felt so soft—glorious. "You'll be okay, Jewel," I whispered. "You'll be okay." She had to be okay damn it.

My stomach turned when I smelled the odor, raw meat mixed with gunpowder and feces.

More blood than I'd seen in my whole life.

I lay by Jewel for a long time, not knowing if she were dying. I only knew she was still alive because the cops kept checking for a pulse. I drifted in and out.

Seconds, minutes, hours later, Tracey's sobs shook my eardrums. The police could not pry her away from Billy's bloating corpse. She'd loved him the way I love Jewel. Guilt spread like a virus in my heart. Billy was dead—big time dead, missing half his goddamn head—and Jewel was, for the moment, still alive. I stuck my nose into her long ginger hair, which smelled like strawberry shampoo.

"Leave him alone," Tracey shrieked.

Huge looked back at us with wide eyes, mortified that Tracey wouldn't let go of the corpse. I laid next to Jewel in a puddle of her blood as they wheeled Huge from the room.

One paramedic tended to my wrist, while the others assisted Jewel before hauling Jewel away. I wanted to go but my body wouldn't cooperate. The last image I had was Jewel's hair floating around the corner.

I loved her.

A big man in a white smock walked over. "Miss?"

Tracey frowned. Snot and tears streaked her face. Her shirt was saturated with Billy's blood. "What?" she hissed, her upper lip arched, exposing her gum line. She held Billy's corpse tighter, like it was her newborn baby. Billy's head flopped back and forth.

"You have to let him go now," the man said. "I'll take care of him."

With trembling arms and unblinking eyes, Tracey handed Billy's corpse to the men. Relieved of her duty, she flopped over, buried her face in the now-filthy floor, and cried, heavy sobs tugging at her delicate shoulders. Sad and vulnerable but not as vulnerable as Jewel. After a few minutes, she got up, no compassion in the hard lines of her mouth, and left the room.

I lay where I was, in shock and clueless what to do next. I must have dozed, because the next thing I knew Mom was standing above me. "Is he okay?" she asked as she bent down to me.

One of the paramedics said, "Caught some lead in his wrist but he'll live."

"Who shot my son?" she said with a white-hot anger I'd never heard before. "Who would shoot at a kid?"

I listened to her ramble and curse, demand information. The cops didn't say much until the Sergeant told her about Huge and Billy. I laid in limbo, still in a pool of Jewel's blood, and thought about her, ghosts, altars, Ouija boards, and dead friends. The rest of the world could go to hell—maybe it already had.

The funny part was nobody asked me any questions. Yet, I felt like a criminal, having led one of my best friends to his death. Billy could still be alive if I made him go home, or if he wasn't so bull headed, or if he'd stayed pissed at me and not come in the first place. In the end, Billy wanted to die, go down in one last blaze of glory, like, perhaps, he was afraid of the life destined him, the one life dealt him. But, now he'd left Tracey behind as well. But the last look in his eyes, the pleading broke my heart most of all. In the end, as he died,

Billy turned to me—not Tracey—for his salvation. I failed him.

I screamed, my fists shaking, "I hope it was all worth it to you, Billy. I hope you found peace and had the time of your motherfucking life." I buried my head in my arms and bawled.

Mom and the cops stared at me like I had gone out of my mind.

I had.

The next twenty-four hours exhausted me. Tracey and Huge were still alive, of course. They didn't let me talk to either of them right away. They said Tracey was too traumatized. Join the fucking club. She loved Billy—I love Jewel.

Maybe not talking to her right away was good. What the hell would I have said to her? What do you say to anybody after going through Hell? I think I might understand what a veteran feels like. At that moment, that's the only person I would've wanted to talk to. Somebody who could relate to how I felt, somebody who, at some point in their existence, had been covered in someone else's blood and guts, whose best friend got his brains blown out, and watched someone they loved be carried away on a stretcher. That wasn't Tracey.

Maybe it should've been.

I thought about the blood on the bushes, the shadow I'd seen leave Jewel's mother, blood oaths and witchcraft, but I tucked those items away for later. There weren't any good answers, anyway.

Harvey'd been a psycho, but got killed by a bigger one. So had Billy.

Chapter 24

I tapped on my cast with a marker, the one everybody used to sign it. I guess the bullet fractured my wrist.

Whatever—who gives a shit, right? I certainly didn't care at the time. I'd been through the wringer.

If the signing helped everyone else, gave them something to do, fine—sign away. I didn't care, didn't want to talk to anyone. I wanted everything to be normal.

Things would never be okay. At least, they would never be the same.

Jewel, in surgery, remained the sole hope I clung onto. She lay in that white sterile room, struggling to live—or die.

An eternity passed before the doctor came out.

"Who represents Jewel Wylander?"

Mom rose but I cut her off. "I am," I said somberly.

"Are you her brother?"

"Jewel doesn't have brothers," I said softly. "She has no family, anymore."

"Poor thing," he said. "Her mother passed—"

"Passed, is that what you call it?"

Mom jumped in. "Jason, he doesn't know, calm down."

I took a deep breath. "Sorry—I've been through a lot."

"Jewel made it through surgery."

My eyes lit up.

He cautioned, "But she's not out of the woods yet." He glanced at Mom.

She shrugged. "Tell him everything, doctor," she said. "He's already been through a bad situation, he can handle it."

I smiled at her, briefly. She did get it, sometimes anyway.

The doctor turned back to me and let out his breath. "Jewel is currently stable. But she's sustained quite a bit of damage to her chest and lungs. Her heart is fine; the blade missed it completely, but not by much. Despite the strength of her heart, I'm still very concerned about her lungs, which could collapse at any time. Please, son, be prepared for anything, okay?"

Sadness ripped at me but my tears were all used up. They'd been all used up hours ago.

He continued, "The best thing you can do is be here. Can you stay for a while?"

Mom nodded.

Dad looked at her impatiently.

I got the impression Dad was more upset than Mom. But I'd already received the worst punishment possible, so whatever he felt like throwing on top didn't matter.

Laying in a hospital bed, struggling to live, Jewel mattered.

I hadn't eaten in a while for days. Eating wasn't exactly a priority. "I'm going to the cafeteria," I said. "I need some time." I choked up.

"Of course, go ahead," she said.

Dad rolled his eyes, like I shouldn't be allowed to even piss by myself.

I walked casually down the corridor, the sterile white in direct contrast to the gore and filth I witnessed. I didn't think I'd ever feel clean again.

People sat at several round white tables, chatting quietly. The gentle hum of discussion eased me.

I perused the contents of a vending machine and picked a bag of Doritos. I removed my change and the bag. I turned around to find an empty table, looking forward to alone time—time to think.

Jewel.

Like an angel sitting at an empty table. My heart swelled until it might burst, the darkness pushed aside and repressed—I hoped never to return. She wore street clothes and I wondered where she got them, because she hadn't worn them here.

I guessed the nursing staff found them for her.

I walked toward her, smiling my fool head off. "I thought you were supposed to stay in bed," I exclaimed. "I'm so happy to see you." I ran and embraced her.

I made a point not to squeeze too hard, protecting her fragile lungs. "How are you?"

"Perfect," she said cheerily.

"You don't hurt at all?" I asked.

"Not anymore," she confirmed. "Let's not waste time talking about being sick."

I opened my Doritos and shared them with her. "I'm sorry, about everything," I said. "You know, what with your mom and all."

Jewel's eyes narrowed, the blacks of her pupils dancing before their light returned. "It's okay," she said. "She's where she deserves to be."

I wanted to ask her where that was but I left it alone. "Did the doctor say when you could?" I wanted to say go home, but Jewel didn't have a home. "Be released?"

Jewel shook her head. "It doesn't matter, Jason," she said. "What's important is the time we have in this moment. We aren't promised forever, Jason."

"I know, I..."

"Kiss me."

"You don't have to ask me twice." I leaned over and met Jewel in the middle. Our lips melted together and it felt like dynamite. All my dread washed from me, leaving nothing but my love for Jewel. We kissed for a long time.

I worried the cafeteria staff might be put out but nobody minded.

Jewel pulled away a little bit so her beautiful blue eyes were illuminated. She said, "You don't ever have to be afraid of being alone, Jason."

"I know," I said. "I won't as long as I have you, we have each other. I'll take care of you Jewel— like family."

"I know you will, Jason," she said.

"What's wrong, Jewel?"

She stared off into the middle distance but nothing was there. "Nothing is wrong at all," she answered. "We've been through a lot."

"I can call a nurse to take you back to your room. We have, you know, forever, right?"

Jewel smiled but looked away. She turned to me and we kissed.

It was my turn to break the embrace. "I want you to know. I love you, no matter what, unconditionally."

She smiled, tears brimming in her cerulean eyes. "Oh Jason, I love you, too," she sobbed. "And you—"

"—make your brain tingle?" I answered with a smile.

"Yes," she sobbed.

I held her in my arms for forever.

She stood up. "Jason, please never forget what we had—not ever."

I was confused. "I won't, but Jewel..."

"Promise." Her eyes bored into mine.

"I promise," I said. "But what's the matter, Jewel?"

The tears spilled out of her eyes, streamed down her cheeks, and dripped off her chin.

I moved to embrace her.

She put her hand up. "No, no, Jason," she whispered. Her eyes, so tortured, broke my heart. "I have to go."

"Let me get you a wheelchair, Jewel," I said, confused, not understanding what she wanted—needed. "I'll take you to your room."

"You—you don't understand."

I did. Ice filled my emptying heart. My own tear slipped down my cheek and I lowered my arms to my sides, dejected, heartbroken. White vapor poured from her mouth and pooled at her feet. She began to fade.

I'll never forget her last words. They still speak to me. "Never forget, Jason."

She left me—forever.

I dropped to my knees, balled my fists, and cried tears I thought all gone, dried up. I guess there were more left in that special place—the place where Jewel lives.

My reservoir spent, I walked into the waiting room, everyone already crying like someone'd died.

I didn't need to ask why.

Mom walked up to me. "Jason, honey, I have to tell you something."

"I know, Mom."

Epilogue

The cop who shot Billy got convicted and removed from duty for his use of deadly force on a child. The cop argued that Billy rushed him but it didn't fly. Perhaps the jury could've understood the one shot to Huge's belly; he killed Jewel's mom after all, bashing her brains in. Who could justify blowing out the brains of an unarmed kid? I think he got sent away because nobody could explain exactly what happened that night.

My parents took me to Billy's funeral, small and attended by hurried people. The pastor said a few inadequate words and almost immediately, the dirt thudded onto the lid of the coffin. I thanked Billy under my breath, but somehow, I think he already knew.

Tracey and I spoke quietly for a while about nothing in particular, and we shared a silent cry. I wanted to talk about the good times, but nothing was the same and we knew it. Blood oaths and dead friends ruined that.

I never went back to Central High. Mom took a therapy job in another town and we moved to a quiet little suburb where nothing much ever happened boring, but also what I needed to heal.

I kept in touch with Huge for a while, over the phone and by e-mail. His stomach healed okay. But one day, he stopped returning my messages. I found out he got put in jail for dealing drugs. I guess I wasn't surprised. But still, it hurts.

Sometimes I can't help but blame it all on Harvey's stupid blood oath, which helped for a while. Then I pick the blame back up, place it square on my shoulders where it belongs.

Harvey's sister attended Harvey's funeral, knocked up like we predicted. At least someone wasn't dead.

It took me awhile to catch back on to girls but it occurred to me Jewel would want me to be happy. I married someone, and we are expecting. Guess Dad was right, there'd be other girls.

It doesn't seem fair I've found happiness and Jewel is dead. It's not fair, but is anything fair in life?

They're screaming—the coyotes, like they did in the swamp. They want blood every day. They're wearing me out. Whether I give the blood to them depends.

This book is for Jewel. On those full moon nights, when the oak trees rustle their leaves just so, I'll think of her and our time together. I'd like to think, someday, sooner or later, when I pass to the great beyond, she'll be there waiting for me at the pearly gates, smiling that big smile of hers.

I wonder if I'll still make her brain tingle—God, I hope so.

As I sit thinking, the wind has picked up; the oak leaves are moving. In the wind's soft murmur, I hear, "Never forget, Jason. Never."

Justin Holley would like to acknowledge the following people…

My beautiful wife, for two reasons besides being beautiful: one, she's patient and supportive even when I'm preoccupied and my mind is in faraway places. Two, she's a helluva shrink. That helps mightily with the psych elements of my stories. What? Oh, I get it. You were all thinking I *need* a shrink. Come on now…

Brian Keene. If he hadn't written Ghoul, Bruised would have remained in my imagination. Period. Thanks for the inspiration. And I wasn't kidding about the drink.

Diane at Novel Website Design. It's like she's in my head running around, and knows what I need before I do.

Editor Heather at HJS for kicking my manuscript's ever-loving –ss. Any errors in grammar are mine, however.

My dad, 'cause if I ever give up on anything he'll kick *my* ever-loving –ss. Even at 67.

My herd: The Goat Posse. The most special group of writers in the world. What? Yes! Goat world-domination is a real thing—it is.

CPSIA information can be obtained at www.ICGtesting.com
Printed in the USA
LVOW04s1636100615

441947LV00018B/1178/P